Just Sing

selena

Cover Design by Starcrossed Covers

ISBN: 978-1-955913-98-0

Blurb

Brody
Yeah, I might just have the most recognizable face on the planet, but that doesn't stop my band from breaking up. Upon returning home from the last show, I run into Laney Tucker—high school sweetheart, next door neighbor, and the girl I left behind when fame came calling. I've made more than my share of mistakes, but that's the one that keeps me up at night.

The moment I lay eyes on her, I know she'll be mine again, whether she knows it or not. Some things are just meant to be.

Laney

No way in hell am I getting back together with the lying scumbag who traded me in for a bunch of groupies. But I'm not above making him think otherwise, if only to teach him a lesson. The problem is, revenge is a dish best served cold, and Brody Villines still makes me so damn hot.

I just have to remind myself that every word of every song is a lie. No matter how right it feels to be in his arms again, some things just aren't meant to be.

May

one

Brody

I looked out over the sea of shrieking, overgrown baby-dolls. That's all I could see—twenty thousand of them. Ever since *Just 5 Guys* dropped our first single, this had been happening. More and more fans dressed up as baby-dolls. The costumes covered the full spectrum, from everyday baby-doll dresses, to those who painted their faces white and lips red, to those who went even further and wore creepy baby-doll masks above sexy baby-doll Halloween costumes.

"I got something very special for y'all tonight," I said, lowering my voice and looking into the front row, as if I were speaking to each girl individually. Of course, some of my fans weren't dressed up—the moms, a few of the gay guys, the occasional dad—but that's what I saw. A sea of creepy faces staring back at me. At first, it had amused me. Now it was both unnerving and titillating. I fantasized about bending that front row of screaming baby-dolls over the railing and fucking them each in turn.

Probably not cool, since ninety percent of them were unquestionably jailbait. Oh well. It was a fantasy. I surely couldn't fuck more than five or six of them in a row.

"It's time we took it full circle," I said when the shrieking had died down enough that I could be heard. "And you know what that means. Our last song will be our first." I added a wink just for fun, and twenty thousand preteens shrieked like they'd won the lottery. In a way, they had. This was the last show before *Just 5 Guys* took a break—indefinitely. Last I'd heard, tickets were a few hundred…for the nose bleeds. How much had these girls in the front row paid?

And then I spotted one girl, standing in the front row, on her fucking cell phone. She wasn't taking pictures or videos of the show. She was just staring at her screen. Probably posting a picture on Instagram or texting a friend, I told myself.

The girl beside her was gazing at me with such rapt adoration that it almost hurt. I met her eyes and gave her my trademark crooked smile, the one insured for several million dollars, and she shrieked and jumped up and down, grabbing the arm of the texting brunette beside her, who scowled in response. The girls around her had erupted into chaos as I smiled at them, too. If I fucked one, I'd ruin her for life. If she lived to be a hundred, nothing would ever compare to the night Brody Villines took her to his dressing room. It would be tragic, really, to peak so young.

I pushed that thought aside a little too roughly. My therapist said those thoughts were self-defeating. Of course I'd keep making music after tonight. Music was in my veins instead of blood. I couldn't stop making music if I lost both hands, couldn't stop any more than I could stop the rhythm of the world turning.

With a dramatic electronic flourish, the music from our first number one single began. The song that had catapulted us to international stardom, the song I'd grown to despise in my very bones.

"Baby-doll."

I tossed my hair out of my eyes, and twenty thousand chicks shrieked like I'd just impaled them on my dick. My feet started moving before I told them to, the muscle memory kicking in when the beat entered my bloodstream. I didn't have to think as I went through the choreography, the lyrics sliding out of me just as easily, without thought.

Be my baby-doll

I ain't even playin' wit' you

I just want a baby-doll

I can hold the whole night through

God damn, did I hate this fucking song. When my quiet refusal to sing the song after our last tour had failed to move our manager, I'd incited Jace into throwing a tantrum. That had worked for a while, but on our very last night, Nash had insisted. It was fitting, I had to admit.

As the song moved into the bridge, I slowed down to grind my hips in that way fans loved, watching twenty thousand chicks fantasizing about being on my tip. It was still a rush, I couldn't deny that. Then it was back into the chorus, my feet finding their way effortlessly. One-two-three-four, spin-spin-spin-plant. Just as I completed one of my triple turns, I spotted the brunette yawning before she went back to her phone. She was fucking yawning.

I was working my ass off. I'd sweated through choreography for years, since I was barely older than my average fan. Drank the nastiest teas and tinctures known to man to keep my throat clear and my voice smooth as silk, that breathy crooning that made fangirls cream their panties on the spot. I'd practiced for hours and then refrained from speech for entire days, whatever my manager required to keep my vocal chords in pristine shape. Kissed the asses of managers, agents, media, labels, paparazzi, other stars. Faked relationships, gotten up at obscene hours, stayed up until obscene hours or entire days at a time, missed holidays with family, went months at a time without sleeping in my own bed or setting foot in my own home. All to please my fans. And this chick was *bored*?

Her thumb scrolled through her phone. I missed a step. Damn it. This was my last show. I couldn't fuck up over some spoiled, entitled phone addict. But when the song slowed and I approached the mic stand to caress it while I crooned the last lines, there she was again. Still scrolling, reading it looked like, not posting or texting, but browsing her social media, no doubt. What a waste of a front row seat.

The song wrapped, and that was it. The last song *Just 5 Guys* would ever play. And not even significant enough to keep the attention of a front row fangirl.

two

Brody

Truth be told, I was exhausted. But before I could go home, disappear into my family's sprawling Kentucky estate, its lands restored to my family thanks to my contributions, I had one last evening to enjoy my celebrity status. Sure, I'd probably be hounded by photographers and tabloids for years to come, based solely on the accomplishments of *Just 5 Guys*, but it wouldn't be the same. There was something to be said for a stadium full of women adoring you. It could get a guy hopped up on a certain kind of energy, one that was more addictive than any drug—unless you were Jace Wilder, that is.

Addictive enough to leave your first love with nothing but an empty promise that, after a while, you almost forgot you'd made.

"Ready for backstage, fellas?" asked Nash, our manager, clapping us on the back as we passed. Our roadies headed onstage to break down the bit of equipment while we went to greet our VIP ticketholders, media, fellow celebrities, and a handful of contest winners whom I would inevitably forget to attribute to the right contest.

"Hey, hold up," I said, grabbing Nash's sleeve. "I need to get a couple girls from the first row back there. You know, make their night. It'll look good for publicity."

"Ask Stacy," Nash said, barely glancing at me. I searched the bustling throng backstage. It wasn't the way people imagined, groupies and orgies and blow. It was all business. But I didn't see our publicist. Instead, I caught the attention of Steve, one of our oldest and most trustworthy security guys who had spent our first tour as a roadie, loading our equipment and chasing off girls.

That was back when I'd been sure that one day I'd marry Laney, that I'd never be with another girl, that our feelings would never change. Before I'd had to fake relationships with other celebrities because real ones became impossible. Before I had the hottest girls on the planet ripping off their clothes and demanding I give them an exclusive encore in the back of my tour bus.

"Hey, man," I said, lowering my voice so only Steve could hear. "I need you to grab a couple girls from the front row. Blondie in a pink baby-doll costume, one of those ballerina things, and the girl with her. Real moody looking. Has her phone glued to one hand."

"Got it," Steve said before hurrying away. One of Steve's greatest assets was his ability to stay out of everyone's business, to do as he was told without asking questions or even looking at you sideways. He had no opinions and knew how to keep his mouth shut.

I talked to a few bloggers, shook hands, signed autographs, kissed cheeks, took selfies, kissed ass.

It wasn't until a good hour later that I saw her standing against the wall, her dark hair in a sloppy bun, wearing jeans and a t-shirt. Unlike most of the baby-dolls, she'd gone for that natural look. And she was still absorbed in her phone.

I made my way over, exhausted but not about to walk away without taking her down a peg. "Must be important," I said, pausing when I reached her.

She looked up from her phone as if startled to find herself among humans. She flashed the screen towards me, fixing me with these crazy purple eyes like nothing I'd ever seen. "Nah, just SnapIt. What's up?"

"I saw you on your phone during the show," I said. "Was it that dull?"

"No," she said with a shrug. "Just not really my kind of music."

"You paid for a front row seat."

"Oh, that," she said dismissively. "My cousin loves you."

"But you don't."

"I got roped into going because her friend got sick," she said. "But I'm not really into the boyband thing. I prefer real music."

"What's real music?" I challenged. If my vocal coaching didn't count, my sixteen years of guitar, my choreography and dance classes, more voice lessons, piano lessons… If all that didn't count, I didn't know what real music was.

"You know, like them," she said, pointing to her t-shirt.

"Pink Floyd."

"Yeah," she said with another shrug.

"So it has to be one of the greatest musical legends of all time to be real music?"

"No, but it has to be something that will stand the test of time. Boybands… Won't."

"The Beatles might beg to differ."

She scoffed. "The Beatles are not a boyband."

"They're the original boyband."

She shook back a lock of hair that had escaped her bun and gave me a challenging look. "You're not the Beatles. You're more like… New Kids on the Block."

"And you're a bitch."

"True," she said, without even flinching. "But I'm a bitch who knows good music."

"Oh, because you listen to some indie shit that no one's ever heard of, you're so superior to the ninety percent of the world that listens to popular music. It's called *popular* for a reason. I think the general population knows what's good."

"I'm sure they do," she said, but her violet eyes flashed.

"What about your cousin? You're so much better than her, too, right?"

"No," she said. "But I have better taste in music."

We stood staring each other down for a minute without speaking.

Then I stepped forward and kissed her, hard. Her lips were warm and tasted like mint gum. Her tongue was wet and minty fresh, and for a minute, it drank mine in. Then she stepped backwards and shoved me, hard.

"What the hell? Do you just go around kissing whoever you want without asking?"

"I don't have to ask," I said. "Do you realize how lucky you are that I even gave you the time of day?"

She crossed her arms and scowled at me. "No. Tell me."

"Are you fucking kidding me? There's twenty thousand girls out there who would drop to their knees and blow me if I snapped my fingers."

"Yeah? So why aren't you out there snapping your fingers, loverboy?"

"There's only one girl I want on her knees in front of me tonight."

"Sorry," she said, though she didn't sound the least bit sorry. "I need a better offer."

"A better offer?" I spluttered.

"Yeah," she said. "Like maybe you on your knees in front of me."

"You got yourself a deal, baby-doll." The word slipped out before I could rethink my usual pet name. The baby-dolls loved it when I called them that, and it simplified things for me, too. That way I didn't need to bother with learning names.

"Is that right?" the girl asked. "You? You're going to go down on me?"

I widened my eyes and said, as innocently as I could manage, "You think I'm afraid of a little pussy cat?"

"It's okay if you don't know how," she said. "There's a learning curve that I'm sure a big rock star like you wouldn't need to master, what with all the girls in line for the job of giving you one."

"Trust me, I know my way around a girl. Every part of her."

"If you say so."

"Now you're backing out? I thought we had a deal," I said with a smirk. "I guess I'm not the one who's scared."

"I'm not scared," she said. "But what's the point, if I know I'll be disappointed in the end? If I'm going to get some, I want it to be good, not some wannabe rock star who thinks he knows how to please a woman because he's fucked a hundred who all faked an orgasm to stroke his ego."

"Yeah, sounds like you're scared to me."

"You're going to go down on me. You. Brady Villines."

"Don't look so shocked, baby-doll. I'm a rock star in more ways than one. And it's *Brody*."

"Alright, fine," she said. "But if I don't get off, I want a refund."

I laughed, surprising myself. "A refund?"

"Yeah," she said. "I want my ticket refunded. The show sure as hell wasn't worth the price of admission."

I grabbed her hand and yanked her out the back door, tension coursing through me. Sure, sometimes a challenge was fun, but this girl was a straight up bitch. Usually, I hooked up with one of the more persistent baby-dolls backstage, a blonde more often than not. At first, I'd been so pissed about their fanatic obsession and my inability to resist it, that I'd picked the faceless ones behind masks. But it had been a while since I'd grudge-fucked a groupie.

But hey, grudge-fucking could be fun.

This was an angry grudge fuck, different from those. Now I wasn't pissed that she'd torn at my clothes like a rapid dog and practically raped me after I told her I had a girlfriend.

This was me proving that, at twenty-three, I wasn't done. I had a lot left to prove.

I pulled her up the steps of my tour bus and back through the cluster of insiders allowed on my bus—my agent, a couple celebrities, Nash, Stacy, and Quincy, impressing his groupie by showing her my tour bus. After being burned once by a fan who took pictures of everything and posted them online, I was very particular about my tour bus, private and choosy about who I let in. My crew was under strict orders not to let outsiders on.

Now I pulled the grunge chick back through the accordion door to my bedroom, which wasn't much more than a bed, a nightstand, and a tiny closet with designer sweats and t-shirts. I never appeared in public without wardrobe pre-approval from my team. Even a trip to Starbucks in sweats required the right branding and accessories.

After yanking the door closed, I tossed the girl on the bed and crashed on top of her. My crew could find their own way out after chasing off the celebrities who wanted to hang.

Without waiting for the chick to catch her breath, I ripped down her jeans, my mouth crushing hers. She kicked her jeans off her feet while I ripped open my own and yanked her knees apart. After wetting my fingers in my mouth, I pushed them into her until she was gasping and squirming under me.

I stood up off the bed and pulled her to her feet, then spun her around, shoved her forward onto all fours on the floor, and dropped to my knees behind her. Then I plowed into her. Her hair had come loose and tumbled around her shoulders and down her back in a wild tangle. Winding my hand into it, I drove my cock into her again. She cried out and arched her back, spreading her knees to let me go still deeper.

"Harder," she gasped, bracing one hand on the wall beside his bed.

I slammed into her with punishing force, expecting her to beg for mercy, but she only grunted in loud, animal bursts and repeated, "Harder," over and over, like a chant. I could feel the whole tour bus rocking under us, but I kept going until my knees ached and my thighs shook with the effort.

When I was close to coming, I grabbed the corner of my bed for leverage and rammed into her so hard she gasped and tensed up, and I knew I'd finally reached the tender spot at the very depth of her pussy.

I started to pull back but she whispered, "harder," one more time. I dragged her head back as hard as I could and drove deeper again, grinding myself into her depths. She let out a strangled cry, one I wasn't sure was from pleasure and not pain until I felt her squeezing around me, then releasing as she came.

Refund her money? Ha. Never.

Then, before I knew it was going to happen, she clenched around me again, milking my cock until I exploded inside her. Fuck yeah. We collapsed together, shudders wracking our bodies, sweat slick between us. Five minutes later, I was halfway asleep when she said, "Ready for round two?"

"Glad the show wasn't a total bust for you," I said, pushing myself up from her.

She rolled over and sat up, touching her knees gingerly while she examined the skin peeling back. "Maybe on the bed this time, though. I'm bleeding."

"I see that," I said. "You got it on my carpet."

"Whoops. Sorry." She stood and tossed my blankets back and dropped onto the edge of the bed, where she peeled off her t-shirt.

I pulled up my pants, picked up her t-shirt, and handed it back. "You can go now."

"Seriously?" She stared at me so incredulously I found my mouth twitching, but I held back a laugh. I'd let her run the show for a while, but it was time she knew who really ran things when Brody Villines, was around.

"Seriously, baby-doll."

"You are such an asshole." She stood and pulled her shirt on, then snatched up her jeans.

I picked up her underwear, hooked them on one finger, and held them out to her. "Unless you want to leave them for a souvenir."

She made a grab for them, but I held them out of her reach.

"I think the words you're looking for are *thank you.*"

"Excuse me?"

"Because I rocked your world like it's never been rocked before. Where I come from, we say please and thank you."

"Where I come from we say *fuck you.*" She flipped me off and then yanked on her jeans, flinging her hair around in a way that was quite sexy, really. When she'd shoved her feet into her black converse with the heels crushed down, she turned to the door.

"Forgetting something?" I asked, letting the panties swing lazily from my finger.

"Keep them," she said. "You know, so you can remember the girl who *rocked your world like it's never been rocked before.* And by the way, you're welcome." With a smug smile, she ducked out of the open bedroom and marched through my bus to the door. I was sure I saw her limping just a little. Oh, well. She'd asked for it.

three

Laney

Laney Tucker was a good girl. Everybody knew it. My teachers at school had known it since the day I entered Kindergarten at the private academy, my little blonde ringlets full of velvet bows that matched my shoes and purse. Yes, I'd carried a purse to school in Kindergarten. It was a black velvet clutch with a sterling silver clasp. Now, as I turned my white Camaro down the long stretch of dirt road that led to my family's farm, I tried to remember what had happened to that little black purse.

Surely it had been gone by the time I was old enough for homework, always turned in on time and with the proper heading, and makeup. Somewhere along the way, I'd traded out cutesy things for serious ones. Serious things like straight A's, music lessons, ballet, horseback riding, and a steady boyfriend at the neighboring boys' academy.

I'd had one of those—all the good girls did. I needed one for Cotillion, for prom and homecoming, for graduation pictures with both our families and trips to the Kentucky Derby. And hadn't we been the perfect pair, the girl with the mane of long golden hair, blue eyes, and just enough curves to be sexy without anyone calling her a slut based on her body type alone; the boy with the sexy smile, bronze hair, and eyes the color of the Kentucky sky. It was this same boyfriend who escaped parental watch with me the night we lost our virginity to each other amid promises of eternal love and forever faithfulness.

A good boy like Brody Villines, he was the perfect match for a good girl like me.

Dust billowed up behind my Camaro, and I sighed in resignation. The bad thing about going home, besides the obvious, was my family's resistance to joining the twenty first century. My father said if we paved the road, hooligans would come onto our property. That was unlikely, but I supposed it was possible that they'd find the dirt road a bit of a deterrent. After all, one couldn't escape at a high speed on a dirt road. One had to know how to drive on gravel.

I wondered if Brody still remembered all the turns, each one seeming to be at a sharp ninety-degree angle. Brody had served me well, from freshman year to senior year. He'd even served as an excuse to avoid what my mother referred to as the "slut culture" of sororities, when I went off to study at Rhodes my freshman year. Yes, a good man was hard to find, and a good girl had to do everything in her power to hold onto him, even encouraging him follow his dreams of fame. It didn't matter that my serious boyfriend, my good guy, had turned out to be a lying, cheating, egomaniacal piece of shit. It just mattered that I'd had one when I needed him.

As I passed the Villines's estate, I sped up, my wheels spinning in the gravel before the tires got purchase and the car roared forward. I'd have to have it washed in the next couple days. It was impossible to keep it clean while driving around on dirt roads. But I didn't want to linger any longer than necessary. Once, my heart had raced every time I neared Brody Villines's place. I hated to admit that it still did. It was from rage now, though, rather than excitement. Or so I told myself.

Yes, a dirty car was the least of my worries. My mother would undoubtedly give the hunky stable boy the job of washing it so she could watch him working in a wet t-shirt. So it all worked out.

My phone buzzed on the passenger seat, and I picked it up, flicked it free of the charger, and looked at the screen. A good girl like me would never ordinarily text and drive. But after twenty-two years of calling this place home, the dirt road was so familiar I could've driven it with my eyes closed. And besides, I only drove twenty miles an hour on it, and the lack of a dust cloud hovering on the road ahead let me know that no cars approached for a good long while.

It was Paul. Of course it was. Nerdy Paul, with his shirt always buttoned up one button too far, with his swampy breath and perpetually slipping glasses. I'd started dating Paul the moment I found out that Brody had turned into the clichéd man-whore I should have known he was all along deep in his evil heart. All men would be, if given half a chance. I hadn't given Paul even quarter of a chance. I wasn't going to make that mistake again. I may have been a good girl, but I wasn't a dumb one.

4:42 pm Paul Griswald: Did you make it okay?

Even his check-in was timid. Paul was not the sort of man who would ever make a woman's heart race, which was probably why I'd chosen him. That, along with the fact that he was about as far from Brody Villines as it was humanly possible to be while still possessing a penis. At least I assumed he had one of those.

Once, when I had been a teenager, I'd overheard my mother—tipsy on sherry during her Sunday brunch-and-bridge club—saying something about Brody Villines that concluded with the word "Me-OW!" This was followed by thunderous hooting and cackling from all the women. The previous winter, at Paul and my engagement party, my mother had congratulated me on making a "safe choice."

I tossed my phone on the seat and pulled my car to the keypad at the end of my parents' long, straight driveway. I could always text Paul later. I pulled through the gate onto the gravel drive that led along a seemingly endless white horse fence on each side. A flock of guinea hens had wandered into the road, and I slowed to let them trundle across. Horses grazed far off in the pasture, but I couldn't tell which was

Pegasus. My father had gotten new ones since I'd moved to Memphis, and I was no longer involved in his equine business.

Finally, I pulled my car to a stop in the four-car garage hidden behind the large, Confederate-style house—an exposed garage was too modern for my mother, who insisted on preserving the sense of the past, and old money, at all cost. Another reason the private road remained unpaved, I thought as I ran a finger through the skim of dust that had settled on the snowy white paint and hot pink trim of my Camaro. I shouldered my duffle bag and headed across the gravel pad that separated the house from the garage and provided parking when guests visited.

Today, I was the only guest arriving. Not that I was a guest, exactly, but after four years at college, I always felt like one for the first few days. I had come home each summer, but this time, a moving truck would arrive the next day with my remaining possessions. This time, I would not be returning to Memphis in September.

"Honey?" Mom called as I let myself in the back door.

"Hey, Mom, it's me."

"I was wondering when you'd make it," my mother said, emerging from the mud room wearing an oversized sunhat and elbow-length rubber gloves along with a bright yellow blouse, a pair of floral culottes, and gardening Crocs. If there was one thing Blair Tucker knew, it was how to dress for every occasion, including a morning of tending her precious flower gardens. She held a spray bottle in one hand, which she held away as she hugged me. "Come out front with me, I'm just finishing up spraying the roses. I've got some news." She gave me a mischievous smile and sashayed out the front door, leaving it open for me to follow.

I dropped my bag and followed my mother down the front steps—freshly swept and recently scrubbed, judging by the redness of the bricks—to the row of rose bushes that served as a hedge along the stone walkway.

"How was the drive?" Blair asked, misting the roses with her spray bottle.

"Good," I said. "How's everything here? You and Dad, the horses all okay?"

"Every one of them," my mother said.

"And the cousins?" I asked. "Has Aunt Cindy recovered from her knee surgery?"

"They're all just fine," Mom said, giving me an expectant, amused look. "Aren't you forgetting to ask about a certain neighbor?"

"Don't remind me," I said with an eyeroll. "Let me guess, the Villines's garage gained a new Lamborghini or something ridiculous like that?"

"No," Mom said slowly. "Haven't you heard? Brody's band broke up."

"Oh, yeah. That."

Of course I'd heard about the breakup of *Just 5 Guys*. Pretty much the whole world was in chaos, according to *Your Celebrity Eyes* and the other gossip channels that I left running in the background while I got ready for school every morning.

"Yes, that," Mom said, watching me over the roses.

"How tragic," I said lightly, unable to hide one hundred percent of my smugness.

"That's very mature of you," she said. "I would have thought you'd be more concerned."

"Why would I care if his stupid band broke up?" I asked, turning to go back inside.

"Oh, I don't imagine you'd care about that," she said, plucking a rose from the bush and pressing her nose into its velvety white petals. "But I thought you might be interested to know that Brody's coming home."

* * *

8:08 pm Laney Tucker: What a day.

8:09 pm Piper Reid: What's up?

8:10 pm Laney Tucker: Mom.

8:10 pm Piper Reid: What did she do this time?

8:11 pm Laney Tucker: She's all innocently gardening and drops a Brody bomb on me.

8:12 pm Piper Reid: It's weird, sometimes I forget you dated the Justin Bieber of boy bands.

8:14 pm Laney Tucker: Too bad I can't forget.

8:14 pm Piper Reid: Sorry.

8:15 pm Piper Reid: I mean, I don't think about it like OMG my cousin dated someone famous. He's just Brody. It's like boyband Brody is not the same person as the guy you dated.

8:16 pm Laney Tucker: So anyway, he's coming home.

8:16 pm Piper Reid: No fucking way!

8:17 pm Laney Tucker: Fucking way.

8:17 pm Piper Reid: Like next door home?

8:19 pm Laney Tucker: Three miles if you go by the dirt road.

8:20 pm Piper Reid: Sounds like a bad country song ☺

8:21 pm Laney Tucker: Don't remind me.

I had once thought we'd be a country duo. How pathetic was that? In high school, we'd played together at church, strumming our acoustic guitars and singing about Jesus. We'd played at school, too, and at the country club. Brody's uncle was some big shot music guy in Nashville, and we'd been in the early stages of planning our career when Brody was "discovered." Being the good girlfriend I was, I'd been ecstatic that he had a shot at major fame so soon. I'd encouraged him to take it, supported him all the way. What a sad sap I'd been back then.

But Piper knew all about that. Piper was the friend who spent weekends at my house when we were kids, talking until one of us fell asleep mid-conversation at dawn. The friend who shared all the memories that girls shared with their childhood best friends, from my first crush (Brody) to my first love (Brody) to my first time (again, Brody). She was the friend who would stand up for me or stand back and let me shine when I got something for myself. But she was more than that, because she was my cousin, so she understood me in a way that only people inside a family could.

It had just about killed me to be happy for her when she'd gone to school in New York for fashion design. It felt like a world away.

8:26 pm Piper Reid: Sorry. I had to switch trains. What are you going to do?

8:27 pm Laney Tucker: I have a plan.

8:27 pm Piper Reid: So what is it?

8:29 pm Laney Tucker: Call me.

I had seen enough movies to know that a good revenge plan centered on never leaving written evidence. I wasn't about to text something that might come back to haunt me. If I was going to get Brody, I couldn't have any secrets hidden in my phone, secrets that would somehow, by the weirdest coincidence, end up in his hands. No, this would be done the right way, without an evidence trail. Because after I got Brody back, I was going to get him back for what he'd done to me.

four

Brody

As I made my way off the tarmac and into my H2, I couldn't help thinking about Laney. I hadn't seen her in three years. I tried not to think about her, and for the most part, I did an okay job of that. But Jesus. She must be home for the summer now that it was June. Or did she stay at school all summer? I hadn't wanted to ask my mother. She'd take it the wrong way. And my dad was in Louisville most of the time and wouldn't know. What did I care if she was home, anyway? It wasn't like she'd want to see me. Not after the shit I'd pulled.

I couldn't blame her. But still. Maybe I could make things right.

My phone buzzed, interrupting my thoughts, and I picked it up. "Hey, Nash," I said, peering out the window at the unsuspecting cars passing the H2. They didn't know that at that very moment, greatness was slipping by them. That one of the most famous celebrities in the world was behind the tinted glass windows in the next vehicle.

Though I was supposed to be taking a break after touring for almost four solid years, I didn't want greatness to slip by me, either.

"Listen, I want you to get some rest," Nash said. "But be thinking about where you want to go from here. I'm going to take you there."

"Oh, yeah?"

I knew what Nash was doing. Not that he couldn't live without *Just 5 Guys.* He could make another band the way he'd made us and a dozen other bands, creating something out of nothing. There was a reason the dude's nickname was "the Wizard." Making the band was his favorite part, he'd told us a million times. That was his passion—the challenge of putting the group together like a puzzle, melding our sounds, building our public personas, bestowing upon each a unique personality to show the world. But he'd never had the kind of success he'd had with us. That kind of success could be addictive.

"Listen, I could call Zane or Quincy, but I chose you," Nash said in his weird accent. Brooklyn? Italian? He reminded me of Danny Devito—short and round, loud and energetic, and with an accent. But Nash had olive skin and tight, wavy black hair instead of a bald head.

"That's real nice of you," I drawled. Was my own accent thickening now that I'd entered Kentucky? "But what do you really want?"

"I want to make some money," Nash said, never one to mince words. "And I think you're the one who's going to make it with me."

I sat up straighter in the back of the H2. Now I was paying attention. Technically, Nash wasn't my manager anymore. He'd been the manager for *Just 5 Guys*, which didn't exist anymore. If Nash wanted to make an offer, he should have called my agent, and we both knew it.

"I'm listening," I said.

Nash laughed, that short bark of a laugh. Like a cough. *Ha-ha-ha!* "Listen, you just get some rest, take the summer off," he said. "I bet you haven't had a month off in five, six years. Am I right?"

"You know you're right," I said. "You made the schedule. But how am I going to make money for you?"

"Like I said, you take a couple months off, let me figure all that out. I'll call you when it's all set up."

I bit back my frustration. That's how life had been in *Just 5 Guys*. Never knowing what came next, blindly having to trust the producers, the managers. I understood why N'Sync had made that video where the band members were puppets. To be fair, Nash had done a great job. How many boybands lasted more than five years? We'd milked that one for every penny it was worth and disbanded just when interest had barely begun to wane. Nash said no one would remember that, because we were still the most popular boyband in the world. We'd gone out on top.

But I would remember.

I started to argue, but Nash had already hung up, and before I could call back, I noticed that we were passing the Pic-Pac, where my mother had told me to stop and get her some toilet paper. She did that every time I came home, to make sure I didn't get "too big for my britches." With resignation, I tapped on the driver's shoulder.

Of course my mother couldn't ask me to get bread and milk. It had to be toilet paper. Inevitably, someone would take a picture of me with a huge pack of Charmin' under one arm, and it would end up in a gossip rag or "Stars, They're Just Like Us." But what else could I do? My mom was still my mom, and no matter how old I was or how much money I made, she wanted me to remember it.

I could have gone home to one of my houses—I had one on each coast—but my grandfather had had a mild stroke, and though he was supposedly back to normal, I couldn't have lived with myself if I didn't go home to see him. If it wasn't for Grandpa Othal, I would never have picked up a guitar. My grandfather had passed the music business to my uncle instead of my mother, but he'd always been around to hear my latest song, to record something and pass it around to his old friends in the business.

At the Pic-Pac, I climbed out of the car and headed in. My agent wanted me to take a bodyguard everywhere, but that made me even more conspicuous. Keeping my head down, I hurried to the aisle and grabbed a twelve-pack of rolls.

I made it all the way to the register before anyone accosted me.

"Oh my God, are you who I think you are?" the pimply teenage cashier said. I could practically see her panties moistening as her voice rose to a squeal.

I gave her a half smile and handed her a twenty.

"I heard you were from around here, but oh my God, I never thought I'd actually see you. Or that you'd come to my register, or buy your own… Toilet paper." Her face had gone beet red, matching most of her pimples.

"Just a regular guy," I said, waiting for her to finish freaking out so I could get my toilet paper and get out of here. The squealing had drawn a little crowd of four or five store employees and the same number of customers.

"Do you think I could, like, get a selfie with you?" the breathless cashier asked, her eyes bugging.

"Sure thing," I said. "But I gotta bounce after that. I left the car running." I didn't mention that I had a driver. People liked it when stars were just regular guys. That's why we'd named our band *Just 5 Guys*. It had started out as Just 4 Guys, but then Quincy pointed out that it sounded like "just for guys," which might lead audiences to believe it was an all-gay boyband. So we'd added Isaac, who, coincidentally, was the only gay one.

After taking a selfie with the cashier, and another with the manager, and then a group picture with the store employees, I made my escape before anyone else could grab me. On my way out, though, I saw an adorable little girl of about four staring at me with big round eyes. She was holding onto her mother's leg with one hand while sucking the thumb of the other, and she wore a hot pink *Just 5 Guys* t-shirt.

I couldn't help myself. I stopped and crouched in front of the girl. "Hey, little lady," I said while the mother grinned a huge airheaded grin but stayed silent, as if afraid she might wake up from her dream if she spoke. "Cool shirt," I told the little girl. "You know who I am?"

She shook her head without taking her thumb from her mouth.

"I'm that guy," I said, pointing to the guy in the middle of her shirt.

She hid her face in her mother's leg.

I laughed and stood to shake the mom's hand. "Want a picture?" I asked.

She nodded mutely, that dreamy smile still plastered across her face. I held out my phone and snapped a selfie with the little girl before taking one on the mom's phone of the three of us. When I'd finished, a couple more people had come in and were staring at me, smiling and looking uncertain. I needed to get out of here.

"Y'all have a nice day now," I said to the mother, returning her phone. I ruffled the girl's hair, grabbed my shopping bag, and scooted out the door before anyone else could ambush me. I nearly ran to my Hummer and climbed in. Every girl in the Pic-Pac would be texting her friends, and if we didn't get out of there soon, we'd be stuck there for hours. It wasn't L.A., but there were enough girls in Kentucky to mob me.

As we pulled up to my gate twenty minutes later, I checked the mirrors as a matter of habit. In L.A., people might follow me home every day. But here, no one. I relaxed a little and punched in the code for the gate. Since *Just 5 Guys'* success, I'd had a taller gate built, along with a new security system, and a high privacy wall around the house and garden. But we had much more land outside the wall, thanks to me. I'd made sure we recovered all the land our family had owned before the Civil War. My father had his tobacco fields, too, but this was our personal property.

I unloaded my bags and carried them all onto the porch, where I found the door locked. It had been strange to say goodbye to my tour bus, but I was relieved to be home. I'd spent way too long living in a moving vehicle. It would be nice to be on solid ground for a while. But only for a little while. I wasn't done making music yet.

Inside the house, I found the rooms empty. Leave it to my mother to make sure she had plans the day I was coming home. She'd never want me to think she gave up something from her own life to be there for me. I hauled my bags inside the big brick house and up the stairs to the room that no longer felt like mine. I'd been gone for so long, over five years, only home for a night or two at a time every few months—if that.

I spotted my acoustic guitar on its stand in the corner, the same one I'd played in high school, back when I'd dreamed of being a country star with Laney. With Grandpa Othal and my uncle both in the music business in Nashville, I'd already had a foot in the door. Back then, I'd never dreamed that I'd become the lead in a multi-platinum selling boyband. I'd been content to play harmonies with my high school sweetheart.

Standing at the window, I tuned the guitar while I gazed out over the back wall, across the rolling fields of bluegrass. Over those fields, two miles away, stood the Tuckers' house with its stables and horses, with feisty Mrs. Tucker and her dashing husband. Somewhere closer, on the border between the properties, was a row of weeping willows. And beyond that, at the halfway point between our houses, was the gazebo where my and Laney's mothers used to sit drinking iced tea and chatting while Laney and I and sometimes my brothers played. Where, later, we'd met on our morning runs, rushing to each other in our adolescent urgency, full of the ache of missing each other after only hours apart.

We'd planned to get married in that gazebo, even planning where the bridesmaids would stand, which horses would pull the carriage that would serve as our getaway car.

In that same gazebo, we'd given ourselves to each other for the first time, and many times afterwards. Maybe we'd meet there again now that I was home. I'd tell her how it had been, and she'd forgive me. She had to. Laney was always the sweet, forgiving type.

Like the first time, I'd kiss her tenderly, undress her slowly, and lay my shirt on the bench before laying her down on it. And just before I entered her, she would look up at me with such vulnerability in her eyes, and maybe a shadow of fear, and whisper, "Be gentle." And I would push inside her slowly and make love to her like I had before, our eyes never leaving each other.

I set down my guitar and turned away from the window. Every time I came home, I spent a grotesque amount of time reminiscing about Laney. Nash wasn't the only one who kept me from home. I stayed gone, stayed busy, for a reason.

Snagging my phone from the bed, I hit the band manager's personal number. "Hey," I said when Nash answered. "I'm not in the band anymore. You don't get to call all the shots. I'm ready to start working again. What do you have?"

"Whoa, whoa," Nash said. "These things take time, Brody-boy. Let me work my magic. You just take it easy, rest your vocal cords, and don't eat too much of that southern food. I can't sell a fat act."

I picked up my guitar again. "Okay, I'll rest for a week. But I can't waste the whole summer here. Getting fat is the least of my problems. By September, some other boyband will have come along, and no one will even remember my name. I've got to get out there now, while my name is still on everyone's mind."

Nash laughed. "I knew I picked the right guy."

"So what are you thinking? Solo album?"

"I'm thinking you let me worry about that. Keep the look, though. You got the right combination of feminine and masculine to give both the gays and the teeny boppers wet dreams. You don't want to lose that."

"You're saying I look like a girl?"

"You don't want to be *Just 1 Guy*, though. You need to grow up a little. You could shave your head, maybe get a tat on those virgin arms."

"Fuck you," I said. "Needles aren't my thing."

"I'll call you in a month."

"A week." I picked out a chord progression on the guitar, then added, "If you can't do it, someone will. Summer is too long to wait. I want a solo album. It worked for Justin Timberlake."

"We'll see," Nash said. "You're no Timberlake."

"Name me one of the Backstreet Boys, and I'll wait a month."

"I'll call you in two weeks," Nash said before hanging up.

I went to the window, still strumming my guitar, and looked out over the fields again. I'd go running in the morning. A mile to the gazebo and a mile back. After all, I couldn't get out of shape from all the southern cooking. Manager's orders.

June

five

Laney

"Brody Villines stopped by this morning," Blair said one morning over breakfast on the veranda. She poured fresh squeezed orange juice into her glass before passing the pitcher to me.

I accepted it and filled my glass. "Oh, yeah?" I asked in the same off hand tone my mother was using, as if he were any other neighbor. "What did he want?"

"Oh, he wanted to take one of the horses out."

"Did you let him?"

"Of course I let him," Mom said, arching a manicured eyebrow as she helped herself to a bowl of tropical fruit salad. "The only person I trust with a horse more than Brody is you, my dear."

"Did he take Pegasus?"

"Of course not," Mom said. "He knows that's your horse."

Leave it to a man to respect my horse but not my heart. I popped a grape into my mouth, letting its juice sweeten my tongue before I spoke, a smile on my face. "Good."

"He asked about you," she said, a twinkle in her eye.

"Good for him," I said, spreading butter on an English muffin.

"You should stop by," she said. "It's the neighborly thing to do. In fact, why don't we all go over. Now that you're home, and he's home…"

"I don't think that would go the way you're hoping it would."

"There's nothing wrong with making a boy wait," Mom said. "Just don't make him wait too long. A boy like Brody Villines, he's got a lot of options."

"You don't think I've got options?"

"Of course you do, dear," she said, reaching across the table to pat my hand. "A pretty girl always has options. But it never hurts to marry a man with money. Marry a man like that, and you'll never have to work a day in your life."

"Mom, I didn't spend the last four years getting a degree so I could marry a rich guy and sit around the house dying of boredom."

"There's plenty to do to run a house," she said, withdrawing her hand from mine. "And not a lot of boredom."

"I'm sorry," I said, setting down my fork. "I didn't mean to imply that your job isn't as important as Daddy's. But I went to school for a reason. I got a degree so I could use it."

"There's nothing wrong with learning," Mom said, spearing a piece of kiwi. "But you're also supposed to meet a husband there."

"In case you've forgotten, I did meet a husband there. His name is Paul. You threw us a lovely engagement party not six months ago. Does any of this ring any bells?"

Mom arched an eyebrow. "You aren't really going to marry him, are you, dear?"

"So you do remember," I said. "I was beginning to think I should call a doctor and have them check for early Alzheimer's."

Mom patted her mouth with a napkin. "My memory is just fine," she said archly. "I suppose I thought that was a phase. I'm not sure I'm ready to call Paul a Tucker."

"Well, lucky for you, you don't have to. You'll have to call me a Griswald." I had almost as hard a time saying that as my mother had hearing it. I had to take a swallow of juice to get the taste out of my mouth.

"Honey," Mom said, shifting her fruit salad around before choosing a piece of mango. "If you can look me in the eyes and tell me that man is going to make you deliriously happy, I'll…well, I'll get used to calling you a Griswald."

"I'm not looking for deliriously happy," I said. "I'm looking for acceptable. And Paul is acceptable."

"Why don't you try that online dating thing? Your cousin Piper did that, remember?"

"Trust me, I know all about it." I finished off my orange juice and muffin before scooting back from the table. "Should I take in the plates?"

"Just think about it," Mom said. "We could have a little welcome home gathering for you."

I sighed. "You don't have to plan a party. The Villineses would know why you were doing it, anyway. They're arrogant enough. I'll go say hello."

"Good," she said, rising from the table as well. "You can have a degree and still marry well. A little nest egg for security never hurt anyone."

I bit back my retort and took the plates in. My mother had married well, so she'd know. I was expected to follow in her footsteps—go to Rhodes, be a legacy at her sorority, marry a rich guy the moment I graduated, and move out to wherever he lived to help him with his business behind the scenes, uncelebrated and unrecognized. But to paraphrase the great Miranda Lambert, this wasn't my mama's broken heart.

Unlike my mother—and *thanks to* my mother—my family had enough that I didn't have to marry well. Blair had a good family name, but by the time I was growing up, it was a name only. Her family had struggled to maintain the air of prosperity, but they'd been nearly destitute when she married into the Tucker family.

I had no intention of becoming a Villines. Still, I was getting tired of waiting for Brody to come knocking. If he was too cowardly to come right up and ask to see me, I'd have to orchestrate it. Obviously, I couldn't do something so brazen as to go knocking on his door. There was an art to it, a way the game had to be played.

After breakfast, I went up to my room. I pulled my blonde hair into a high pony, slicked on a coat of deodorant, and refreshed my lipstick—nude, so a boy might be fooled into thinking I wore none; long lasting, so my lips would stay pink through a workout. Brown mascara because black was too harsh for a blonde trying to look natural. I pursed my lips and turned my face to check it from each side. My skin was clear, and the exercise would serve as blush.

I wiggled into a pair of black yoga shorts and a hot pink sports bra, pulled on my grey and pink running shoes, and headed downstairs and out the back door. I crossed the gravel pad where the gardener's truck sat, and the stables, empty now. When I'd gone through the little white gate and closed it behind me, I took off jogging down the wide footpath that led through the fields towards the Villines's property. Horses dotted the rolling fields further off, but I wasn't riding this morning. Though it was only nine, it was already hot, the sun blazing over the grass and drawing up the warm, green smell of my childhood.

Our childhood. Brody and I had traveled this trail all our lives—at first with our parents and his brothers, and later, when we were old enough to be trusted to stay on the path, by ourselves. And then, suddenly, we'd been too old to go alone. That hadn't stopped me from sneaking out at night, racing across these fields in the dark to throw myself headlong into Brody's waiting arms. Into love.

I *had* loved him once. I still believed—even now, after everything—that he had loved me, too.

Too bad he hadn't loved me more than pussy.

Not that he hadn't gotten that from me. We hadn't snuck out to meet at midnight to talk about the weather. Sure, it had taken a few months of kissing, of being sure and unsure, of backing out at the last minute, wanting to preserve some imaginary virtue. But finally, in the heat of the moment, I'd forgotten Good Girl Laney and all the things I'd learned in Sunday School. I'd forgotten everything except the feeling of

Brody's warm breath caressing my neck, the pulsating hardness of him in my hand. In that moment, I had wanted nothing in the world more than to make Brody Villines my first and only one, forever.

Unfortunately, Brody had other plans. Plans to get famous and fuck his way through the Western world. Or maybe he just couldn't resist "gettin' some strange" as Piper called it. Whatever it was, he'd ripped my heart out, stomped it into the dry Kentucky dust, and spit on it. He'd told me that my forever wasn't enough. My heart wasn't enough. My body wasn't enough. He had to have all the girls, those creepy girls in their baby-doll masks. I shuddered at the memory of seeing them on TV for the first time.

Your Celebrity Eyes again, of course, as I got ready for class. They'd been talking about *Just 5 Guys'* first sold-out stadium show after their first Platinum single, "Baby-Doll." Even then, it had creeped me out to see all the painted and masked faces. Later, after he'd dumped his "hometown honey"—that's what a magazine had once called me—they'd creeped me out even more.

"Do you think they keep those on when they're hooking up with Brody?" I'd asked Piper over the phone.

"Probably," Piper had said. "That way, when he gets arrested, he can pretend he didn't know they were twelve."

Though of course I'd made lots of friends in my sorority—it was true, we were like sisters in a lot of ways—none of them would ever replace Piper, the closest thing I'd had to a real sister. None of them could be as close. Even after Piper had gone off to New York City, we'd talked on the phone at least once a week for four years, having midnight coffee dates since Piper was a night owl. Now, I couldn't believe she wasn't coming home for the summer. How was I going to make it through a summer with Brody Villines if I couldn't run to Piper's when I needed her?

When the gazebo came into view, my feet tangled, and I stumbled. From so far, I couldn't tell if he was there. Waiting for me. I wasn't sure anymore that I wanted him to be. But I was sure he would be, and if he'd seen me and I turned around and ran, I'd lose everything I'd come for.

I pushed myself onwards, hoping he hadn't seen me stumble. Memories of our nights in the gazebo rushed up at me, but I pushed them back. This time, he'd be the one who came and lay in the gazebo crying over me when I was gone.

six

Brody

I stopped at the end of the Tuckers' driveway for only a moment to peel off my shirt and mop my sweating face with it. I punched in the gate code and strolled through. It hadn't changed much. Guinea hens and peacocks warbled and waddled about, the smell of horse manure still hung in the air, and the big white house still stood regally over the place like a Confederate manor. Which, I supposed, it had been.

As I made my way up to the house, I debated putting my shirt back on but decided against it. I wasn't all tatted up like the Wilder brothers, but I knew I looked good.

"Speaking of the devil," Blair Tucker said with a grin, standing up from behind a hedge. "You say his name and he appears."

I looked around. "Who were you talking to about me this morning, Mrs. Tucker?"

"Oh, don't you Mrs. Tucker me," she said, sashaying around the hedge to give me a hug. "You didn't know me from your own mother when you were knee high to a grasshopper."

"It would be hard to confuse you two," I said, giving Blair time to really hug me good. "You look at least twenty years younger."

"Oh, you," Blair said, swatting me with a pair of gardening gloves. "Stop that before you make me blush."

"I don't think you know how," I said with a wicked grin.

Blair gave me a knowing smile. "You come for some more of my sweet tea?"

"That's just why I'm here. How'd you know?"

She swatted me on the ass with her gloves and, cackling all the way, led me onto the veranda. "Have a seat, Brody. I'll be right out."

I looked around for signs of Laney while Mrs. Tucker was inside. I couldn't find many, but I knew she was home. The last time I'd come, Blair had said as much. She'd told me to have patience, that Laney would come around. But I wasn't so sure. Since we'd broken up, we hadn't spoken even once. At first, I'd called to ask her forgiveness, though I knew I didn't deserve it. After having my calls refused a few dozen times, I'd given up. I wasn't too proud to beg, but I'd be damned if I was going to keep groveling forever.

Especially since I knew I'd make even worse mistakes if she took me back. That realization had finally cured me of the urge to keep calling. I couldn't keep hurting her, filling her with doubts and insecurities, making her think she wasn't enough. She was. I could have been faithful, no matter how many temptations I faced. If only she'd believed me.

For a while, I had been sure she'd call me once she calmed down. That she'd break down and forgive me. But I'd given up hope of that. She would never understand what it meant to be on the road like that, lonely and missing her, and to have those baby-dolls tearing at my clothes like a hungry mob of cannibals. Eventually, it was either succumb to them or be eaten.

I hadn't succumbed. Not at first. I'd held them off even when the other guys hadn't, even when they gave me shit and my manager threatened to kick me out of the band if I didn't pretend to date some starlet in our opening act. But too many nights on the road without talking to Laney had taken their toll. I couldn't expect her to understand, and eventually, her trust was worn away and she no longer believed my promises. There were too many suspicions, too many missed calls, nights when I hadn't charged my phone, nights when pictures of me with scantily clad fangirls draped over me surfaced after I'd told her I'd been too busy to call back.

And the worst part was that even if I hadn't cheated, I might as well have. I hadn't held out for her after the breakup, hadn't kept myself pure and fought for her. She'd told me to go be a rock star, and I had. I'd been pissed when she dumped me, and that very night, I'd succumbed to the thirsty mob. Anything to fill the void she'd left, anything to numb the soul-rending pain. I was just a man, and what man wouldn't do the same when faced with hundreds of girls eager to fulfill his kinkiest fantasy at the snap of his fingers, rush to obey his every whim, more than willing to be his sex slaves for the night—his baby-dolls.

seven

Laney

When I arrived at the gazebo, I could hardly believe it was empty. I looked around, as if he might be hiding nearby. But he was nowhere to be found.

For the first time since hatching my plan, doubt crept in. What if he didn't want me back? I hadn't considered that. When we'd broken up, he'd called almost nightly, leaving messages begging for my forgiveness and swearing he'd never miss a call again, that I'd never see pictures of him at parties with flawless starlets, while I kept my head down and studied hard. There had been the last night, when he'd stayed up all night partying with the band and I'd stayed up all night studying for finals. He said he'd never strayed, but the pictures told a different story. In the end, I had to believe the facts. He couldn't be trusted, and I couldn't keep driving myself insane with doubts and fears. But I'd believed the earnest words he'd left in those messages begging for me to take him back.

That had been three years ago, though. A lot had changed since then. Maybe he didn't want me back anymore. After all the girls he'd fucked in those three years, I was probably the last thing on his mind. How could one girl compare to all the girls? Even if I'd been an insatiable contortionist porn star with no gag reflex, I couldn't add up to the things that a hundred girls and more could do. Why would he want sweet little Laney Tucker, with one notch on her belt, when he could have all the pussy in the world?

After a few minutes of stretching and cooling down, I started back toward my house. He couldn't have all the girls, I reminded herself. Not anymore. His band was done. His brief but glorious career was over, and he would go the way of all boy bands. What had happened to the members of O-Town, or Boys II Men, or New Kids on the Block? They'd go the way of jelly sandals and acid wash mom jeans, crimped hair and blue eyeshadow. In a decade, they'd be nothing but nostalgia porn.

Just 5 Guys would be no different. Brody's band was done, and he'd come running home to mama to wallow in memories of the good old days like an old man, knowing the best of his life was already behind him. And here I was, heading off to travel the world for a year before starting grad school. I was just getting started. At twenty-three, Brody Villines was already a washed-up has-been.

When I reached my house, I ran up the brick steps to the veranda before I even noticed my mother sitting at the outdoor breakfast table, the one that overlooked the garden, where we sat almost every warm summer morning. She was not alone.

Brody Villines was sitting with her.

I fought the many competing urges that raced through me when I saw that painfully familiar face after so long—run away, throw a plant pot at his beautiful face, faint dead away…

"Well, hello, darling," Mom said, pulling out the chair beside her. "Come and sit."

"I just ran," I said, struggling to compose myself. After the run, sweat streamed down my neck, and I must look a mess.

“Hello, Laney,” Brody said, his voice lower than I remembered. He wasn’t all smirky and confident, as I’d expected. His eyes locked on mine, intense and unsmiling.

“Hi.” I gave a little half-wave.

His eyes never left mine. “How have you been?”

“Let me just go inside and grab you a place setting,” Mom said, pushing her chair back and patting the seat beside her.

“No, Mom, it’s okay. I’m not hungry. I need to shower.”

“Nonsense. Sit. I’ll be right there. I’m sure you have some catching up to do. I’ll be back in a jiffy.” She smiled and gave my hand a quick squeeze on her way past.

I shook my head, rolling my eyes at Brody as Mom closed the sliding doors behind her.

“Same old Blair,” he said with a chuckle.

Without intention, I felt the corner of my mouth start to twitch into an answering smile. What was I doing? My body had taken over, the muscle memory coming back like getting on a horse after three years instead of seeing the boy who had ripped my heart from my chest and eaten it raw.

"What are you doing here, Brody?" I asked, ignoring my racing pulse and facing him squarely. I planted my hand on my hip for good measure, hoping to come off as stronger than I felt. A new round of sweat broke out on my body as I looked at Brody sitting there in a sweaty old t-shirt, one leg sprawling from under the table. God, I still remembered the smell of his sweat, how much it turned me on. Those summer nights in the gazebo, how breathlessly and completely we'd given ourselves to each other…

"Just dropped by for a spell," Brody drawled, leaning back and resting his arm across the chair beside him, spreading out the way only a guy could. "Aren't you going to join me? You're not going to leave a guest outside by himself, are you now?"

There was the smirk, the one I'd seen on TV. Not in person—he hadn't been like that when I'd known him. Yes, he was gorgeous, but we'd been in high school. Even gorgeous guys weren't that confident in high school. Some pretended, but it was all a front.

"I wouldn't dream of it," I said, sweeping over and sitting down opposite him, crossing my legs primly. I would not be the one to back down.

"That's the Laney Tucker I know," Brody said, smiling bigger. "Always a lady."

I bit back a scoff and smiled demurely instead. I was rewarded for my efforts when I caught Brody's eyes following a bead of sweat as it trickled down the side of my neck, along my collarbone, and finally, down my chest, where it disappeared into my cleavage. I could practically see the bastard salivating.

So I *did* still have an effect on him.

"Y'all okay out there?" Blair called from inside the house, her voice getting louder as she approached the door.

"Listen," Brody said, leaning forward so quickly that my stomach dropped. "I want a chance to talk. When can we see each other again?"

"I don't know what ever you mean," I said, widening my eyes. "We're talking right now."

"Without your mother."

"Now, I don't think that would be appropriate, Brody Villines," I said. "Do you? What with us having the history we do, and me being an *enfiancéd* woman."

I almost laughed out loud at the shock on his face. It was almost too perfect. I'd fantasized about this moment more often than I'd fantasized about anything in my life. More than I fantasized about my fiancé, that was for damn sure. But in real life, things never worked out the way they did in fantasies.

Except this once.

Brody's mouth didn't literally fall open, but it might as well have. He recoiled as if slapped, his eyes narrowed, his nostrils flared, and the muscle in his jaw twitched as he clenched his teeth. His hands closed around the edge of the table, gripping so hard his knuckles went white, and for a second, I thought he might hurl his glass of freshly squeezed orange juice.

He got control of himself just as Blair appeared, and his face smoothed into its usual easy expression. God, I'd missed this boy.

He's not that boy anymore, I reminded myself. *He's a big star now, a player, a man-whore. A cheater.*

When my mother appeared, I slipped from the table. "Thank you, Mama," I said. "I'm just going to rinse off. It's unseemly to eat in such a state." I turned to Brody and offered him my most placid smile. "It was nice seeing you again, Brody. Have a good summer." With that dismissal, I turned, flipped my ponytail back over my shoulder, and walked into the house.

Laney Tucker, 1. Brody Villines, 0.

eight

Brody

After breakfast, I hung around only a few minutes, as it was apparent Laney would not be making another appearance. I said my goodbyes and started across the field on foot. Now that the morning's fleeting cool had worn off, the sun beat down mercilessly, and a sweet green smell rose from the grass as it warmed. If I'd been sure that no reporters would be sniffing around my place, I would have taken the road, which had some shade trees. But I wanted solitude. My old Hanes t-shirt wasn't exactly a brand name my manager would approve, and I'd been too distracted by my determination to see Laney to grab designer shades before leaving my house that morning.

The thought itself seemed ludicrous now, as I jogged along the trail, gravel crunching under my feet. What did the name on a pair of sunglasses matter when the only woman I'd ever loved was going to take someone else's name? I'd known she had a boyfriend off at school. Our mothers had remained friends even when we hadn't. But I'd always known that someday, I'd come home to Laney. That she would wait for me.

I'd never imagined her breaking my heart in return for the heartbreak I'd caused her. I'd never imagined that her revenge could be so cruel. Because it had to be that—it had to. She couldn't really love this clown, whoever he was. I was somebody, and who was this asshole? She'd couldn't feel about him the way she had about me.

The way she'd delivered the news was almost more heartless than the words themselves. It wasn't that she'd enjoyed watching my illusions shatter. That would have been better. At least then I would know for sure that she'd only done it to hurt me. That she still felt something for me. But she'd told me in such a calm, offhand way, as if she didn't for a moment consider how I would feel about it. As if that no longer mattered to her.

But it would. I would get her back. She wasn't yet married. I had to find a way to stop her before she made the horrible mistake. I had never stopped loving her, and I wasn't going to let her go until she loved me again, too.

* * *

As soon as I was through the door, my mother rushed out of the sitting room. “Brody, I’m so glad you’re home,” she said.

Instantly alerted by the choked sound of Virginia’s voice, I stiffened. “Mom, what’s wrong?”

“You’re grandfather—he—.” She stopped speaking, her breath hitching.

“Oh, Mom, I’m sorry,” I said, pulling her into a hug. Hugging was usually reserved for funerals in our family. “Is he…?”

She shook her head against my chest, then pulled away and dabbed at her eyes with a silk handkerchief. “He’s still with us,” she said. “But he’s had another stroke, and it’s… It’s not so minor this time.”

“Does Dad know?”

“Yes,” she said. “But he’s in Louisville. He won’t be home until the weekend.”

“Okay,” I said. “Let’s go see Gramps.”

She patted her eyes dry, took a breath, summoned some of her usual poise. “Not in those clothes,” she said. “Go and take a shower. You can't go running into a hospital looking like that."

"On it," I said, jogging up the stairs. I grabbed some slacks and a polo shirt, not wanting to dress too casually and piss off my mama. I didn't mind showing Gramps the respect he deserved. My grandpa had been as big a part of my life growing up as my own father. While my dad was often away on business, Grandpa Othal was always there, fixing things, taking care of his "little girl," a name he still called my mother to this day.

Even though he'd amassed a fortune as a producer in country music's early days, he came from nothing. At eighty, Gramps still knew how to roll up his sleeves and get under the hood of a car, could diagnose an engine problem by ear, and prided himself on having never had a professional oil change in his life. As a boy, I had looked up to my grandfather, with his big, firm handshakes and tough-guy attitude. He'd taught me to be a man.

After a quick shower, I got behind the wheel of my H2, and we went to see the man who had taught me to play the guitar and to get while the getting was good, encouraging me to pursue the opportunity Nash offered. Gramps had also been there to teach me to suck it up and not cry after skinning a knee—"put some salt on it"—falling from a tree—"rub out the sore spot"—or wrecking my bike—"if you can still move it, it ain't broken."

Now, life's problems were so much bigger.

nine

Laney

I didn't go back downstairs for breakfast until Brody was gone. I watched him out the window as he took off down the path, running like he had something to prove. He was probably just showing off, knowing that I'd watch from my window as I always had while he drew further and further away. A moment of nostalgia overtook me, and I had that same unbearable urge that I'd always had—to throw open my window, lean out and blow him kisses, call down that I loved him.

But the love was long gone, and the urge was just a silly moment of weakness. No, not weakness. Laney Tucker did not have time for weakness. This was a simple case of *déjà vous.* I turned from the window and descended the stairs to join my mother on the veranda.

"What are you doing having Brody Villines over for breakfast?" I demanded, placing a hand firmly on my hip.

"Oh, don't be so hard on him," Mom said, looking up from her gardening magazine. She'd put on her bifocals now that Brody wasn't around to notice she was getting older. It gave me a slight pang to see them. Mom had worn reading glasses for some time, but I'd never seen the bifocals. The sight of my lively mother wearing something I associated with the elderly tugged at my heart.

"I'm not being hard on him," I said, joining my mother at the table. Not every mom still made her daughter breakfast when she came home from college.

"Maybe a little," she said. "He may be famous, but he's still the boy you loved. If you talked to him, you'd see that. He's not so much different than when he left."

"I don't have to talk to him to know that he's not the person I loved. Not anymore. And even if he was, I don't love that person anymore."

Mom peered at me over the top of her glasses, an old habit from when she'd worn reading glasses only. "You can't change who you loved in the past," she said. "That can't be erased, no matter what happened afterwards. Cherish that memory, darling. If you're planning to go through with a loveless marriage, that memory is all you'll ever have."

I sighed. My mother was being unusually serious, but I wasn't falling for Brody the way my mother had. He may be able to charm the pants of every other woman in America—hell, in the world—but he couldn't charm me. Not this time.

"Mom. He cheated on me. Remember? I'll always have that memory, too."

"Of course he did," Mom said, flipping a page in her magazine. "You know what they say. Boys will be boys."

"Don't give me that shit," I snapped. "That's no excuse."

"No," she said, laying her magazine flat on the table. "Men are weak when it comes to temptation. And I doubt if he was the one doing the chasing. He's a star. And girls will be girls, too." She gave me a conspiratorial smile, the way she had all my life, whenever my dad said or did some asinine thing. It was a smile that said we were a team, me and my mom. An "us girls stick together" kind of smile.

"I don't buy it," I said. "He had a choice. He could have chosen to be faithful to me."

"True," she said. "But don't forget, you looked at him that way when you were teenagers and you heard him playing the guitar. You may not remember it, but I do."

"I get it," I said. "I was a stupid, gullible girl like every other girl he screwed over. Except I'm the one who's going to do something about it. For all of us."

"Oh, honey. Cut him some slack," she said. "He was a rock and roll star, on the road, alone. And he was barely more than a child. Men much older have done the same. Even country singers do it. Even when their wives are on the road with them." She gave me that no-bullshit look.

"He doesn't deserve my forgiveness," I said, standing. "But you're right about one thing—I couldn't have done anything about it. Cheaters are cheaters. If I'd gone with him instead of going to college, or if he'd turned down the band and we'd become an idiotic country duo, the same thing would have happened. I know it's not my fault, Mom. You don't have to tell me that."

"I know," Mom said lightly. "But I like to. Maybe one day you'll believe the rest of it, too."

Upstairs in my room, I dropped onto my bed and picked up my phone. Majesty, my father's beloved Maine Coon, lay on the floor at my feet, purring and digging his claws into my Persian rug. I called Piper and filled her in, then noticed I had a text from Paul. With a sigh, I opened it. We hadn't talked since I'd gotten home two weeks ago, and I really owed him more than an occasional text. But we didn't have flourishing conversations, and the feeling of obligation to call annoyed me.

If I wanted to marry this man, I'd have to learn to make those compromises, though. So I called, my mind drifting as he told me about his summer internship at a law office in Knoxville. I wondered what Brody was doing right then, what plans he had for the future. While he'd been in *Just 5 Guys*, it was easy to think of him as a permanent part of boyband culture. But now what? Surely he had some plans beyond bumming around his parents' house for the rest of his life, wallowing in vats of cash.

I realized the line had gone quiet later than I should have. "I'm sorry, what?" I said.

It struck me then that I really, truly did not care. "I think we have a bad connection," I said. "I didn't hear you. I'll call you later." I hung up the phone feeling both relieved and guilty. A bad connection was exactly what we had.

ten

Brody

After returning home with my mother, I needed to get out of the house. I needed to do something, to get my mind off my grandfather, lying in a hospital bed with the thin, threadbare blanket pulled up under his arms. Once, he'd seemed impossibly strong as he clutched my hand in a crushing handshake or turned a wrench under the hood of a car while I stood on the front bumper, watching, eagerly awaiting a turn.

Now, those forearms looked stringy and brittle, the skin spotted and delicate. His hands were gnarled in ways I didn't remember happening gradually. Granted, I hadn't seen my grandfather in a year, and probably hadn't spent much time looking at his hands. But now, suddenly, as if it had happened overnight, he was old.

I made my way through my mother's meticulously manicured gardens behind the house, wandering aimlessly down one path and another, going nowhere. Gramps had worked hard his whole life, but he never denied that luck had played a part in his success. It was his way of staying humble, of giving credit to God for working in his life. Without a lucky break, Gramps said, he would never have met Hank Williams, Sr, in his short life, and through him, gone on to make connections with dozens of other country legends.

When Nash had contacted me, Gramps had urged me to take the lucky break when it came instead of stubbornly holding to my own ideas of the future. Now, I was adrift.

What if I hadn't joined Nash's boyband? Without *Just 5 Guys*, I'd be nobody. Nobody but Laney's husband, probably. By now, we'd have a baby and another on the way, and Laney would be hating me because she'd never finished college.

I punched in the code at the back gate to leave the fenced portion of property around the house. For a while, we hadn't protected that gate since it was hidden from the road and quite a distance from photographers. But eventually, some crazy fan had found the gate, snuck inside, and taken pictures through the windows of my childhood home. After that, we'd installed a tall iron gate with a keypad.

When it swung open, I stepped through. Instead of following the trail all the way to the gazebo, I stopped at the row of weeping willows that had once served as the dividing line between the properties. Because the Villines's estate had ruined the aesthetic when we created the monstrosity of a brick wall around our house, like some kind of medieval castle, we apologized by giving the Tuckers all the weeping willow trees. I wouldn't have made that concession. The willows added ambience and would have added to the property value.

The Tuckers would have forgiven us eventually.

I chose my favorite tree, the largest one, whose branches draped all the way to the ground. Parting the curtain of branches and leaves, I slipped through and sat against the trunk, between two twisted roots that protruded from the ground slightly at the base of the tree. As children, Laney and I had played under these trees, had climbed into the branches, heedless of our mothers' warnings. The last time I'd been with Laney had been under this very tree, an urgent, breathless, almost desperate attempt to hold onto something that had already begun to slip away.

Not our love, but our innocence, our illusions. It was before our breakup, before I'd fucked anyone but her, but I'd let two of the baby-dolls grope me after a show. They'd refused to take my excuses for an answer, and after a while, I hadn't been able to keep their hands off my dick. I hadn't told Laney, but she'd already lost faith in my promises of fidelity. I'd sworn to myself it would never happen again, that I would hide out in my dressing room or my tour bus until they disappeared. I hated every one of them, hated that goddamn song, hated Nash and the songwriter and the rest of the band.

But the show went on.

I'd gone home to see Laney one weekend, a rushed visit where we barely saw each other after her drive up from school and my escape from prying eyes. When we'd managed to sneak away, we'd met under the willow tree. Even then, she must have known it was ending. I remembered the frantic way she'd undressed me, how she'd told me not to wear a condom. She wasn't the kind of girl who would trap me into marrying her, but in that moment, I knew that she'd been trying to hold onto me, have a piece of me that would last forever.

She'd cried afterwards as she lay in my arms. But she hadn't gotten pregnant. Shortly afterwards, she'd said it was over, and I'd gotten wasted and hate-fucked a baby-doll. And I hadn't stopped since. I wondered if my grandfather had done things like that in his day, as a producer. If he had known the temptations I would face, and if he was disappointed in me for not resisting. Othal loved Laney like his own granddaughter, having seen her almost every time he visited me since we were children.

I shifted against the rough bark of the tree, resting my head back against it and closing my eyes. In the distance, I could hear horses' hooves as they ran one of the fields, and in the tree overhead, the insects had begun to play their night song. The evening was dispelling the heat, covering the countryside in a warm, damp, oppressive stillness.

And then, cutting through the buzz-saw song of the crickets in the tree surrounding me, a horse's hoofbeats approached, pounding the earth until I could almost feel their vibration. I sat up, alert now. Had I fallen asleep thinking of that last night, and now I dreamed Laney was on her way?

When she stepped through the curtain of branches, I knew I wasn't dreaming. She was here, in the flesh, just as she had been that last night.

But this time, she didn't run to my arms and fall to the ground with me. She stopped short, a look of confusion flitting across her face before quickly disappearing. "You're on my property," she said frostily.

"Actually, I'm on your father's property."

She rolled her eyes. "Don't be a dick."

"You came all the way here to tell me not to sit under my favorite tree? I'm not the one being a dick."

"I didn't know you'd be here," she admitted. "I was just…"

A smile tugged at my lips. "Coming to sit under my favorite tree?"

"Not because it's your favorite tree," she assured me. "I didn't think you'd make yourself so at home on our property anymore."

"Grandpa Othal would never have given you all of them. Maybe half. Not all."

"Well, Grandpa Othal didn't have that hideous wall built around your place. You did."

It was true. Although we'd never hurt for money, Grandpa Othal wasn't famous. Sure, a few crazy country music fans might drive all the way out here to take a picture, but it was different than the kind of fame I'd achieved.

I sat silent for a minute, not sure if I wanted to tell Laney this news. But she'd hear it somewhere.

"He had a stroke," I said at last, picking at the bark on the protruding root.

"What?" Laney cried, her expression changing from confrontational to stricken. "Oh my God. How bad was it? Is he…?"

I shrugged, trying not to show that it bothered me, but something pulled tight inside me. Any other girl would have given an insincere, awkward condolence. But Laney knew me, and Othal, and what Othal meant to me. She understood exactly what it meant without me having to explain it.

"He's okay for now," I said after a pause.

“How okay?” Laney asked, inching closer. “Is he coherent? Can he talk? Is he… Paralyzed?”

“He’s not great,” I admitted. “But you know Gramps. He’ll pull through. He can make it through anything.”

“Brody…” Laney hesitated, then sank onto her knees beside me. “This isn’t anything. This is different. You can’t fight age.”

“He’ll be okay,” I said again, but this time, I wasn’t sure if I was trying to convince myself more than Laney. She wasn’t buying it. But I was still trying to.

“Is he home? I’ll go see him.”

“He’s at the hospital,” I said. “He’ll be home in a few days.”

Laney folded her legs and sat down in the grass. Her voice was softer this time, tinged with kindness. “Did the doctor tell you that?”

“I don’t remember.” I crossed my arms over my chest to keep them from reaching for her. She was so close I could have reached out and touched her, and I wanted to. Damn, I wanted to. To pull her into my arms and bury my face in her hair, to feel her soft hands moving up and down my back as she told me it was going to be okay. But I could no longer rely on her to reassure me when I needed it. I'd had her love, and I'd wasted it.

"Oh, Brody," she said, and she reached out and touched my knee. "I'm so sorry." Again, I thought I had to be dreaming. No way in hell was Laney Tucker ever touching me again. Not if she could help it. She'd made that abundantly clear.

None of this was real. It had nothing to do with me, and everything to do with her overreaction to the news about my grandfather. Death was literally the only thing that could convince her to touch me.

"Stop acting like he's dead," I said, shifting away from her. "I don't need your pity."

"It's not pity," she said. "I loved him, too."

I gave her a hard look. "Yeah, well, I still do."

"I didn't mean..." Her lovely, sweet face turned a little pink, and she shifted, curling her legs beside her on the sparse grass beneath the tree. When at last she met my eyes, I saw something there... Something... But I wasn't sure what. Once, I would have known, would have been sure.

"I didn't mean I don't still love him." Her voice was soft, but an edge of hurt and accusation colored it, and suddenly, I wasn't so sure we were talking about my grandfather.

"Then what?"

"I don't know." She shifted again, pulling her knees up under her chin. She wrapped her arms around her legs and stared off in the direction of Pegasus, who made a soft whinnying sound in the gathering dark.

"You taking him back?" I asked, nodding to the dark shape outside the curtain of leaves.

"I probably should," Laney said, unfolding herself and standing. She looked down at me, and again, that inscrutable expression crossed her face. When had Laney Tucker, as sweet and sure a thing as iced tea at her mother's house, become a mystery to me?

After a moment's hesitation, she turned and ducked through the curtain of willow, leaving me sitting alone again.

eleven

Laney

I took Pegasus's bridle and pulled his head down, resting my forehead against the bony ridge of his face. Closing my eyes, I ran my hands up and down his jaws, under the soft skin of his chin, along his neck. He stood motionless, absorbing my confusion and sadness. Othal Carter was a man to be reckoned with, a big personality with a big voice. He'd made big things happen for both his family and many others in country music. And he'd been more than generous with advice, sharing his connections and donating to local charities. He was the kind of guy people referred to as a "pillar of the community."

He wasn't dead, I reminded myself. Lots of people had strokes and went on to live long lives afterwards. But the shock of hearing that someone so respected and well-known in the area, someone larger than his own life, was laid flat in a hospital bed by something out of his control, had gotten to me.

And then there was Brody.

I knew I was treading dangerous ground, that I should swing back into Pegasus's saddle and ride home, leave him to himself. Because if I didn't, I might do something I'd regret, something that would ruin all my carefully laid plans. It had been all I could do not to wrap my arms around him, a memory burned into my muscles after twenty years of doing just that. Three years hadn't made my body forget.

But I was the master of myself, my body. I could keep it from doing the things it wanted to do—to be there for Brody, to comfort him and let him comfort me until we both forgot our sorrow and shock. And he was vulnerable now, malleable, despite the defensive act. This was the perfect opportunity to move forward with my plan, to get him on my hook.

A flare of guilt went through me, though. I couldn't take advantage of someone when his grandfather had just had a stroke, take advantage of his loss. Brody and his father had always had a strained, distant relationship. But he loved his grandfather, even idolized him.

Wasn't Othal the exact person who would say to strike while the iron was hot, though, to take advantage of a lucky break? Othal took care of his family, was always friendly and smiling at church picnics when he visited. But he hadn't gotten where he was by being a pushover.

Othal would have told me to go back under the tree and do whatever I had to do to get what I wanted. I knew from Brody's reactions that he wasn't going to chase me. I'd made it clear years ago that I wanted nothing to do with him, and he'd finally respected it. If I played hard to get now, he'd leave me alone. He thought that's what I wanted, that nothing had changed. I had to give him something first, to plant a seed of hope in him. Throw him the worm and let him swallow the hook before I reeled him in… And ate him for dinner.

I looped the reigns back around a bar on the gate, gave Pegasus a few more strokes, and turned to the tree once more. I wished I could see Brody behind the curtain of leaves, wished I knew if he could see me psyching myself up for this. But all I could see was the strands of leaves draped from each magnificent tree, could hear only the rise and fall of insect songs like a shifting wall of sound. With one more deep breath of the warm twilight air, I approached the tree again.

When I parted the hanging curtain, Brody was sitting just where I'd left him, with his head leaned back against the tree trunk and his eyes closed. For a second, I stood watching him, fighting my guilt at what I was about to do. Of course he deserved this. The fact that his grandfather lay in a hospital bed didn't excuse what Brody had done. It didn't make him less of a lying, cheating piece of shit. He'd done what he'd done, and he should pay for that, whatever state his family was in.

But he was so beautiful. God, he was beautiful.

I shook the thought away and approached, trying to hide the hard determination in my eyes. I didn't want to look like the wolf going in for the kill. I wanted to look like the sweet little lamb, harmless and innocent and dumb, just the way Brody had always seen me.

"Hey," I said softly, sinking down beside him.

"I thought you left," he said, but he showed no sign of surprise. He didn't even open his eyes.

"I just… I'm really sorry, Brody. I wanted to make sure you were okay."

"That's big of you."

"I know we ended on bad terms," I said. "But we've been friends our whole lives. You can't think that all just goes away."

Now he opened his eyes, turning to me with a bitter smirk. "You're saying you want us to be *friends*?"

"I never said I didn't want that. I can't hate you, Brody. Believe me, I've tried."

"So now you care about me?" he asked. "After avoiding me for the past three years, suddenly you want to be friends? What do you really want, Laney?"

I took a moment to compose myself. No, I wasn't the same girl Brody had cheated on and dumped. But he wasn't the same guy I had loved, either. As much as I'd changed in the past three years, he must have changed, too. I wasn't ready to excuse his behavior the way my mother had, but fame had to do funny things to a person's head.

"I don't want anything," I said. "I'm not one of those gold-digging girls you date."

His shoulders stiffened. "What do you know about it?"

I rolled my eyes. "Believe me, more than I want to. It's not like I could just forget you, the way normal girls do. I can't pretend you don't exist. You're on the TV, you're on the radio, you're at the grocery store, the drugstore, everywhere I go. There's your face on the front of some magazine, with some other girl. Do you think that's been easy for me?"

"It's not real," he said. "None of it's real, Laney. I haven't been with anyone else."

I bit back a cutting retort at his choice of words. I'd bet my very life that he'd been with plenty of girls, probably hundreds of them. In the very first month after the breakup, when I'd kept up with him partly out of habit and partly to torture myself, paparazzi had caught him 'canoodling' with a B-list movie star at a premier, 'cozying up' to one of Taylor Swift's squad in the VIP section at a club, and partying with the up-and-coming pop singer who had been opening for *Just 5 Guys*. The pain of it had been addictive, almost pleasurable, like worrying a sore tooth with your tongue.

That was when Piper had staged an intervention, and I had forced myself to turn off *Your Celebrity Eyes* and step away from the gossip magazines for a while. Just until I'd picked up the pieces of my shattered heart and cultivated the appropriate image. Suffering in silence, carrying on bravely and with ladylike composure like I was a fucking Kennedy or something.

"It was pretty convincing from the outside," I said after a short silence. Beyond the tent-like shelter of the tree, Pegasus snorted and stamped a foot, no doubt irritated by a horsefly.

"I'll tell that to my team," Brody said. "I'm sure they'll be thrilled to hear it."

"I saw an interview on one of the late-night shows."

"Yeah?" Instead of pushing me, he waited for me to speak. It was something he'd always done that I hadn't appreciated until I met Paul.

Paul was quick, impatient with those who weren't, and always asking *what, what, what?* If I needed time to think of an answer, he said I wasn't being honest. He wanted my gut response to everything, even the most thought-provoking questions. He'd wait three seconds, and then repeat the question, or say *Well? What do you think?*

When he'd proposed, he'd done the same thing. *It's a yes or no question, Laney. So what's it going to be?*

When Brody didn't press me, I went on. "You were talking about the popstar you were dating, I can't remember which one, but you were saying she really understood the pressures you faced because she had the same ones. And that made for a great relationship. Was it Selena Gomez? Amy Bedgood?"

He scooted up a bit, shook out his legs and adjusted his slacks. Even though he was sitting in the dirt, he hadn't changed into old jeans or sweats. He was still wearing what he must have worn to the hospital—designer slacks, an Izod polo. He looked good, too, with his shoulders filling out the polo shirt in a way I didn't remember them doing in high school. I had an absurd urge to reach out and squeeze his deltoids. Even brushing his knee earlier had ignited a spark inside me.

"You have to say that shit," he said. "They give my guys the interview questions ahead of time, and then my guys give me the answers. None of that's real."

"You can't even answer your own interview questions?"

He shrugged. "No. You're a pawn. Maybe some people, but Nash was meticulous about image. I don't think he even sleeps. He's like a telepathic vampire. I swear, if we were even out at the wrong place in the middle of the night, he'd be calling like, *What the fuck are you doing there? Get out of there. You don't go to places like that.*"

I didn't ask what places. I could guess well enough. Still, as much as I hated to admit that I cared, a seed of pride swelled inside me when he said no one else had taken my place. Sure, he was famous, and he could fuck whoever he wanted. But he'd never loved another girl. Maybe never even dated one—not in a real way. And even if he had, I knew without having to be told that he'd never felt about anyone else the way he felt about me. He never would. I was his first love, and more than that, the only girl who would ever date him for himself, not for "Brody Villines, Boyband Popstar."

Even if one day someone loved him for who he was, she could never separate the Brody Villines of *Just 5 Guys* from the one he'd been before the cameras, the fame, the fake shit that he'd only begun to explain before we broke up.

"Well, for what it's worth, I'm glad you never found anyone better," I said lightly.

"Better than you?" he asked with a little laugh. "Nah, Laney. That's not possible. There was never anyone even close."

"Good."

Our eyes locked, waiting for what came next. Waiting for the other to speak, to move. I could see the hunger in his eyes as they moved over my face, lingering on my lips. My lips, which he'd always said were irresistible. Remembering that, I let my lips part just the slightest. As if on cue, he leaned forward.

Hooked, I thought triumphantly, trying to drown the wave of heat that bloomed over my body at the thought of his kiss. His hand tangled in my hair as he drew me forward until our noses were beside each other, our lips just a breath apart.

"What are you doing to me, Laney?" he whispered, his hand tightening in my hair. "Are you fucking with me?"

Suddenly, I didn't know what I was doing. Inside my chest, my heart was pounding louder than a drum, drowning out the evening song around us. I couldn't swallow, couldn't breathe. I was caught. It had all slipped through my fingers in seconds. I'd been in control. Everything had been going according to plan. How had this happened?

"Let me go," I said, trying to pull away but only succeeding in pulling my own hair.

"Let *me* go," he growled back.

"I can't," I whispered, my voice catching. It was true. All this time, I'd never answered his phone calls. I'd avoided coming home when he was home. If I saw him, if I gave him the closure he deserved, I'd have to admit it was over and let him move on. And I couldn't do that. If I could have, I wouldn't be here now.

His lips grazed mine, his breath hot on my mouth. Without stopping to consult my brain, my mouth responded hungrily, pressing against his. "Then let me have you," he whispered against my lips. Then his mouth met mine again, his tongue tickling my lower lip before his teeth bit down lightly, stopping just before the point of pain. A gasp escaped me, and I pressed forward, melting into him instead of running away as I should.

That spark that the barest touch had ignited was now glowing, rekindled so many years after I thought it had died.

The heat inside me pulsed brighter as his tongue slid over my lip, pressing into me, pressing my lips open and entering my mouth.

My hands spread out across his chest, exploring muscles that were new to me. I could feel the pebbles of his nipples hardening through his shirt and an erotic charge shot through me, trembling in my lower belly. The heat inside me grew, almost painful in its intensity, the way a baby must feel upon seeing light the first time. I felt like that, brand new, burned clean.

Still gripping my hair with one hand, he raised his other hand to cradle my cheek, caressing my skin while his tongue explored me, teased me, until I couldn't help letting out a moan into his kiss.

I felt his body shudder in response, and he slid forward, wrapping me in his arms and lowering me onto the grass. Somewhere inside, a faraway voice was warning me to stop, that I needed to stop right this instant. But I couldn't. I clung to Brody, afraid he'd pull away at any moment, leave me to die of starvation for his touch. My insides were blooming with emotion, but all my body wanted was to revel in every stroke of his fingers over my skin.

He lowered himself with me, never breaking the kiss. Cradling my head, he deepened it, his tongue moving over mine, stroking it faster as our breathing mingled, coming faster now. I slid my hands down his body, over those broad shoulders, his shoulder blades, down the ridges of muscle on both sides of his spine. I couldn't get enough. Seconds later, my hands were under his shirt, against his warm, smooth skin. I sighed with pleasure at the sensation, so long forgotten, of touching a man's body. Heat bloomed between my thighs as my fingers explored his muscled body, his velvet skin.

He groaned into my mouth and nudged my legs apart with his knee, settling his body between my thighs. I gasped against his lips at the delicious pressure. He crushed my hips with his own until the seam of my shorts bit into my flesh. I arched up against him, craving more, even if it hurt. Hoping it hurt.

And then a thought billowed up from the depths of my mind, not a reasonable thought, because I was far beyond reason, but a memory. It bubbled up like a black cloud, filled with pain and betrayal. The memory of the last time we'd lain here, frantically devouring each other. The last time we'd been together, when I'd known something was wrong, even before the pictures came out, the pictures taken on the night when I'd called and called, torn apart with worry that he'd missed our video chat once again. The pictures of my drunk boyfriend and his friends hanging out, with girls all over their laps, their hands in places they had no business being.

Afterwards, I'd looked back on that moment under the tree and cried until I couldn't breathe, knowing it had already been over, even before I knew, before I had to say it. That last time, things had been different. He had been different.

Now I pushed him away, gasping for breath. In the darkness, I could feel his breath on my face, but I could barely make out his features, those strong bones and soft hair falling over his forehead, tickling my face. Tears threatened to burst forth from my eyes. I was out of control, everything spinning away from my grasp. How could I have been so stupid? How could I be lying under that same boy who had crushed my heart so thoroughly I'd never trust a man again?

"What about Paul?" Brody asked, his silky voice rough for once.

Sure, now he was concerned about cheating. Now he was worried about faithfulness, when it wasn't his to worry about. With a frustrated cry, I shoved him away, lifting my hips and rolling over, jumping to my feet before he could catch me.

"Nice of you to worry about my fidelity but not your own," I snapped before whirling around and storming out from the canopy of the tree. Outside, it wasn't quite so dark. Pegasus huffed his breath into the blue twilight, shifting toward me.

"Laney," Brody called after me, emerging from the tree. "That's not what I meant. But I'm not going to take what's not mine to take."

"Then it's your loss," I said, thrusting my foot into the stirrup after untying my horse from the fence. I swung up onto Pegasus and turned him down the trail toward home.

"Stop and talk to me," Brody said, stepping onto the trail in front of me.

"Fuck you, Brody," I said, shaking my hair back and nudging the horse forward. "I'm not Paul's to give. You should have taken what I offered."

"Laney," he said sharply, letting Pegasus step around him. "Can we talk reasonably? I'm not going to chase after you."

By now, he was calling after me as I urged Pegasus forward. "There's nothing to talk about," I called back over my shoulder. "Moment of weakness. Won't happen again!" I didn't know if he heard all that I'd said, because he really wasn't chasing after me, though he called my name one more time. That was fine. Let him call. Let him beg. Let him get so worked up that next time he *would* chase after me.

When I was halfway home, rounding the gazebo, I slowed Pegasus to a walk. I needed to clear my mind. That had all happened so fast, too fast. One moment I'd been set on my goal, everything going according to plan. The next, I'd been lying on the ground, ready to be the one begging for him. Just the thought of that hoarseness in his silky voice made me wet. I remembered that edge of desire well, the only thing that roughened the coveted silky strains of Brody Villines's voice.

That hoarseness meant one thing only, and I could not let that one thing happen. I'd kept Paul at bay for three years, and it had worked marvelously. Now I had a ring on my finger. If I refused Brody, gave him blue balls for a little while, maybe I could get him to trail around after me like a dog, the way Paul did. But I had to be careful with that, had to play him just right. Like Blair said, he had options. He might take his blue balls to some other girl for emptying.

Or I might give in. I squirmed in the saddle at the tangible memory of his body on top of mine, burning me up like a match to gasoline. I shivered, a delicious, giddy shiver. I hadn't accounted for that hazard.

I tamped down the thought fiercely, the sensations coursing through my body, burning through my veins. I was stronger than that, could control myself. I wasn't some dumb animal who couldn't control my libido. That's what Brody was. Not me.

Laney Tucker was poised, polished, and in control. I would never be the kind of person Brody was, too consumed by lust to control myself. I would never give in.

twelve

Brody

It had been two weeks since I had heard from Nash, and I'd started to relax about my future. Now that I'd been away from it, I realized exactly how exhausted I'd become over the past five years. Maybe Nash was right—he usually was—and I could use the whole summer off. Surely the world wouldn't forget me in three months. My shrink assured me as much, and even my agent had only given me two interviews, both over video chat.

And then there was Laney. Just thinking about that kiss made my head spin and my cock twitch. But it was too good to be true. I couldn't believe that Laney would want me back after what I'd done to her. The thing was, Laney wasn't the kind of girl who played games. She was smart as hell, not simpleminded, but the kind who liked things simple. Straightforward. So what had the kiss been about? Nostalgia?

A moment of weakness, she'd called it. Which meant that only by her own determination was she keeping herself from me. Pride and hurt might make her standoffish, but she still felt something for me. I was sure of it.

If I was a good guy, I would have walked away. I would have accepted that she was engaged to someone else, that she was going to marry that bastard and live happily ever after. If I was a good guy, I'd admit that maybe I hadn't changed so much in the three years since I'd broken her heart, and it was possible that I could break her heart again. Not in the same way—I had learned from my mistakes—but in some other way. If I was a good guy, her moment of weakness wouldn't give me hope. But I wasn't a good guy.

Amy Bedgood had told me that, right after she threw a bottle of Grey Goose at my head in a London hotel room. Laney was right about that interview. It had been Amy I was talking about. I might have even halfway meant it. We'd hung out a while, my blazing stardom supposed to dazzle the world into forgetting her stint in rehab. I still remembered Nash shoving her number at me. "Take her out a few times, but for fuck sake not to a club. She'll be passed out on the dancefloor in five minutes."

"I'm supposed to be dating this lush?" I had asked.

"I don't give a damn what you do with her," Nash had said. "Fuck her, don't fuck her, I don't care. But for fuck's sake wear a rubber if you do. You knock her up, and the baby's coming out pickled in vodka."

It was hard to forget that image.

My squeaky-clean reputation hadn't relaunched Amy into stardom as intended. Everyone loved to watch a train-wreck rise from the ashes, Britney Spears style. But they liked the train-wreck better. Amy had been fun, a lot of fun. What had started as a favor to Nash had become something almost real, or as real as any relationship I was allowed to have.

But a train-wreck by any other name was still a train-wreck. Eventually, it became clear that she wasn't ready for sobriety. *Just 5 Guys'* European tour ended, and I'd gone home. Still, she'd been fun for a while. Most of them were. Only Laney lasted longer than that, the notes of her song etched into every broken piece of my soul. A constant reminder of what could have been, what had been, before I'd fucked it all up.

Life could be good, if I could just figure out how to get back to the place where I'd gone wrong. I was determined to do just that. After spending the day writing a song, I called Nash. Of course, he didn't answer. He liked to do things on his own terms. By evening, I was pacing my room like a caged lion. I set my guitar in its stand and stood staring out the window, my hands buried in my hair. I couldn't leave now, not if there was a chance. Before I put my career on hold, though, before I risked throwing away everything I'd worked so hard for, I had to make sure.

From across the fields, I could feel Laney's presence, could almost smell her there, waiting for me. Calling to me. I had to see her. I'd been denying it for weeks, but I couldn't pretend any longer. I needed her, and if I didn't try now, it would be too late. This was my only chance, and I'd be damned if I was going to let some lame-ass college boy stand in my way.

That guy didn't know Laney like I did, didn't know the taste of her like the ocean, the salty wildness that even she couldn't tame. He didn't know the whisper of his skin on hers inside the song of a Kentucky night, with the grasses sighing in the fields that stretched to eternity around us. The siren song of her didn't call to his blood the way it called to mine, the music of Laney that only I could hear.

It was time I answered.

July

thirteen

Laney

I found Oscar in the stables, cleaning the brushes. "Good evening, *senorita*," he said when I walked in. "Nice day for riding, wasn't it?"

"Yes," I said. "Now that the heat's finally broken."

Though Oscar wasn't the best groom we'd had, my mother had saved his job more than once when my father tried to fire him. I had a pretty good idea that it was because of his penchant to work shirtless, and to call everyone *senorita* in his sexy accent. More than once, I'd caught my mother admiring the scenery from the veranda when he was outside spraying down the equipment with his brown skin shining in the sun, water droplets clinging to his shoulders, his tight jeans wet from the spray.

"Saying *buenos noches* to your horse?" Oscar asked.

"I think I'll take an evening ride," I said. "Saddle Pegasus, please. I'll be back in a few minutes."

"*Si, senorita*," Oscar said, giving me a little mock salute. I returned to the house, wishing I could ride now instead of doing what I was about to do.

To stall, I called Piper first. As usual, she gave me sound advice and encouragement, but eventually, I had to hang up and make the call I did not want to make.

Rationally, I knew I shouldn't make it at all. I should leave well enough alone. But I had never loved Paul the way he deserved. It had always been a plot, from the beginning, meant to lead me here, to this moment. After all, I'd accepted Paul's first invitation for two reasons—he was everything Brody was not, and he was infatuated with me. That would show Brody.

And now, I had something else to show Brody—how it felt to fall madly, irrevocably, shamelessly in love, only to have your heart wrenched straight through your ribcage, pinned to a billboard, and used for target practice.

But there were lines I was unwilling to cross, and cheating was one of them. If I was going to give Brody enough hope to fall in love with me, I might have to do things that would cross that line. I'd already done one thing. And though I did feel a little guilty about what I'd done with Brody under the tree the night his grandfather went to the hospital, I felt more guilty about how little guilt I felt.

That was what had sealed the fate of this engagement. Because I should have been wracked with devastating remorse. Our relationship had never been one that could devastate, but I'd thought my love for Paul would grow with time. But that wasn't fair to him. Once, when I had expressed my concerns about the imbalance of emotion between us, my mother had told me that it was more than fair. I got to marry a man with a good, stable, respectable job, who would never cheat. Paul got to marry a beautiful, intelligent, well-bred woman, the perfect accessory for a lawyer starting out at a new firm. "Honey, that's the way things have been done since the beginning of time," Blair had said. "You've got nothing to feel bad about."

I did feel bad, though. I'd felt more obligation to make my mother happy by getting engaged than I cared about making Paul happy. My mother had understood my choice to marry Paul, even if she preferred the cheating, lying manwhore next door. I suspected that mostly, Blair just wanted an excuse to throw a ridiculous party.

But I couldn't keep up the pretense any longer. It was one thing to mutually benefit from our relationship, as my mother had said, and another to cheat. No matter how little I loved Paul, I was never going to do to him what Brody had done to me. No one deserved that. And if I didn't do this now, I'd be no better than Brody. I needed to focus on Brody's downfall right now. Maybe, once I'd gotten Brody out of my system for good, I really could fall in love with Paul.

I hit the call button.

After three rings, Paul answered. "Hello?"

"Hey," I said. And I realized that's all I had to say to him. Even after a month apart, I didn't miss him. I wasn't bursting with things to tell him or dying to know what he was doing.

"What's up?" he asked. "How are you? Your parents?"

The longer I let the conversation go on without telling him the intent behind it, the worse I would feel. And Paul was not a southerner. He would appreciate my straightforwardness. "So, listen, I was thinking maybe we should take a break."

The silence stretched on and on. Five seconds, ten.

"Break off the engagement?" he asked after the eternity.

"Well. Yes and no."

"You can't have it both ways, Laney. Yes or no?"

This was what I hated about talking to him. How he made me feel stupid and scatterbrained. I knew what I wanted, but before I could articulate it, he jumped in. "So which one is it? You can't *sort of* break off an engagement. Once it's broken, it's broken. There's no halfway on this."

"I didn't say break up," I said. "I said maybe we should take a break. Take some time apart."

"We've been apart for over a month," he said. "I'm coming to stay next weekend. Remember?"

"Yes, I remember," I said. "That's why I'm calling now. I think you should… Not."

"Is this your mother's doing?"

I scoffed. "It has nothing to do with my mother."

"Are you sure? Because I know how you idolize her. Did she tell you I'm not good enough again?"

"She never said you weren't good enough," I said, my back stiffening. "I already told you that."

"I know, I know. It's my fault, like everything else, because I took it the wrong way."

"She said we all make compromises in a marriage. Both of us. Not just me," I said with as much patience as I could muster. We'd had this fight too many times.

"I'm not blind, Laney, and I'm not stupid. I know what she meant. You know what she meant. Everybody at that engagement party knew what she meant."

"Well, maybe she had a point."

"She had a point?" he asked. "So now you think you're too good for me? I thought we were on the same side here. A wife should always have her husband's back. I should have known better than to let you go home for the summer."

I drew myself up even straighter, as if he could see me. "Let me?"

"She's never appreciated what I can offer you," he said. "But I thought you had enough sense to make your own decisions."

"Oh, trust me, Paul. This decision is all mine."

"Spending the summer with your mother is obviously influencing you in a negative way. Otherwise you'd be smart enough to recognize this for the mistake it is. I hope you'll really think it through before you make this decision."

"That's what I'm trying to do," I said through gritted teeth. "That's what I called to tell you. I'm not saying never. I'm saying we take a break, and we'll talk again in... I don't know, another month. At that time, we can evaluate where we want to go from there." I was sure that Paul would appreciate my very practical proposal. Which just went to show that maybe I wasn't as smart I'd thought.

"I don't think so," Paul said coldly.

"You don't think we can talk in a month?"

"No. That doesn't work for me. I'm half of this relationship, so I make half the decision. And I don't agree to this separation."

I took a deep breath. I was shaking a little. I'd been prepared for him to fight it, but not quite so unemotionally. I'd thought he might beg a little, maybe even cry. He'd always held onto me when I was unsure, had always pleaded his case in his lawyerly fashion. But I forged onwards, jumping off the cliff without a parachute in sight. I hadn't been single for more than a month since I was sixteen. Maybe it was time.

I stood from where I'd been sitting on my bed, almost stepping on Majesty, who yowled a loud reminder at me. "Then I guess this is goodbye."

"No," he said. "I don't accept your terms."

"Don't be ridiculous," I said. "We're not married. You can't refuse to sign breakup papers."

"No, but I can refuse to accept your proposal for a separation," he said. "I'll be there next weekend. We can talk then, without your mother's interference. Then maybe I can talk some sense into you."

"Paul, I said no. I don't want to see you right now."

"We aren't going to be like your parents, where your mother has your dad by the balls. You might be just like your mother, but I'm not your father."

"You better not show up here," I said, pacing to the window. "Or you'll learn a thing or two about how fathers react to men who don't take their daughter's no for an answer."

Paul clicked his tongue. “Laney, Laney, Laney,” he said. “I expect more of you. I thought you could stand up for yourself, not hide behind threats of your daddy’s big gun. Such an antiquated tradition, from back when fathers owned their daughters’ chastity.”

“Don’t worry,” I said sweetly. “I know how to shoot Daddy’s gun, too. I hoped it wouldn’t come to that. I simply thought that maybe, since you didn’t respect my answer when I said not to come, that you might respect another man’s.”

“I respect your answers when they’re yours, not some silly idea your mother put in your head.”

“I never took you for the type who wouldn’t respect my wishes, Paul,” I said. “But now I see that you are. So I guess it’s a good thing we had this conversation. I’d hate to have married you before I figured it out. Then I really would have to accept your refusal of an amicable ending. As it is, you don’t have to agree. I haven’t promised you anything. I don’t owe you anything.”

“The ring on your finger tells a different story.”

“Come on, Paul, you’re in law school. You know that doesn’t count. An engagement isn’t legally binding.”

"You told me you'd save yourself for me."

I winced, remembering that conversation, how important it had been to Paul that I be a virgin before he gave me a ring. So I'd lied. At the time, I'd found him ridiculously stuffy and old-fashioned. Now I wondered if he wasn't just a controlling pig. Here I'd thought he was such a nice, logical guy. Our relationship was so different from mine and Brody's that he must be different from Brody. But he was just a different breed of asshole.

"I said a lot of things," I said, sinking to the edge of my bed and mindlessly stroking Majesty, who had made himself at home on my pillow. "But I thought it might be nice to reevaluate those promises before we put them in writing. And now I see I made the right choice. So thank you for that."

With that, I hung up.

Ready to get out of my room, but not for the reasons I'd expected, I jumped up again. Whatever my feelings for Paul, I'd thought I'd be wracked with guilt after the breakup. Instead, I was furious.

I threw on a pair of jeans, knowing I'd need a longer ride tonight. I was in no mood to play games with Brody, so I didn't bother with makeup or even brushing my hair. I'd had enough of men for the day.

When I entered the stables, Oscar was on his way out. I'd taken longer than expected with my phone call. "*Buenos noches, senorita,*" he said, giving me an oddly shy smile. Coming from a guy who looked the way he did, I always found that smile unexpected and adorable.

I gave him a polite smile. "Goodnight. Thanks for getting Pegasus ready. I'll put him up."

"Of course," he said, but he looked very confused as I passed him. I was aware of him lingering in the doorway, as if unsure if he could go home now that I was there.

Pegasus's stall was empty, so I turned to scan the stable to find where Oscar had hitched him. I couldn't have missed him tied to the hitching post outside, and he usually didn't put him in the corral when I was about to ride. "Where's Pegasus?" I asked, turning to Oscar, who looked panicked and guilty at once.

"I thought you must have meant to go riding with your friend," he said. "He came by just as soon as the horse was ready. I asked if he wanted to wait for you to come down and join him, but he said no."

"What friend?" I asked, my voice brittle.

"Mr. Villines," Oscar said. "I'm sorry, *senorita.* He told me you were expecting him. I can saddle one of the others, if you would like."

"Yes, please do that," I said. "I'll wait."

"I'm very sorry, Miss Laney."

"It's fine," I said. "It's not your fault. In the future, please phone up or text me, not my parents, if anyone asks for Pegasus while I'm home."

"Of course, Miss," he said, lifting a saddle from its hook. I could see why my mother liked to watch him work. He really was nice to look at.

I had too many other things on my mind to pay much attention, though. I needed to ride, to really go, to clear my mind of the swirl of emotions for a while. Of course, just when it looked possible, Brody Villines had stolen my horse, forced his way into my thoughts once more. I was supposed to be thinking over Paul's words, not dwelling on the distant past. But as I set out across the pasture on Thunder, my father's prized black stallion, I couldn't shake my fury and indignation.

He had some nerve coming by now and messing with my head. I was supposed to be relaxing at home for the summer, deciding where to travel on my year off. Brody had come home and ruined it all, getting back under my skin like he had all those years ago, reigniting a fire in me that I'd thought was dead forever. Maybe I'd never gotten rid of it. All these years, it had lain forgotten under the ashes, a coal waiting to burst into flame the moment Brody breathed life back into it.

Or maybe it was just dormant, like a bad case of herpes. Once you had it, you couldn't get rid of it.

Brody had some nerve coming by the house, charming my mother, and God—kissing me again! How had I let that happen? As if I'd forgotten what he'd done. Like he'd never chosen an endless supply of groupie pussy over me. He had some nerve coming along and taking my horse, my only comfort, without even asking, stealing it out from under my nose. It looked like he was ready to play games, too.

It was time for me to take things up a notch.

fourteen

Brody

I was ready for her when she came. When I heard the horse's hooves from far off, I smiled. I still knew Laney well enough to know she'd come looking for her horse. And she knew me well enough to know that I'd be waiting for her at the gazebo. She came thundering up on a black stallion, her blonde hair whipping behind her, like a warrior queen in a fairytale.

I was ready to battle Laney Tucker if her heart was the spoils of war.

"You stole my horse," she snarled at me, swinging her leg over and dismounting in two seconds flat.

"I had to get you out here somehow. You haven't answered my more polite requests to see you."

"Fuck you, Brody Villines."

"I hope you will," I said, smirking at her as she leapt forward, shoving me in the chest. I caught her elbows.

"Never," she growled. "You're probably carrying all kinds of diseases."

"Never say never," I said, pulling her closer.

"I said never."

"You know it's going to happen," I said. "Why are you fighting it so hard?"

"Because you're an asshole," she said, her face losing some of its fury. Her lip trembled, and her voice came out quieter with the next words. "Because you broke my heart."

She may have spoken softly, but her words were a devastating blow.

"I'll never do it again," I swore, my hands moving up to grasp her upper arms.

"What happened to *never say never*?"

"Give me a chance," I said, coaxing her forward. "One chance. I promise you, Laney Tucker. I'll be the best thing that ever happened to you."

"You're already the worst."

"Let me make it right." I drew her in, my eyes on her baby blues.

"Why should I?" she asked, her voice still edged in resentment.

"Tell me you don't remember how good we were together," I said. "Tell me you don't want me anymore, and I'll walk away and never talk to you again. You can go and marry that idiot from school, and I'll send you a toaster."

"I don't want you," she said, but her eyes were pooling with moisture.

"You're lying."

Her pillowy lower lip quivered, and I wanted to lean in and bite it. "You lied to me," she whispered.

"I'm sorry, Laney. I'm so fucking sorry." I eased forward, waiting for her to pull back, to spit in my face, to crush my balls with her knee. But she didn't. Her eyes dropped closed, and I tilted her chin up, my lips caressing her trembling ones. A single tear ran down her cheek, and I stopped it with a kiss. It awakened my hunger for the taste of her, the whole ocean between those thighs.

"I love you," I whispered, my mouth finding hers again, pressing harder. Her lips parted, and my tongue slipped between, slowly this time, drawing her back from the edge. She responded, stepping closer, so our bodies melded together, and her hands found my hair. Her thumb stroked my cheek while her fingers tickled at the back of my neck.

Securing her body to mine, I took a step back, pulling her toward the gazebo. The night sounds swelled around us, urging me on. Wordlessly, she followed, never breaking the kiss until we reached the step up to enter the place where we'd first played as children and then met as lovers.

When she hesitated, I bent and scooped her into my arms, carrying her over the step and inside, where I laid her down on the wooden bench.

"Brody," she whispered, her fingers trembling as they stroked my cheek. "What are we doing?"

"Remembering," I said, lowering myself onto the bench, careful not to press her into the hard wood beneath her back. "Tell me you remember."

My hands cradled her head, my eyes searching hers for a clue, a sign. I tasted her mouth again, pressing my tongue into her deeply this time. She clutched at my shoulders before sliding her hands down my back, pulling me closer still, until I could feel her soft tremble belly under my taut abs.

"Tell me you do," I said, pulling away and smoothing her hair back from her forehead.

"I remember." Her eyes were vulnerable, almost afraid. I reached for the button on her jeans, opening it with one hand while I held myself up with the other, wanting to crush myself into her but holding back.

"I remember, too," I said. "I remember everything, Laney. I've never forgotten a single moment we shared. Have you?"

"No," she breathed.

"Tell me you still want this." I slid down her zipper and touched her, pressed my fingers to the hot pulse of her clit. "I can feel it," I whispered. "I know you still want it."

"I do," she gasped as my cheek brushed hers. I pulled my hand away, not wanting to lose control and waste the chance, to have it end too quickly. Laney dropped her head back, letting my lips trail over her throat and back to her mouth. I sank my tongue into her mouth, devouring the kisses I'd needed for so long without knowing it, without believing I could have it again. Without daring to believe.

I kissed her until I was drunk with it, until her intoxicating scent made my senses disappear and all I could do was breathe her in like I hadn't tasted oxygen in three years. I kissed her until there was nothing but her, and me, and the summer night over us like a curtain.

I didn't stop until she pulled back, her lips swollen, her eyes blurred with desire. "Touch me," she breathed.

I sat up and tugged her jeans down over her hips, pulling of her boots with them. They clattered to the gazebo floor. Her mouth drew me back, hungrily devouring me as her hips pressed up against me, begging for my touch.

Wrapping my arms around her, I stood and lifted her onto the railing. "You're still my girl," I said, spreading her knees. "You've always been my girl, Laney Tucker. You always will be." I peeled off her shirt and then my own, wanting to feel her skin against mine.

She pulled at me, tugging at my shoulders. I held back and undid her bra, drawing it over her arms before stepping forward and pressing my bare skin to hers. Our heartbeats intertwined, weaving together into an old, familiar rhythm.

"Touch me," she whispered again.

My fingers skimmed the silken skin of her inner thighs, then pressed against the wet fabric of her panties between them. I worked my fingers against her for a few seconds before tugging her panties aside. A sharp, shuddering inhalation sounded as I stroked her swollen clit, and her nails dug into my shoulders. I slid my finger lower, finding her slippery opening and sinking a finger deep inside her. Fuck, she was so tight I wanted to feel her take my cock. She gave a shuddering cry, spreading her legs for me.

But when she reached for my belt, I pulled away and knelt between her knees. I'd been waiting for this moment for three years. I didn't want to rush it. She wasn't one of the baby-dolls. She was the girl I'd been dreaming of every day since I lost her. I intended to savor her like the delicacy she was.

My lips moved from her knee, tracing along one thigh and then the other, pulling lightly at her soft skin, until I found her center, her flesh softly pulsing under my tongue. Without knowing it, I had been waiting for this every night I'd been without her. She was my addiction and my savior from it. Everything I needed was right here. Nothing else mattered, nothing else existed. I sucked gently at her, then slid my tongue into her, electric with the sensation of her fingers clenching in my hair, her nails raking across my scalp, her thighs trembling.

Her hand circled the back of my head and she pulled me in, burying my face in her cunt. I pushed his tongue deeper, savoring each taste as she gasped more quickly, coming closer, coming closer, coming…

She cried out and clutched me to her, the pulses against my mouth and the rush of her cum almost enough to drive me over the edge. I tasted the ocean and the whole world in her cunt, the sweetness, the wildness, the awe.

When she finally let me go, I stood and pulled her closer, my mouth finding hers. "Laney," I whispered into her hair. "I didn't know how much I needed you until you showed me."

"Shhh…" She covered my mouth with her fingertips. "Let's not talk more tonight. We've done enough talking for now. Let's just be here, together, like we used to be."

Sweeter words, I'd never heard spoken. I kissed her mouth, her temple, trailing my lips over her ear. "You can run away from me, you can ignore me, but I'll always come back to claim you," I whispered. "Always."

Her body shivered against mine, and she arched her back as my hands moved down her bare skin to her hips. I rocked her forward against me as my lips scattered kisses down her neck.

"Promise?"

"I promise."

This time, when she reached for my zipper, I let her undo my jeans. She guided me to her opening. But when she pressed me against her slick entrance, I paused, not sure I could control myself more than a minute or two, like our first time, when the feeling of being inside her had overwhelmed me. But I wasn't some sixteen-year-old virgin now. I could show her what she'd been missing. I ran my hands over her body, marveling in her soft skin while she squirmed for more. Leaning in, I brushed my lips over hers, my hand cupping her breast.

"I want you inside me," she whispered, tilting her head back so my mouth could move over every inch of her throat while my fingers squeezed her nipple gently. She gasped and arched against me, reaching down to guide me in. Slowly, I began to push into her impossible tightness. She sucked in a breath when I breached her opening and she swallowed my tip. I bit my lip, hard, to hold back. The sound of her gasping breaths reassured me, and I pushed a little deeper.

"Wait," she whispered. "Hold still." Gripping the railing, she lifted herself and slowly lowered onto my cock, sinking further and further until I was buried in her. Her legs circled my waist and she threw her head back and braced herself on the railing. "Now," she gasped. "Now."

I began moving, slowly at first, taking my time with her. Her thighs flexed around my hips, and I moved faster, faster, driving into her tightness until she adjusted to my size, her wetness coating my cock and letting me move more easily. I gripped her hips and slammed into her harder, harder, until she threw back her head again and let out a wild cry that almost did me in. Her walls gripped me tighter as her back arched and helpless cries slipped from her lips into the blackness above as she came. Again, I held back, the throbbing inside her too intense to give up.

When the pulses subsided at last, she sat upright, draped her arms around my neck and kissed me. "Wow," she breathed. "That was amazing."

That was all I needed, the only person who ever needed to tell me that. I didn't need any of the other girls, the money, the fame. All I needed was Laney, and she was mine at last.

"Now you," she said.

"You again," I said. "One more time."

This time, I lay her on the bench, just the way I remembered doing when we'd been teenagers. I kissed her eyelids, her cheeks, moving slowly inside her now that some of our passion had been dispelled. More than anything, I wanted to make it last, make her remember this night forever, the same way I'd remembered the first time. So I made love to her slowly, tenderly, watching her face, tasting her lips, running my fingers over her smooth skin. I came with the taste of her still on my tongue.

Afterwards, we lay in a tangle on the grass outside the gazebo. Laney lay on me, her head resting on my chest, as my heartbeat slowed to normal. I stroked her hair, now a tousled mess, and drew in a breath, savoring the scent of our sweat mingling with the scents on the night—the dewy grass, the horses, the Kentucky earth around us.

It was just like it had been before the band, before all of it. Just us, in the night, with the stars above and the rolling, grassy fields stretching out around us. In that moment, I knew that I didn't need to call Nash again. I had all I had ever wanted right there already.

fifteen

Laney

I was fucked. Here I'd made all these plans, spent all summer formulating my revenge, and now I'd ruined it all. What was it they said about best laid plans? Here I was, lying on Brody Villines's hoodie in the grass, staring up at the millions of diamonds sparkling in the big star-strewn sky, my head pillowed on his arm.

"Remember the first time we came here?" Brody mused. "I'd come all the way to your house to throw pebbles at your window. I thought I was so romantic. Until we got back, and your dad was waiting up for us." He chuckled and turned toward me. "I was so scared I thought I'd piss my pants. I thought he'd shoot me for sure."

"He wasn't mad at me," I said smugly. "He sent me to my room, but I wasn't even grounded."

"Are you sure? He called my parents, got them up out of bed in the middle of the night. I was grounded for months."

“Oh, I’m sure I had to beg Daddy and tell him how sorry I was,” I said, smiling at the memory. “And promise never to do it again.”

“But here we were, the very next night.” His eyes grew serious, and he stroked my cheek. “Nothing could keep me from you.”

“And that time your mom caught us in your room,” I said, stifling a giggle.

“Almost caught us,” he said. “You hid in my closet.”

I laughed, thinking back to all the nights I’d snuck out. Blair had caught me sneaking back in one morning at dawn, but she hadn’t done anything. She’d shaken her head and said something about young love. If only she had stopped me, maybe I wouldn’t have gone on to have my heart shattered into a million shards like a crystal vase.

But no, that wasn’t fair. I would have found a way to keep seeing Brody if I had to break out of a prison to do it. He was right—I was his, and I always had been. He was under my skin, in her blood, smeared on each of those million pieces of my shattered heart. He was inside me, my weakness, the one thing I couldn't resist. Even when I turned away from him, ran away, he could lure me back with one crooked smile.

I'd tried to fight it all these years, because somewhere deep inside, where only Brody could touch me, I'd always known it. I'd known that I wouldn't be able to resist, so I'd avoided him. And now that I couldn't, he'd proven it. No matter how strong my resolve, I was helpless when it came to him. He tore down all my defenses, each and every wall, and claimed me for his own.

And what a reclamation it had been.

* * *

Later, I sat on my bed, a tray balanced on my lap. On the tray sat a mug of foamy cappuccino, decaf, three blackberry shortbread thumbprints, and my phone. The midnight coffee-and-video chat date had become a tradition for Piper and I our freshman year of college, when Piper had her first real boyfriend. In high school, she'd been too busy and focused for a boyfriend.

"So, what's on the agenda for tonight?" Piper asked, her face blurring as she adjusted her laptop for the video chat session ahead. She snuggled down into the mountain of pillows she'd made at her headboard and smiled teasingly. "Any new Brody gossip?"

I considered hiding what had happened for about one tenth of a second. Yes, I was so ashamed of it I'd actually considered flaying myself as penance, but Piper was the one person in all the world I trusted enough to share my most humiliating moments, like when I'd gotten my period on the bus to church camp and bled through my white shorts.

"I ruined it all," I blurted out. As I spilled the story, Piper nodded sympathetically and sipped her coffee, certainly not decaf. Piper lived on coffee and seemed to be one of those rare superwomen who needed almost no sleep.

"Do you still want revenge?" she asked when I had finished the story.

"Of course I want revenge," I said. "More than ever. I can't believe he wore me down again. I swore I'd never even speak to him again. I'm so weak."

"Maybe it could work to your advantage," Piper said. "Maybe you've got him hooked now."

"How? How do I have him hooked? I already gave him what he wanted."

“What do *you* want, Laney?” Piper asked, sliding a hank of red hair back over her shoulder. “I mean, what’s your end game?”

“My end game is to destroy his life the way he destroyed mine,” I said fiercely. “He can’t just do that to girls and get away with it. Someone has to teach him a lesson. And you know it’s not going to be one of his groupies.”

“And you’re sure you don’t like him anymore?”

“Yes, I’m sure. He’s disgusting. Oh, God, but he’s so sexy.” I groaned and shoved a cookie into my mouth.

“I still think, if you’re sure that’s what you want, it could work to your advantage,” Piper said. “Now he’s had a taste, make him want more. You know he’s always been crazy about you. Y’all are perfect together, and he knows it.”

“Maybe,” I admitted, remembering the way Brody had held me in the grass afterwards, told me he loved me. Surely he didn’t do that with his fangirls. This wasn’t a part of my plan, but that didn’t mean I had to give up entirely. Maybe it could be salvaged. I’d have to play it even more carefully now, though, do everything I could to speed things up. I’d already gone miles beyond the line I’d sworn to never cross. Now, I was in too deep to stop, to abandon the whole plot. If I did that, I was just one more sucker who fell for Brody Villines's twisted smile and lying eyes.

sixteen

Laney

I managed to avoid Brody for the next few days while I regrouped. Sunday morning, I joined my parents at the little country chapel with a belfry on top that I'd gone to all my life. I'd been baptized beside this very building, and I knew everyone in congregation by name. We stood around talking for a few minutes as people greeted me and asked about school, the weather in Memphis, my sorority, the Tigers, and the Grizzlies. After the usual pleasantries, I made my way inside and sat in the familiar pews while my father, one of the deacons, greeted people on their way in.

Someone slid into the seat beside me, and my skin prickled with heat before I even turned to see Brody giving me that panty-dropping crooked smile.

"What are you doing here?" I asked through clenched teeth, turning back to stare straight ahead.

"This is my church, too."

"I'm surprised they even let you in after everything you've done."

"Good thing they don't know," he said with a grin.

"This isn't funny," I hissed. "You can't be here."

"Can we talk about what happened the other night?" he asked, lowering his voice to that silky purr that made my knees threaten to clench.

"We're in a *church.*"

"So?" he said. "It's not a sin if I'm gonna marry you."

"You're not going to marry me, Brody," I said, but my heart was pounding. This was it, everything I'd always wanted. Although, I'd wanted it for different reasons back when we were together. Now… It was so easy I wondered if he'd figured me out, if he was playing me right back.

"If I have anything to do with it, I am," he said, taking my hand. "I meant what I said. I love you, Laney. I've always loved you. I know I made mistakes, but I'm going to keep trying, keep making it up to you, until you forgive me."

"Stop lying to me. If this church had holy water, it would be boiling right now." I tried to pull my hand from his, but he gripped my fingers and refused to let go.

"Too bad it doesn't have holy water," he said. "Because then you'd see that I mean every word I'm saying. I'm not lying. You're going to be my wife one day, Laney Tucker. I promise you that."

"What makes you think I'd want to marry a cheating bastard like you?" I asked, just as my mother appeared in the doorway.

"That's no way to talk to a fellow parishioner and neighbor," Brody said, scooting closer so that Blair could squeeze in next to him.

"Well, hello there, Brody," she said, giving him her big, mischievous grin. "Isn't this a nice surprise."

"Laney was just saying the same thing," Brody said, gripping my fingers even tighter, until I was wincing. "Weren't you, baby?"

I relaxed my hand in his and smiled adoringly at him. "Of course I was."

"I wouldn't expect anything less," Mom said, arching an eyebrow at me. She must have seen the hand holding. As Brody's hand relaxed around mine, I tried to calm the fury in my mind. Yes, I'd made an unplanned detour. But it could still work out. In fact, it was working out perfectly. I just needed to go along with it, pretend it was mutual, until he was in too deep to back out. Not a wedding, but maybe an engagement, if he asked me properly.

I couldn't have asked for things to work out better. Brody hadn't just fucked me. He'd shown up at church the next Sunday and sat with me. That was what I wanted, his groveling, his commitment. I just had to remember that it was all staged, that it wasn't real. Brody was falling for me so easily it almost took the fun out of it.

I had to remember that at any moment, it could all fall apart. Just because it was easy now, that didn't mean I could get comfortable. If I slipped and showed my hand, he would win. He'd leave with another notch on his belt and that smug smile on his face, knowing he'd gotten what he wanted one more time, and I'd gotten nothing.

But as he stroked my hand, sliding the pad of his thumb between each of my fingers, I had to scold myself for the thoughts entering my mind in a church. This was worse than him finding out I was playing him. This was something too close to what I'd felt before, what I'd felt again the other night.

No, I reminded myself sternly. *That was only lust.*

I'd had to give him something to get him hooked on me again. One night, and he was already talking about marriage. So maybe it hadn't been a mistake. It had gotten him where I wanted him. The only danger now was keeping myself in check. The moment I started to believe his lies, started to trust him, to feel anything in return, it was all over. I would not let that happen again.

Now I just had to get a real proposal out of him. If he really meant it, he'd have to ask, and I'd have to say yes. So I'd do whatever I had to do to make that happen. To bring him to his knees in an even grander fashion than I'd planned. A public humiliation. It was almost like he was taking my plan a step further than I'd taken it myself. That was fine, though. When it all came crashing down around him, it would only make my victory that much sweeter.

* * *

Brody

When I rose from the pew, I had to adjust my trousers so I wasn't walking around startling all the older ladies in their Sunday best. It was the kind of church where women still wore hats, where people stood around on the lawn afterwards, chatting and inviting the pastor over for lunch. As I followed Laney out, my eyes lingered on the curve of her hips, the roundness of her ass, and I remembered gripping it as I thrust into her.

With some satisfaction, I saw that she was walking a little funny, too. I'd noticed her squeezing her knees together in there when I slipped my thumb between her fingers, into the soft flesh of her palm. Something as innocent as holding hands became erotic with her. She wasn't the sweet, passive girl I remembered. She was even better. Now she was feisty, passionate, driven and stubborn, but I knew that sweetness still lingered somewhere inside her. I just had to get deep enough inside her to reawaken it. I was up for the challenged.

As we emerged into the baking heat of summer, I saw a couple missed calls from Nash on my phone, and suddenly, it felt like I was looking at a call from the wrong number. In the midday Kentucky sun, my world seemed small and simple, and the days of waking up hungover and unable to remember the things I'd done with strangers the night before seemed like another lifetime. I was too close to getting Laney back to worry about Nash right now.

While my own parents were accepting condolences from well-wishers who had heard about my grandfather's stroke, Blair hung on my arm. I hadn't been to church since I'd come home, and people crowded around to see the prodigal son, returned at last. When I finally broke away, I couldn't find Laney's car among those left.

My phone buzzed with another incoming call from Nash, but I rejected it for now, smiling to myself as I thought of Laney leaving without a goodbye. She was jealous of all the attention I was getting, much more than she'd gotten when she came home from school. But she couldn't blame people in a small town for being excited to have a star in their midst.

As I walked to my H2, I spotted two preteen girls surreptitiously taking pictures of me from inside their car. I grinned and jogged over, watching the girls inside squealing and grabbing each other as I approached. I tapped on the window, and one of the girls rolled it down, her round, pimply face going red all the way to the ears. "Want a picture with me?" I asked.

After they were done taking a dozen selfies with me, I headed for my vehicle, turning to blow the girls a kiss. They shrieked so loud I could hear them across the parking lot. Granted, it was a pretty small parking lot, but I was happy to make their day. They'd have something to brag about when school started, maybe even to propel them into popularity. Not every girl had a picture on her phone of Brody Villines with his arm around her.

My phone buzzed again, and I sighed and answered at last. Nash was a persistent little bastard, I'd give him that. "Hey, Nash. You do know it's Sunday, right?"

"What's that got to do with anything?" Nash asked in his barking voice. "You at a funeral or something?"

"I'm in the south," I said. "And in the south, we go to church on Sunday."

"While you're down there trying to save your unsalvageable soul, other people are wheeling and dealing. And I got you a deal."

"Really?" I asked, stopping short beside my H2. "A solo album?"

"Just like you wanted," Nash said. "I got you a studio in Chicago to record. Then I'm thinking small American tour, and if it takes off, we'll add some more dates, maybe extend it for an extra leg or two. Then we'll talk about international, but I don't think it's going to happen for this one. I liked your EP idea. The tour can be a smaller, more intimate experience. Get those girls in there close to you, where they want to be. They'll pay the big bucks for that. We'll start recording next week."

"Next week?" My mind returned to the night with Laney, and my cock stirred inside my slacks just thinking about it.

"That's what I said. I'll send you over the contract tonight."

"But—I haven't written enough songs."

Nash laughed. "You don't write songs, Brody. You stand up there and look good while you sing them. That's your job. I've already got a songwriter, and we've got some songs that'll be great for your new solo persona. A definite break from the boyband. Show your maturity a little. You're all grown up now, Brody-boy."

I felt the familiar frustration set in, the helplessness, the loss of control.

"I don't think I can do that," I said. "I have some things in the works here."

"What things?"

When I didn't answer, Nash said, "Are you working with another manager?"

"No, nothing like that," I said. "Personal matters."

Nash laughed, his barking ha-ha laugh. "A girl, Brody? You know that's not how it works."

"No, that wasn't how it worked before. I call the shots this time."

"I don't think so," Nash said. "Be in Chicago next week or it's the end of your career. I didn't waste the last month lining this up for a no-show. If you aren't there, someone else will be."

"I could find another manager."

"And I could find twenty more Brody Villineses. I'll see you next week." Without waiting for an answer, Nash hung up. I tossed my phone in the passenger seat and jumped up into the Hummer. How was I going to break this news to Laney?

seventeen

Laney

I stood before the mirror, adjusting my sundress and checking my hair. I couldn't decide if the dress was too much. I wasn't the kind of girl who would ride a horse in a dress, but then, I'd done a lot worse things for Brody. Even after that morning, I'd been surprised to get his text, asking me to meet him under the tree. I didn't have to ask which tree.

I'd made him wait until evening, telling him it was too hot during the day. But now I'd run out of excuses. It was time to make him beg, make him crazy for me. Deciding the dress would work for that purpose, I turned from the mirror and headed downstairs.

"Going out?" Blair asked when she emerged from the house.

I turned to where my mother was trimming the rose bushes along the walkway. "I thought I might take an evening ride."

"Going to be out late again tonight?"

My stomach tightened. So, my mother had heard me come in the other night. If she knew where I had been, she wasn't giving it away that easily. Instead, she offered me a placid smile. But her eyes took in my sundress before going back to her pruning shears. Mom knew I was not the kind of girl who rode horses in a dress as well as I knew it.

"I won't be gone long," I said, returning my mother's smile. "Did you need me home for something?"

"Oh, no," she said. "Take your time."

I turned to go to the hitching post, where Oscar was brushing Pegasus, shirtless as was his custom when Mom was outside. I'd never been sure if anything had happened between him and my mother, or if he was simply indulging her fancy.

"Is he ready?" I asked.

"*Si, senorita*," Oscar said, stepping back. Pegasus swung his head around and nuzzled me, snuffling at my hands for a treat.

"Sorry, boy, I didn't bring you anything," I said. He huffed against my shoulder and tossed his head. I smiled and took Oscar's hand as he helped me into the saddle. When he'd handed me the reigns, I squeezed Pegasus with my knees. He started off for the gate, which Oscar ran ahead to open. I walked Pegasus for a few minutes, then nudged him into a trot. When he was warm, I leaned forward and gave him his head.

Pegasus liked to run, and I liked the rhythm of his hoofbeats and the wind in my hair. The warm evening streamed past, fireflies dancing over the swaying grasses, the buzz and shriek of insects all around us. When I came into view of the wall—a hideous monstrosity, according to my father, and I couldn't disagree—I slowed the pace so Pegasus could cool down. Soon we reached the line of willows, and I slipped off, leaving Pegasus free to graze.

"Brody?" I called, approaching the hanging curtain of weeping willow branches. I ducked under to find Brody sitting against the tree trunk, wearing a pair of jeans and a t-shirt with the sleeves torn off. Just the sight of him made me want to sink to my knees, melt at his feet like butter.

"Hey," he said, patting the ground beside him. "I'm glad you came. I thought you might stand me up."

"Now would I do that?" I asked sweetly, tucking my skirt under me before sitting in the grass beside him.

Brody grinned. "I think we both know the answer to that."

"Fair enough," I said, folding my legs beside me. "What did you want to talk about?"

"Us," he said, taking my hand. "Laney, I know I did something unforgivable, but—."

"Then why are you asking me to forgive you?" I blurted out before I could stop myself. I had planned out my every move, how demure and well-mannered I was going to be when I saw him, a true lady. And as soon as I saw him, the raw pain of it swept all that away. It was like no time had passed at all, like I was having my heart ripped out all over again.

"I'm not," he said, his jaw set. "I know you can't forgive the way I behaved five years ago. I'm a different man now, Laney. I learned my lesson."

"By screwing your way around the world? That must have been tough."

Brody flinched, but he pressed on. I had to give him credit for his persistence and for the fact that he didn't defend himself. "I'm asking for a chance to set things right," he said. "Just one chance. I'll never hurt you again, Laney. I promise."

"You can't promise that." Even though I'd tried to shut off my heart, already he could hurt me. And the longer I kept this up, the more likely it would be that I would end up crushed, not him. I could see that now. But I couldn't stop.

"I still love you," Brody said.

"You don't love me," I snapped. "You love the fantasy of me you have. But that sweet little girl doesn't exist anymore, Brody."

"That's not true," he said. "You'll always be that girl to me."

"Don't you see, that's just it," I said, throwing my hands up. "She only exists in your head. She's not real. I'm real, and I'm right here, and you blew it. Because the girl you love, she's dead. And you know why? Because you killed her."

"I'm sorry I hurt you," he said, his eyes begging me to understand something I never would. "But I think that girl is still there. I think you know it as well as I do. And if you're not that girl anymore, I don't care. I want you, Laney, no matter who you are."

"Oh yeah? And why would you want me if you don't even know who I am."

"I do know," he said quietly. "And I want you like I had you the other night, every night. And more than that. I want all of you. The sweet and the salty. And I want to give you all of me. I want another chance. Please, Laney. It's killing me to be away from you."

"I don't know if I can give you that," I said stiffly. If I let myself get drawn in, I'd drown in him all over again. My heart was ripping in half with every word he spoke.

"You can," he insisted. "Only you can. And someday, when you've learned to trust me again, I want you to be my wife. I won't give up until you are."

"Are you asking me to marry you?" I asked, my throat thick with emotion. It was all I'd dreamed of since the moment I noticed he was a boy and I was a girl. It had always been Brody.

"I know I fucked it all up," he said, reaching out and taking my hand, his blue eyes burning with earnestness. "I was young and stupid. But I learned from losing you, Laney."

I swallowed hard, staring at our linked hands. "A promise of a promise isn't much, Brody."

"It's what I have to give you," he said. "All I'm asking for is a chance to make it right."

I took a deep, unsteady breath. "Okay."

"Okay, you'll be my girl again?"

I nodded, and Brody leaned forward, pulling me in. My heart was racing as his lips touched mine. Could he tell? His hand circled my waist, and he pressed deeper, his lips crushing mine, his mouth searching mine for a truth I kept hidden. As his tongue teased my lips apart, that heat began to grow inside me. This time, I would leave him wanting, would leave him with only a kiss.

A few kisses wouldn't hurt. I let myself have it, my tongue dancing inside his mouth until I thought I would burst into flame if he didn't take me right there, under the tree, like he had before. My mind warned me to pull back, to stop before it went that far, but my body refused to obey. After three years of celibacy, all it wanted was to be full of him again. And again. And again.

Finally, he pulled away and stroked my hair back, cupping my face between his hands. "I have to go to Chicago for a while."

"What?" I asked, jerking away, my head spinning. "You make me promise, and now you're leaving?"

"I'll be back."

"You asshole," I said, jumping to my feet. For one moment, I'd let myself believe he cared. "You can't do this to me again."

"Laney, I didn't have a choice," he said, throwing up his hands.

"I hate you," I cried, turning on my heel and fleeing. I couldn't believe he'd played me again, so easily. Tears stung at my eyes as I raced toward Pegasus.

Before I reached my horse, Brody caught me from behind, his arms circling me, jerking me to a halt.

"Let me go," I growled, prying at his arms. I kicked at his legs until he stumbled forward, crashing to the ground with me.

"Laney, wait."

"You asshole!" I said again, rolling away and onto my knees. When he tried to rise with me, I shoved him back, hard. He landed back on his elbows. "You think you can just come here and ask for a promise, ask me to dump my fiancé for you, and then you're going to leave? I've been there, done that. I know how it ends."

"Things were different then," he said, pushing himself up to sitting. "I was an immature idiot. I didn't know what I had to lose. Now I do."

"Fuck you, Brody." I shoved him back again, but this time he grabbed my wrists and pulled me against him.

"And this time, you'll be coming with me," he said. "Now that I have you, I'm never letting you go."

I wrenched my wrists free and shoved his shoulders this time. When he rocked backward, I threw a leg over him, straddling his hips. Just as I raised a hand to slap him, he caught my wrist and pulled me down to him, his free hand circling my waist. He lifted his lips to mine, and my body responded, that fire racing across my skin like the wind over the bluegrass around us.

I couldn't make it stop. I'd played the game, gone all in, and now I didn't know how to get back to where I'd been. Back to the place where I loathed the very name of Brody Villines. Now my body ached for him, my skin begged for his touch. Now that I'd gotten a taste of him, it wasn't enough. I needed what he'd promised me—all of him, every night.

"I mean it," he said. "Come with me. Tell me you're mine again."

"If I'm yours, then show me you're mine," I said, yanking his belt undone. "I'm not sharing you with a bunch of fangirls."

"I never asked you to," he said, rolling over onto me. His mouth crushed down on mine, and I bit at his lip hard enough to taste blood. He growled and yanked up my skirt while I shoved down his jeans. His hardness filled my hand, and a shudder of desire rocked through me. I squirmed under him, opening my legs, hungry to feel him inside me. To be part of him, to let him be part of me again.

I gripped his cock, my cheeks flushing with desire at the raw heat of it, the demanding hardness. "Then fuck me like I'm the only one," I demanded.

He shoved my underwear aside, and with one quick thrust, he was inside me, filling me. I cried out, arching up against him as he ground me into the dirt. My hands found their way under his t-shirt, and I raked my nails down his back, over his tight, round ass. His muscles flexed as I gripped him, driving him deeper as I thrust my hips up against his. He growled and slammed into me harder, his palms braced on the grass as he drew back and then filled me again and again, filling me in a way I hadn't known I needed so badly until he'd come back into my life.

I opened myself to him, giving myself to the moment, to the anger and pleasure that gripped me. I ground my hips up against him shamelessly, my heels digging into the grass as my body begged for more, for his cock to fill me in ways his empty words couldn't. He growled in response, pounding me back to the ground with a brutal thrust that made my core clench in protest. I cried out, and he pumped into me in a frenzied, desperate rhythm, as if he could somehow erase what he'd done if he just fucked me good enough. As if his body could prove the truth was a lie, as if it could turn back time and undo the things he'd done.

"Come for me, baby," he said, and his pelvic bone crushed down on my sensitive bud. My body responded to the command in his voice, and I cried out again, the warm evening shimmering around us as I climaxed, my nails still dug into his skin. Warmth filled me as he came, and I gasped, unable to catch my breath as waves of pleasure rolled through me in quick, blinding spasms. When I finally started breathing again, the world came back to me, and I saw the most beautiful man I'd ever seen leaning over me, his breath coming as hard as mine, his eyes filled with warmth and concern and a love that made me ache.

Brody's lips touched mine so softly I could hardly stand it, and he slid a hand under my head, cradling it. "Are you on birth control?" he whispered.

I laughed shakily. "Now you ask."

"Better late than never. And if you're not, I don't think I mind."

"I am," I said, frowning. He'd probably given me twenty different STDs, but a baby wasn't going to be one of them.

"So you'll come with me?" he asked, picking a damp lock of hair from my forehead. "I need you, Laney Tucker. Please come with me."

I hesitated, my heart still pounding against his, both of us damp with sweat. "I'll come," I said at last. "How long are you going to be there?"

"I don't know," he said. "We're making a new album. How long can you stay?"

"I'm taking a year off before grad school," I said slowly. "But I was planning to travel."

"Come with me," he said. "I'll be on tour. And I can take you anywhere. I just want you there with me. We'll figure something out, Laney. We'll make it work. I'll make it work. I promise."

"You make a lot of promises, Brody Villines."

"Only to you," he said, kissing my nose. He pulled away slowly, rolling over onto his back.

The air was suddenly too cold, the distance too far. I scooted over to him and lay my head on his chest. "If you ever cheat on me again, I'm going to rip your balls off with my bare hands," I said, running my hand down his stomach.

"Noted," he said, lifting his hips to pull up his jeans with his free hand.

I laughed. Maybe I wouldn't get to make all the rules to this game. And if I couldn't resist him, maybe it wasn't such a bad thing. Everyone had at least one weakness. He didn't seem able to resist me, either.

And I was having sex again. Orgasms, even. I'd forgotten how good they were. And Brody had definitely gotten better. I had to admit, as much as I didn't want to think about it, that all those fangirls had been good for something.

August

eighteen

Brody

I couldn't believe my luck. Several times, as I packed my bags, I had to stop and wonder if it was real. I was getting a solo deal, and Laney Tucker was back where she belonged—mine again, after all this time. It had been so easy, as if she'd been waiting for me to come home and claim her all these years. I suppose she had.

She wasn't like anyone else I'd ever known, but she was still a girl, after all. Even she wasn't immune to my charms, to the rock star allure.

When I had packed and said goodbye to my parents, I took the H2 out of their garage and down the winding drive to the gate. The media wasn't hanging around anymore, which was both good and bad. Good for me, bad for my career. Once they forgot about you, you were toast. Unless you made a comeback.

And Brody Villines was about to make a comeback. It had only been a few months, but it felt like forever. This time, I'd be making music the way I wanted—or at least closer to the way I wanted—and Laney would be there with me, a reminder to avoid temptation, a reminder of the cost.

I turned right and followed the flat dirt road to Laney's. For a second, I let off the gas, hesitating. If I went knocking on her door, and she'd changed her mind, I was going to lose my fucking mind. But I pulled into the drive anyway, because the thought of going to Chicago alone was worse than the chance that she'd say no.

Pulling onto the gravel parking area, I shut off the engine and circled the house to the front door. I knew better than to come over and get Laney without paying her parents the proper respect.

Mr. Tucker opened the door. He'd revoked my right to call him by his first name when I'd started dating his daughter. He was tall, though not as tall as I remembered, with light brown hair and a large red mustache.

"Come in," he said, standing aside.

"Thank you, sir," I said, stepping into the foyer.

"I hear you've come to take my daughter off to the city," Mr. Tucker said. "I guess I always knew this day would come, but it's still too soon."

"Oh, Daddy, don't be dramatic," Laney said, appearing behind him. She took his arm and pulled him aside.

Blair came sashaying in and hooked an arm around Laney's waist. "I, for one, am happy this day has finally come," she said. "Could have come a little sooner, if you ask me." She gave me a wink. "Now you take good care of her, you hear? I better not get news of any funny business."

"Yes, ma'am," I said.

"Oh, come here and stop that 'yes ma'am' nonsense." Blair stepped forward and pulled me into one of her thorough embraces. "Now," she said, pulling back and looking up at me. "You going to stay for breakfast?"

I gave Laney a questioning look, but she shook her head. "I already ate."

"I think we'll be on our way, then," I said. "But thank you for the offer. Rain check?"

While I loaded her bags, Laney went to say goodbye to her horse. When she came back, she was glowing. "I don't know if I like that look on your face when I didn't put it there," I said, wrapping an arm around her waist and pulling her in.

Laney smiled and stood on tiptoes to give me a quick kiss. I flattened my palm against the small of her back, pressing her body to mine. "You better stop that," she said, but she was grinning. "My parents are right inside."

"I don't care," I said. "We're not teenagers anymore. Besides, this big car has advantages." I pulled her behind the vehicle, my lips already skimming over hers, dropping to the hollow of her throat.

"Quit," she protested, pushing at me weakly. I trailed my lips up her neck to her ear, and she dropped her head back, sighing.

"You're the one who needs to quit teasing me," I said. "If you let me keep this up, I'm going to have to fuck you up against the side of this car."

"If you keep *this* up, I'm going to have to let you."

I growled and nipped at her earlobe. "Don't tempt me." Giggling, she tried to pull away, but I pinned her against the car. "You think that's funny? You think I won't do it?"

"I have no doubt you would," she said. "But you were tickling my ear."

"In that case," I said, smiling and leaning towards her ear again.

She wiggled free and ducked sideways out of my grasp. "I guess we'll have to save the Hummer sex for another day."

"If you call it that, I don't know if I can wait."

"Hummer sex," she said, grinning. When I lunged for her, she darted around the back of the car with a shriek. I shook my head and climbed into the driver's seat. Breathless with laughter, Laney climbed up in the passenger seat. "My goodness, this thing is huge," she said, leaning out to snag the door handle.

"You know it, baby."

"You know people will say you're compensating."

"And you know I have nothing to compensate for," I said, smirking at her. "What everyone else thinks doesn't matter."

"I don't think you'd drive a Hummer if you didn't care what people thought."

"Oh, yeah? Why's that?"

"They're pretentious eyesores."

I shrugged. "I like being up high, away from the crowd. I've had it mobbed before, and trust me, you don't want to be in some cute little convertible when people are literally trying to tear off pieces of your car as souvenirs."

"Wow. I hadn't thought of that. Am I going to have to deal with that?"

"Depends," I said, glancing sideways at her. "Are you going to go public as my girlfriend, or sit back in the shadows and avoid the shit storm?"

"I hadn't thought about it."

"I'll get you some bodyguards either way."

Laney laughed and craned her neck as we passed between the seemingly endless rail fences bordering the pastures on either side of the dirt road. "I don't think I'll need a bodyguard."

"You never know," I said. "What if some crazy kidnaps you for ransom?"

"Then you'll kick his ass?" Laney asked, grinning.

"Her ass, more likely."

"I'd like to see her try," Laney said. "If one of your groupies comes up to me, I'm the one you'll need to worry about."

A few minutes later, we pulled up in front of Grampa Othal's house. He'd been discharged, but he had around the clock care from the best private nurses in the state. Anyone else would have been in a rehab facility, but Othal wanted them to come to him, not the other way around.

I climbed out, then went around to open Laney's door and help her down from the high seat in the H2.

"I guess you haven't totally forgotten your manners while you've been away," she said.

"I told you, I'm going to take care of you," I said, lacing my fingers through hers as we made our way up Othal's front steps. I stopped on the front porch and turned to face Laney, squeezing her hand. "I meant it. I take care of what's mine. And you're mine, Laney Tucker."

I searched her blue eyes for understanding. She swallowed and nodded, dropping her gaze. Before releasing her hand, I pulled her in, circled her shoulders with my arm, and gave her forehead a quick kiss.

Inside, the big house was bright as always, decorated opulently with wood and leather everywhere. Vases of late summer wildflowers graced the tables instead of the hospital flowers. Othal wouldn't like to be reminded of his weakness. From our left, the steady beep of a heart monitor gave away his location and served as more than enough of a reminder.

I led Laney into the living area, where Gramps sat propped up on a cot that looked exactly like a hospital bed. But he was wearing a flannel shirt and his face was freshly shaved. A nurse sat in a chair nearby, reading on her device.

"You look good, Gramps," I said, stepping forward to hug my grandfather.

"I look like garbage," Othal said, his voice slurred. One corner of his mouth was turned down from the stroke, and saliva glistened in the wrinkles there.

"Fine, you look like garbage," I said, grabbing a napkin off the tray beside the bed to dab at Othal's chin. "But you don't look like dead garbage, so that's an improvement from the last time I saw you."

Othal grinned with all but one corner of his mouth. For one terrible second, I thought I was going to burst into tears in front of my tough old grandpa and my girl. But I took a deep breath and laughed instead.

"And who's the girl you brought me?" Othal asked, peering around me. "Is this my new nurse? Damn, each one is better than the last. I'm going to have to keep firing them until they bring me a Kardashian."

Laney laughed and stepped forward to hug him. "You're sweet, Gramps," she said. "But it's me, Laney Tucker, from next door."

"I know that," Othal said. "I'm just joshing you. What are you kids up to this morning? Out for a drive?"

"I got a call from my manager," I said. "He wants me to do a solo album."

"You got a deal with a label yet?"

I couldn't help the smile of pride from finding my face. "I think so."

"I don't suppose it's country? Because I've still got ties."

"No country, Gramps."

"That's too bad," Othal said, lifting a big hand and pointing at me with a gnarled finger. "I always said you'd make a good country duo, the two of you. Could have been the next Johnny and June."

"There's still time," Laney said. "You never know."

"You get her on your record," Othal said, shaking a finger at me. "She's got the voice and the looks. Not everybody's got the right combination."

"She's the whole package," I agreed.

"I ever tell you I offered to get her plugged in with some of my Nashville people after you left?"

I shot Laney a look, but she'd put on a poker face. "No," I said, turning my attention back to Othal. "I didn't know that."

"I did," Othal said. "But she wasn't having it. Y'all two always were a stubborn pair. Couldn't keep you apart once you made up your mind to be together."

"I guess not," I said, taking Laney's hand. "Because here we are, together."

We stayed a bit longer before bidding Othal goodbye. I leaned in to hug him, and though my grandfather's hand shook slightly when he reached for mine, his handshake was still firm.

nineteen

Laney

"This is where we're staying?" I asked, looking around the spacious high-rise apartment we had managed to get to without too much fuss. A few people had seen Brody and run over to get selfies and hug him, but it hadn't been too bad. I thought I could handle it. And the apartment was gorgeous—all clean lines, stainless steel appliances, and a killer view.

"Did you think we'd be in a motel on the south side?" Brody asked, coming up behind me and putting his arms around me. "How many times do I have to tell you I'm going to take care of you before you believe me?"

"Maybe a few more," I said, wiggling my bottom against him.

He growled and rubbed his chin against my neck. "You better stop that, or I'm going to have to take you to the bedroom."

Pressing harder against him, I squirmed around even more. "Don't make promises you can't keep. I know you're going to call your manager first thing."

"Then you don't know me as well as you think," he said, bending to scoop me up. He threw me over his shoulder, and a little shriek escaped me as he ran into the bedroom and tossed me on the bed. Pouncing on top of me, he pulled my hands over my head and nuzzled my neck until he found my ticklish spot. He mercilessly rubbed his scratchy chin against it and growled against my ear until I was giggling uncontrollably.

"Stop, I can't breathe," I gasped at last, and he pulled back and looked down at my face with amusement.

"All this writhing around is making me want to do a lot more than tickle you," he said, his hips grinding slowly against mine.

"What about your phone call?"

"Fuck Nash," he whispered, bending to press his lips to mine.

"I don't know if that's allowed," I teased. "But I guess if you're okay with it…"

"Never." Still holding my hands over my head, he stroked my cheek with his free hand. "You're mine, remember? All mine."

His lips found mine, and I tried to remind myself again that this wasn't real, that I didn't feel anything for him except hatred and revulsion. But it was no use. His mouth skimmed my cheek and a shiver ran through my body. Once again, I was helpless to stop my body's response. Worse, he seemed well aware of it. With a grin, he sat up and tugged at my shirt, drawing it slowly over my head and dropping it to the floor.

His mouth met mine again as he leaned down to give me a taste of his tongue, just enough to make her want to scream when he pulled away a second later. After peeling off his own shirt, he slid onto me again, smiling down at my face. "I think I owe you," he said. "I've been waiting for this since we left Kentucky."

I'd been waiting for three years. But I'd die before I admitted that to him. When he reached under my back, I arched up, letting him unhook my bra and then slide it over my arms.

"You're so beautiful," he said, his mouth moving from my ear, down my neck. My nipples hardened against him as his chest skimmed across mine. His warm hand cupped my breast, massaging it gently before taking my nipple between his thumb and finger and giving it a little tug. A jolt went through me, as if an invisible tie led directly from my nipple to my clit. Brody grinned and did it again, watching my face for reaction. I gasped and reached for him, wanting him inside me again.

"I need you," I whispered, my hands sliding down his back, pulling him against me. But he only slid down further, his mouth descending onto my nipple. I tried not to cry out from the wet heat of his mouth as he sucked gently, then pulled back, letting his teeth graze across the sensitive nub. He blew softly at my wet nipple, and a chill raced across my body.

His mouth traveled further south, sucking at the skin of my stomach, his tongue dipping into my bellybutton, then circling it until I started giggling again. I stopped when he looked at me with those hooded eyes as he drew down my skirt and panties and tossed them aside, then knelt between my knees. Just watching him look at my body, naked on the bed before him, imagining what he was about to do to me, made me wet with desire.

He licked the pad of his thumb and touched it to my pearl, massaging it gently and then circling it with his thumb. My thighs quaked, and I squirmed with need, which only made him smile. He slid his thumb down and pushed it into me, then used my wetness to slicken my clit again.

"Oh, God, Brody," I moaned. "Fuck me already."

"I'm going to make love to you this time," he said. "Nice and slow." He continued circling, then pushing his thumb into me again, at first slowly and then faster, and then circling his thumb while he slid a finger into me as deep as it would go. I gasped and arched up, wanting something more, wanting all of him.

"I need you," I said again, but when I tried to sit up, he gently pressed my back onto the bed, his eyes almost dazed as he watched his finger pumping into me.

"What do you need, baby," he breathed. "Tell me."

"I need—I need all of you."

"You got me," he said.

I bit my lip, squirming against his hand, frustration building inside me as he wound me tighter and tighter.

"I need your cock," I blurted out at last, spreading my thighs and bucking my hips.

"You're going to get it," he said, working a second finger into me, pumping them faster while his thumb slicked back and forth across my tender clit until I wanted to scream. "But not until you come for me."

As if I'd been waiting for permission, my body rocked upwards, and a wave of pure ecstasy washed over me. I bit my lip to keep from screaming when he stopped. Before I could, he'd slid down his jeans and pushed his cock inside me, filling me as I throbbed around him. I choked out a wordless, helpless moan. He drew back, bracing his palms on the bed and holding his body still, pressing the head of his cock directly against the spot inside me that was pulsing. This time, I couldn't stop myself, and I cried out, my whole body wracked with pleasure. Waves crashed over me from head to toe, and I lost all control, sucked down by the raw ecstasy of the moment.

When it finally ended, I felt like I was coming to after a faint. My hands were clenching the blanket, my feet cramping from flexing while my toes curled. And worst of all, Brody was watching me, his eyes locked on my face with burning intensity. I felt exposed suddenly, embarrassed to have let go so completely. Laney Tucker did not lose control easily. I prided myself on that. But I'd just had a screaming orgasm for minutes at a time, in broad daylight, while Brody leaned over me watching.

"I don't think I've ever made anyone come that hard," he said, which did not comfort me one bit. I reached for my clothes, something, to cover myself, but I couldn't find anything, and it was kind of pointless while he was still inside me.

I scooted up the bed and grabbed a pillow to cover myself. Brody sat back on his heels, his cock still hard and glistening with my cum.

"You didn't finish," I said, my tone accusatory.

"I was enjoying the view."

To my horror, I felt her lip start to tremble. I bit down on it hard.

"Hey," he said, dropping onto the bed beside me and propping himself up on one elbow. "What's wrong?"

"Nothing."

"Come on, Laney. I know you better than that. Just tell me."

"It's stupid. Just finish." I tossed the pillow aside and turned to him, threw my leg over his hip, and reached down to guide him back inside me.

He cupped my cheek in his palm, his guitar-calloused fingers stroking my cheek. "Laney?" His lips skimmed over mine, then tugged lightly at my bottom lip. "Are you sure?"

I nodded, and he began to move slowly, his hips flexing as he pushed into me. This time, I wasn't thinking about myself, and I had time to run my hands over his sculpted shoulder, his side, his hips, that gorgeous ass I liked so much. After a few minutes, I forgot my insecurity and instead, enjoyed watching his cock slide into me and out again. My fingers trailed up his muscled arm, down his chest, and I scratched my nails lightly over his pecs, flicking at his nipple.

He began to move faster, and I pinched his nipple this time. Brody growled and rolled over onto me, his lips pressing mine apart. His tongue slid into my mouth in perfect rhythm with the stroke of his cock. There was something to be said for sleeping with a musician. I wrapped my legs around him, sliding one leg up his back and then down, over his ass to his thighs. Flexing my leg, I used my muscles to pull him in harder. He hit that sensitive place deep within me, and I gasped, raising my hips so he'd hit it again.

I gripped him with both legs as he drove into me. With one powerful thrust, he plowed me up the bed until my head hit the headboard. He groaned, and his whole body went rigid when he came. I could feel the pulse of his cock thickening inside me, the strain of taking him all in, that last little swell that hit a nerve. A pinprick of pain darted through me, and the pulse came again as he filled every last bit of me. The tightness inside me broke loose in response, answering his shuddering breath with my own, and my walls clenched around his length. He sucked in a breath a spasm went through him, delivering another spurt of cum to my pulsing depth.

For a minute, neither of us spoke. This time, Brody lay his head on my shoulder, keeping himself propped on his elbows enough to keep some of his weight off me. At last, he lifted his head and brushed his lips across mine again.

"Are you going to tell me what that was?" he asked.

"What?" I asked, hating the position he had me in, so unbearably intimate with his cock still buried to the hilt inside me even though we'd both come; so impossible to look away with his forearms framing my head as he looked down at me.

"You know what. A minute ago. What happened?"

"We had sex?"

"Laney… Don't lie to me. I'm going to keep doing this until you tell me."

I sighed. I would have teased him more if we hadn't been going for an hour. Before he even pulled out, I could feel the swollen tenderness between my legs. When he started flexing his hips a little, the heat stirred inside me again. I had no off switch with him. Just being near enough to touch him made me squirm with desire.

"I can't do it again," I said, when I felt him starting to swell inside me.

"That's why you looked like you were about to cry?"

"Uncle," I said, pushing at his chest. "You win. I'm crying uncle. I surrender."

He laughed softly and moved off me, lying on his stomach beside me. The air-conditioned air in the room chilled the sweat from our bodies, and I reached for the blanket again. I had to sit up to pry it loose from where it was tucked rigidly under the mattress. While my back was turned, it was easier to tell him. "I just don't know how I can keep up with you," I said. "Obviously, I can't."

"What are you talking about?"

He waited while I slipped under the sheet, throwing the lush comforter off. "I can't make you do what you made me do."

"I don't think guys can do that," he said. "It's kind of over and done when we come. You can keep going for a while, apparently."

"If you smirk right now, I'm going to throw something at you," I said, pulling a pillow into my arms and meeting his eyes at last.

"I don't smirk."

I rolled her eyes. "Oh my god, you're the king of smirking."

"Zane's the king of smirking. I'm just smiling."

"Riiiight."

"Seriously, Laney," he said. "I love you. You're amazing. You don't have to do anything other than be yourself. I love everything about you. I love kissing those gorgeous lips, I love being inside you, I love tasting you..."

I felt my face warm as he spoke, and I had to force myself not to stop him. I wasn't a total prude. Was I? If even hearing him say it could make me blush, how could I be enough for him? He could have all the other girls combined, or just me, little barely-more-than-a-virgin Laney Tucker. Every move I had, I'd learned from him. He had a million moves I'd never even seen yet.

"You're all I want," he said, as if he'd read my thoughts. "Now move over so I can lay with you. I love holding you, too."

I opened the sheets, and he slipped under, pulling my body against his. As much as he loved holding me, I loved it ten times more. After a few minutes, he began to relax and breathe deeply, and I realized he'd fallen asleep. I had him exactly where I wanted him. Wrapped around me and wrapped around my little finger.

So why was I suddenly looking at his gorgeous, lying face, so innocent in sleep, and feeling guilty? Why did I feel like I was the one doing something wrong? And why was I feeling a warm swelling in my chest, an overwhelming urge to reach out and brush a soft strand of dark hair off his forehead, kiss his sculpted cheekbone?

I needed to do something about that, and fast. Careful not to wake him, I slipped from under the sheet and dug my phone out of my bag. Piper was my emergency contact for situations just such as this, where I'd crossed the line into certifiably insane. If I stepped any further, I might not be able to uncross that line.

Giving myself a stern pep talk all the way, I ducked into the other room and hit Piper's number. "I have a confession," I said as soon as Piper answered the phone.

"You're still in love with Brody?"

"Not exactly." I wasn't in love with Brody. That was ridiculous. In lust, sure. But love? Never. It had been temporary insanity, that was all. "But…I did move to Chicago with him," I admitted.

"What!" Piper shrieked. "What do you mean, you *moved* to Chicago?"

"He got a call from his manager, and he had to come. It was very last minute."

"And what does that have to do with you?"

"I have a plan," I said, unable to stop an edge of defensiveness from creeping into my voice. "I wasn't going to abandon it just because he left."

"Why the hell not? I thought you never wanted to see him again."

"He asked me to come, and I thought it would be a good chance to further said plan."

"Uh-huh. Sure. Your plan to marry Brody Villines?"

"Don't even joke."

"No judgement here. Brody's hot as hell, and he must be, like, a billionaire at twenty-three. And you're the lucky lady who stole his heart, not to mention you've been in love with him since you were in a training bra. I don't think anyone on earth is going to blame you for it. Even me, and I remember what he did to you."

"It's not like that," I said, but it sounded hollow even to my own ears. Maybe it was exactly like that.

twenty

Brody

Later, I met with Nash, who was in Chicago to greet me. When I entered the restaurant through a side door, I was escorted by two bodyguards, Laney, and her bodyguard. "This is so weird," she whispered. "He's just breathing down my neck."

"You'll get used to it," I said. "You'll forget he's even there." I didn't mention that I knew this because one of my tabloid girlfriends had used the same bodyguard. He was good, though. I wasn't going to risk Laney's life just to keep her from having the same bodyguard as one of my exes. That would have ruled out half the guys in the industry. A single guy could easily end up dating twenty girls in a few years.

"There's Nash," I said, nodding to the table where my manager sat. A hostess greeted us in the back of the restaurant and led us to the corner where he sat. She didn't show the slightest recognition, which meant she was a good one. It wasn't like I could just go out and eat at a regular restaurant. There were certain places, though, where they had a better shot at going to eat without being bothered. Where the employees didn't ask for autographs and the other patrons were as sick of being hounded as I was.

"Who's this?" Nash asked, nodding to Laney as he fished an olive from his martini glass with two fingers.

"This is Laney Tucker," I said. "She's my girl."

"I didn't say to bring a girl," Nash said through his bite of green olive.

I pulled out Laney's chair. "But I did."

"Huh." Nash swiped his fingers across the napkin in his lap and held out a hand without rising. Laney shook it quickly before sitting. I sat down as well, scooting in at the round table as the bodyguards melted back against the wall. "Get all set up in your new place?" Nash asked.

"Yes, thank you. We did."

Nash pushed aside his menu and scanned back and forth between his two dinner companions. "You're both living there?"

"Yes," I said, taking Laney's hand. "We're getting married. No more celebrity setups."

"That was fast," Nash said.

"When I know what I want, I don't waste time."

Laney was looking at me with an appreciative shine in her eyes, obviously impressed that I was laying down the law with no question when it came to where we stood.

"I think I could make it work," Nash said, scratching his slick curls as he squinted at us. "Like I said, this is grown up Brody Villines. This is Nick Jonas, not the Jonas Brothers. Settling down for a while might not be a bad idea."

"Good," I said. "Because if she has to go, I go. That's the deal."

Nash must have heard something in my voice, because instead of scoffing, he held up his hands. "Now calm down, nobody's getting rid of your girl."

"She can sing, too," I said. "I'd like you to hear her. Maybe she can do some background vocals."

"We'll see," Nash said. He gestured for the waitress, ordered a round of cocktails, and ducked off to the restroom.

"Who said I wanted to be your backup singer?" Laney asked.

"You love singing," I said. "I thought you'd want to."

"I guess I won't be annoyingly famous like you," she said with a smile. "Sure, why not. It might be fun to be part of your album, see how it all works."

"It's not as glamorous as you think," I said. "It's actually tedious as fuck."

"That's not very tedious," she whispered, giving me a sultry pout. "Is it?"

"You better stop that." I took her full, soft bottom lip between my finger and thumb and pinched it gently. Just touching the plumpness of it made my cock stiffen.

"Or what?" she asked, her blue eyes going wide with innocence.

"Or you know what," I said. "You're going to get it later."

"Get what, Brody?" she asked, smiling her sweetest smile.

Nash returned to the table before I could answer, but I sent Laney a warning look. She responded with that same wide-eyed innocence.

I took her hand and moved it into my lap, under the edge of the black tablecloth. The restaurant was dimly lit and private, but I still expected Laney to pull away and be terribly shocked. Instead, she squeezed my cock through my dress slacks, moving her hand subtly, slowly, from base to tip.

"Let's talk about the tracks," Nash said, leaning down to pull a packet out of his briefcase. He slid it across the table, and I picked it up, as if my girl wasn't running her nails lightly along my rigid length at that very moment. I could hear the rasp of her nails on the fabric, the sensation enough to make me bite his tongue to keep from moaning.

"That's the track list right now," Nash said. "They're in order. Look it over and get yourself ready for the first one. We've got the studio booked the day after tomorrow."

I flipped through the pages, pretending to look while trying not to squirm or make any sound as Laney cupped the head of my cock, then flattened her palm and moved it in slow, agonizing circles. It was all I could do not to grab her and bend her over the table, lift up that little black dress and give her what she was asking for. Instead, I scanned the music and lyrics to the first track on the album.

"Will do," I said.

When the waitress arrived, again I was sure Laney would stop her torment, but she continued as I ordered for us both.

If the waitress knew what was going on, she kept on the same poker face she'd worn since we walked in. At last, the food arrived, and Laney needed both hands to eat with.

"You're going to get it later," I said under my breath.

Laney gave me her sweetest smile and swung her hair back over her shoulder, the same way she'd been doing since we were kids. "We'll see."

On our way out, no one bothered us, though I met the eyes of a few celebrities—a new actor giving an interview over dinner, a famous director with his aging movie star wife, an indie-pop singer with a name that sounded like a whole band though it was just him. I recognized them, but out of mutual respect, we only smiled at each other. I'd been approached for movie deals, but it would have interfered with the band's rigorous, non-stop recording, touring, and press events.

When Nash stopped to chat with the director, I felt that familiar rush of time passing me by. How much longer could I keep going? I was so young, but I felt ancient, older than Grandpa Othal. It had hit me at odd moments over the past few years. The superficial relationships, the tours, the groupies, the restrictions… They were all part of my life, but they were all designed to be temporary, fleeting. They changed as quickly as the opinions of fickle fans. Nothing in the business lasted.

I may have been many things, but I wasn't stupid. I knew I was lucky to have the life I did. That's why I had wanted to go back so soon, to grab the opportunity before it shot past me and disappeared forever. And yet, this wasn't my life at all. I was a pawn, doing what I was told, going where I needed to go, singing this song, performing this choreography, and all the time feeling like the real Brody Villines was not here. I was giving my life to these people, but even when I enjoyed it, it wasn't for me. And I could never get it back. How many years of my life would I give away before I started saving some for myself?

"Can we ditch him and just go?" Laney whispered, squeezing my hand. This is where the real Brody Villines was and had always been. Not on a stage in front of thousands of fans, not filling Madison Square Garden or signing autographs until my hand cramped around the pen and couldn't let go, not showing up to this movie premier and that awards show with a preapproved celebrity date. I had been with Laney all along, sleeping somewhere next to her while the clone of Brody did all this. Already, I could barely tell one event from another in the long blur of *Just 5 Guys'* history.

"I should stay," I said reluctantly. "Nash might need something else before I go."

"Nash can text you," Laney said, leaning in to look up at me with those baby blues, her pillowy lips forming a little pout. "And don't you have something to give me?"

"Nash who?" I said, wrapping my hand around hers and pulling her out of the restaurant, trailed by our bodyguards. With my free hand, I pulled out my phone and thumbed a text to my driver. I'd used the front door this time, but the couple outside was too classy to pounce on me, though I could tell by their barely repressed grins that they recognized me. I was hard to forget. I shielded my face to stave off recognition as I hurried towards the lot where my driver waited.

"Come on, let's get out of here," I said, pulling Laney to where my driver was waiting. We slid into the town car, and

I let out a breath. I'd almost forgotten, or blocked out, how stressful this had all been, how exhausting. Just when I was about to lean my head back against the seat and try not to freak out that I was back here, back in the real world, Laney's warm hand slipped into mine.

Laney, who was part of that safe world back home, where things moved impossibly slowly in the country heat, where people and cars didn't rush at reckless speeds in every direction, stopping short of running over each other only to avoid a lawsuit. The lives of others were of no consequence or concern here. Only business mattered, making the next buck. It didn't matter how you made it.

Back home, everything mattered. Taking off your hat at the table, remembering to talk about the weather and the Kentucky Wildcats and your cousin's health before you got to the real reason for a visit, remembering to offer a beverage to guests. In the city, nothing mattered but money money money. But with Laney there, it was as if a little piece of home had come with me. I could recapture that warm summer breeze over the grass even when the sweltering stench of exhaust and asphalt made my eyes water.

When we reached the apartment, I punched in the code and let us in. In the elevator, I pushed Laney against the wall, trapping her hands beside her head. Then I kissed her, hard.

"What was that for?" she asked when the elevator stopped and I pulled away.

"That was for earlier," I said. "I told you not to tease me. There will be more later."

"How much later?" she teased as we stepped out of the elevator and let ourselves into the apartment. *Our* apartment. Laney and I were living together.

"Keep it up, and you'll find out," I said, locking the door behind us.

"Am I in trouble?" she asked with her little pout. "Are you going to spank me?"

I grabbed her and pulled her roughly against me, crushing her mouth with mine. My tongue drove into her mouth, the kiss bending her backwards as I held her hips firmly against mine. "I've been waiting for hours to rip this little thing off you," I said, spinning her around and bending her over the end of the couch.

I threw up her skirt and dropped my jeans. "I thought you were going to spank me," she said, turning to give him a smoldering look over her shoulder.

I gave her bottom a quick smack.

She batted her eyes at me. "More, please."

She giggled as I gave her a playful smack on the other cheek. I growled and pressed my hardness against her nice round ass. I ran my hands up her back, still sheathed in the silky black dress, then reached around to cup her breasts. She arched her back and squirmed against me as I slid my hand down her belly and into her underwear. When my fingers found her clit, she moaned and pushed back against me, stepping away from the couch to brace her hands on the arm and spread her legs wider.

I leaned over her back, covering her hands with my own. Nuzzling her ear through her hair, I dropped kisses along her shoulder, down her shoulder blade, to the center of her back, just above the dress.

She sighed and arched up against me again. "I'm ready," she said. "Don't make me wait. I need you inside me now."

I pulled her panties aside and pressed my tip against her wetness. She gasped and pushed back against me, her pussy swallowing my tip. I pulled back, then slid all the way in with one deep thrust. Gripping her hips with both hands, I watched myself plunging into her. With a cry, she arched her back, her blonde hair tumbling around her shoulders.

When I felt her tightening up, I pushed myself even deeper, easing her legs further apart so I could reach her depths and move faster, driving into her harder.

"Now," she begged. "Come now. Oh please, Brody, now."

We both gripped the edge of the couch, and I slammed into her, burying myself in her wet flesh as she came. When she was done, I pulled her onto the couch with me, kissing her forehead and lips. "You," I said, touching the tip of her nose. "Are one hell of a lady."

"You didn't even come."

"I'm not done with you yet," I said, rolling onto my back and pulling her on top of me. My cock throbbed at the contact with her wet thighs, but she didn't sit up and ride me like the cowgirl she was.

"I don't know how," she whispered. Her confident, playful mood disappeared, and she looked about to cry. She buried her face in my chest.

"You've never been on top?"

"No," she said, her voice muffled by my shirt. "I've never been with anyone but you, and we were in high school. We weren't exactly adventurous back then."

"Are you sure we never did this?" I asked, running my fingers through her long hair. "Because I have some fantasies about it, and I don't think they're all in my head." I'd been fantasizing about her for years, though, so it was entirely possible. So many predatory groupies had climbed on top of me, they all blurred together. I wanted to make something real from it, something to hold onto, a picture of Laney moving on top of me.

"We didn't," she said, lifting her face from my chest. "You always asked, but I never wanted to because I didn't know how."

"That's no reason not to try," I said. "If you want to do it now, I'll help. It's easy, I promise."

"Okay," she said, but she looked doubtful. "I just don't know how I can measure up."

"Laney," I said, cupping her face between my hands. "How many times do I have to tell you, you don't have to measure up to anything. You're already the gold standard, okay? No one could measure up to you in a million years."

"But you've been with all those girls. I'm the furthest thing from a porn star groupie."

"I love you. Don't you think that matters?" I asked, sliding my arms around her and pulling her tight to my chest, my heart that died to hear her say those things. "It's a million times better with you than it could ever be with anyone else. And I don't even remember them. There's only been you all along."

"No one else?"

I kissed the top of her head. "No one else."

We lay there in silence a while, Laney's cheek on my chest while I stroked her hair. At last, she sat up and shook her hair back. "Okay," she said. "So how does this work?"

She turned and positioned herself in my lap, between my thighs with her back to me. I slid down the zipper of her dress, revealing her tanned back. I kissed her shoulders while she ran her nails up and down my legs. When I peeled down her dress, letting it fall around her hips, she leaned her head back against my shoulder. My hands moved over her belly, her ribs, and cupped her full breasts. I squeezed her nipples gently, delighting in the gasp the move elicited.

"Okay, you asked for it," she said, standing abruptly. She dropped her dress and kicked it away, then pulled off her panties and climbed on top of me, that little crease of determination between her eyebrows that I loved so well. I pulled her down for a kiss, then held still while she wrapped her small, soft hand around my cock. When she guided me to her opening, it was all I could do to hold still and not thrust up into her slick, tight cunt. But this was the Laney show, and she had to be comfortable, so I held back, biting my lip to keep from groaning as she lowered herself onto me. My cock throbbed inside her, and I had to hold back from coming the moment she began to move.

I held her hips gently and began to guide her, helping her find her rhythm as she rode me. "Is this okay?" she asked, her breath coming quicker.

"More than okay," I said. "You're galaxies past okay, Laney. I don't need a porn star, I need you. You're every star in every galaxy to me."

She leaned down to kiss me, and I ran my hands down her back, gripping her hips and moving her faster. When she'd found her rhythm, she relaxed a little and her hips pumped up and down, sinking her slippery cunt over my cock again and again. I couldn't tear my eyes from her—her perfect, tight nipples pointing at me, her blonde mane tumbling around her shoulders, her face moving from determination to ecstasy. I pushed himself up to take one pink nipple in my mouth, giving it a quick, hard suck. Her walls clenched around me, and I groaned against her tit. She gasped and arched her back, and I repeated the motion, this time more slowly, before turning my attention to her other nipple.

I could feel her cunt's grip tightening on me, gliding over my shaft quicker and quicker. Sliding my hands from her hips to her round ass, I added a slight rocking motion to her strokes. Her breath came in little gasps, sweat glazing her skin as she began to bounce and rock, biting her lip and moaning.

Finding her clit, I pinched it between my thumb and forefinger and rolled it gently. She tensed and cried out, throwing her head back, her walls pulsing around me. She squeezed her eyes closed and gripped my biceps, biting her lip. Watching her cum undid me.

A moan escaped my lips as I wrenched her hips down and drove myself upwards, slamming my cock home, my cum spurting into her depths. Another cry burst from her lips as she continued rocking against me, her walls squeezing and fluttering, milking every last drop from my cock until we were both spent.

At last, she collapsed onto my chest with a little laugh. "So that's how it's done."

"God, yes," I said, stroking her damp hair back from her forehead and planting a kiss there. "Can we do that again every night of our lives?"

When she fell asleep on my chest, I lay awake, running my fingers through her hair, thinking maybe this time, it would be okay.

The outside world could stay out there, but in our apartment, it couldn't touch us. As long as I had this little bubble of safety, I'd be okay. They couldn't take pieces of me, chipping away at me until there was nothing left of me, because they'd taken it all, piece by piece, each one demanding something different.

This time, I'd save it all for Laney. I was never going to let anything come between us again.

September

twenty-one

Laney

We spent the end of August and into September recording. The recording process was not at all the way I had expected. Sure, Brody had warned me it was tedious, but I'd thought we would be doing a few takes, changing up a line here or there. Instead, when we got to the studio, I was taken to a separate room, and although I knew Brody was there watching me through the glass in the sound booth, it was unnerving being in that room alone with the microphone.

After my first day, I asked to watch Brody's session before doing any more. I only had to add a few 'oohs' and 'mmms' anyway. They would add them all to Brody's tracks later.

Brody, at least, seemed to know what he was doing. "So we're doing all the vocals before any of the guitar, right?" he asked, sinking onto the stool and securing his headphones.

"Music's in the making," Nash said to the glass in front of us. "Don't worry about that."

"I thought I was getting to do my own guitar on this album. I'm a musician, Nash. I want to play, not just sing."

"Brody, I know what I'm doing," Nash said. "Does Harry Styles whine about his guitar? No. He sings his ass off and lets his producers worry about the rest. And that's all you gotta do, too. Don't make more work for yourself."

"This sounds like what the band did," Brody said. "I thought this was going to be a different sound."

"It is," Nash said. "Now start making it. If I want you to play guitar, I'll let you know. For now, just sing."

Brody looked miserable, but he adjusted the microphone and did a line. Then he did it again. And again.

"That one," Nash muttered. One of the producers jotted down something. I didn't even know who the other three people in the sound booth were. There were other producers, some of whom I'd already met. And people to mix the music, choose which of the three takes made the cut, add in vocal tracks, background vocals…It was all very dry and businesslike, with no passion or spontaneity. There was no improvising, just doing each line one by one and taking the best one.

Sometimes, we did the line five or ten times. Sometimes, we left it at three but then came back to it another day and asked for him to do one or two random lines that weren't even in the same song, all over again.

After I wrapped my vocal contributions on my last day, I watched Brody do his lines for a while, thumbing through a stapled packet of lyrics and chords. No wonder he had thought he'd get to play the guitar, too. Nash had included the guitar portion, too, the sneaky bastard. He'd probably planned all along for Brody to just sing. After all, that silky croon was his moneymaker.

"What is this shit?" I asked after a while, turning to Nash, who had come down every few days to hang around and tell Brody what to do.

"That's your bread and butter, sweetheart," Nash said. "Those songs are going to pay your bills, your kids' bills, and your grandkids' bills."

"This is crap," I said. *"I know you like it/ when I treat you like shit.* What is that supposed to be? Your 'power' anthem? Or the theme song for domestic violence?"

"I told you. This is Brody Villines. He's gotta find his own voice, away from the band. He's not cutesy little Justin Bieber this time around. He's grown-up. He's got a grown-up sound."

Brody stopped repeating his line and pushed the mic away. "What's going on, Laney?"

I had to mic up to speak to him through his headphones. "These songs are really offensive, Brody. I know this is your grown up sound, but this is promoting violence against women."

"Damn feminists," Nash muttered.

"It's just a song, baby. You know I don't think like that," Brody said.

"Yeah, but are you really okay saying this to the world? Telling the entire world you think that way? All those little girls who crushed on you in *Just 5 Guys* are going to hear this, Brody. Their parents are going to hear it. Your mother is going to hear this."

Brody removed his headphones and stepped out of the studio. A second later he was in the sound booth with us. "Laney, you know it's just business," he said pleadingly, taking my hand. "I didn't get to write the songs."

"It's bad business," I said. "Those parents who buy their teenage girls songs for their iPods are not going to buy this. You're alienating your fanbase."

Not that I loved his fans. But the song was appalling.

"I'd never treat you like shit. I'm not that kind of guy."

"That's not what I'm saying," I said, pulling my hand away. "Why aren't you listening to me? This isn't about us. It's about what message you're sending."

"Come on, Laney," he said, his eyes flicking to Nash, who stood behind me, and then back. "The guys who would take the song to mean that, well, let's face it, they're not going to be buying a Brody Villines EP."

"If he thinks this is a good business move, you need a new manager," I said, turning to glare at Nash.

"Brody, I'm paying by the hour for this," Nash said. "You need to get her out of here."

"You're kicking me out?"

"I'll come, too," Brody said. He turned to Nash. "If she goes, I go."

"I don't have the studio forever," Nash said. "Get your ass back in there and make me my album. Laney, you can wait outside. Don't come in here trying to run things. You got no idea what you're talking about. Sex sells, honey, and this is a sexy song."

"These are shit songs," I said, picking up the packet and flipping through it. "A hipster anthem romanticizing youth, a dance song about dancing, a sappy love song about idealizing an image instead of a real person… These are worse than your *Just 5 Guys* songs."

"Nice to know how you really feel," Brody muttered.

"It's pop music," Nash said. "I know what sells. We're not trying to change the world. If you don't like how the business works, find a different business."

"Fine," I said. "I will. You can forget using my vocal tracks. I don't want to be any part of this shit."

"Baby," Brody said, reaching for my hand again. "Let's go outside and talk about this."

One look at his earnest face, and my lip started to quiver. "No, you're right," I said. "Go finish your day. I'll walk around and cool off."

"I'll come with you."

"No, finish your session. I'll be home when you get there."

He hesitated, then sighed. "Bring Dan."

I nodded, fighting to hold back tears. Everyone was staring at me like I'd lost my damn mind. Maybe I had. I turned and walked out quickly, without looking back. Dan, my bodyguard, didn't stick too close, which I appreciated. We took a cab to Hyde Park, and I walked around, aware of Dan walking a dozen yards behind me. I didn't think I needed him when I went out without Brody, but of course Brody insisted.

After a while, I found a bench and sat by the river. Watching Brody sitting in there repeating his line over and over, looking miserable and trapped like an animal at the zoo, made me feel awful about what I was doing. I knew he didn't like what he'd signed on for, either. All I wanted was to go home, to have a place of our own, like we did now but in Kentucky. To have a little stable with our own horses, just a couple for riding, and a few rose bushes out front. Like a starter version of what my parents had.

I sat up straighter and sucked in a breath. Here I was, thinking about having a home with Brody. Thinking about having a family with him, a real relationship. When had I stopped playing?

I reminded myself of my revenge plan, but it no longer held much appeal. Still, never one to give up, I tried to convince myself I would still do it. When he asked me to marry him, I would say no.

During the next few weeks, I lost sight of the end goal more and more often. There were press junkets, photo shoots, interviews. When I went places with Brody, he was inevitably recognized, even when he wore shades and a hat, which he always did. More often than not, I found myself with time to explore the city, eat at local landmarks, and go to museums while Brody worked. It was freeing to be able to go out anonymously, though Brody insisted my bodyguard trail after me as unobtrusively as possible. If anyone noticed a hulking mountain of muscle trailing fifteen feet behind me, no one alerted me.

I went to see Piper over the last weekend in September, and when she asked about Brody, I found myself talking about him and our apartment as if it were all real. As if he were my boyfriend, and we had a future. I could go days without reminding myself that I still meant to break his heart. When I returned to Chicago, I realized I didn't. Our apartment was home now.

I liked cooking with Brody, even cooking for him. I'd always been too focused on getting somewhere to enjoy being exactly where I was. But now, with time on my hands, I found I enjoyed trying out recipes I found on Pinterest, making our apartment a home, buying throw pillows for the couch and frames for photos of the two of us together in Chicago. I didn't clutter the place, knowing it was temporary, but a few nice, expensive pieces that I could take with me when I left gave it an elegant charm.

I'd been ready to marry Paul, but I'd never realized how much fun being domestic and playing house could be. Even buying groceries or cleaning supplies suddenly made me happy. And then, of course, there was the steady supply of orgasms Brody provided. That didn't hurt, either.

October

twenty-two

Brody

One night, when we were lying in bed after satisfying each other, I rolled over and ran my fingers down Laney's belly. "We're done with the album," I said. "The tour starts in a week. We're going to have to move out of here."

"Where to?" she asked.

"To the tour bus," I said. "I know it's not this. It's shit, really. But we'll be in nice hotels, too, whenever you want. You are coming with me, right?" Even now, I couldn't read her all the time. A part of me still expected her to pull out at any moment. This wasn't a life most people would choose. Even I got tired of it, and I was the famous one.

For her, it was worse—not being able to do things most couples did, like walk in the park or go shopping together, having to leave restaurants because people wouldn't stop interrupting our meal to ask for autographs. I was used to it, but she wasn't.

"Damn straight I'm coming with you," she said, grasping my hip bone. "You think I'm going to throw you to the wolves again? Fuck that. If one of your fangirls tries to get with you, they're going to have to come through me first."

I grinned and leaned in to kiss her. "I kind of like your jealous side."

"I'll remind you of that when I'm turning away the naked contortionist Swedish model twins inviting you to have a threesome."

I laughed and tweaked her nipple. "These are the only twins I'm interested in."

"Then you'd better show them some appreciation," she said with a pout. "I think they're feeling insecure."

"Now that's an invitation I can't turn down," I said, scooting down and closing my mouth over her nipple.

* * *

Laney

I had no idea what to wear to a Brody Villines show. Sure, I'd gone to a few when he'd first joined *Just 5 Guys*, but that had been a long time ago. He hadn't been a mega-famous star then, with fans about to rip out each other's hearts for a front row seat.

I settled for a classic Chanel little black dress—simple, elegant, a little sexy. It irritated me that Nash had already asked what I'd be wearing, and that I found herself questioning whether he would approve, would find it suitable for grown-up Brody's new girlfriend. Not that I'd be up on stage, but he'd insisted we arrive together and that I be with him backstage, where he'd deal with the media. And, of course, a photographer was going to take pictures of me at the front of the VIP section, his devoted new girlfriend.

Or, more accurately, old girlfriend. The magazines were all loving the story, how he'd gone home to visit his ailing grandfather and reunited with his high school sweetheart in the process. Since I'd been in a couple photos with Brody back when *Just 5 Guys* first hit it big a few years ago, they were digging up old stories for any mention of me. No one mobbed me when I was alone, but when I was with Brody, they seemed to think I was a minor celebrity, too.

Even Nash had started to begrudgingly approve of me. After a teen music magazine had asked me to be on the cover with Brody, he'd even agreed to change the lyrics to the song I hated if I'd let him use the background tracks I'd recorded. Which was nice of him, really, because he could have just used them. I'd signed them over before he let me in the studio to record them. And the new lyrics weren't much better—*I know you like it/ when I treat you like this.*

Nash was at least trying to be civil, though.

"Are you okay?" I asked Brody as we waited in the dressing room for his opening act—a teenage popstar trying too hard to be Miley Cyrus—to finish.

"No," Brody said, sinking onto the arm of a leather settee. "What if they hate it, like you said? What if the moms won't buy it and the girls hate me?"

"I thought you only cared about one girl liking you?" I said, winding my arms around his neck.

Brody looked up at me, his eyes close to panic. "It's just, when I had the others, the focus wasn't just on me. I could fuck up a little. I wasn't the only one out there."

"Sweetie," I said, sinking onto his knee. "You have eight backup dancers and two backup singers. You're not alone out there. And I'm right back here."

"I need you on that stage with me," he said, putting his hands on my shoulders. "You're the only thing that grounds me. The only thing that feels real in this crazy mess."

"Then maybe it's good that I'm not going to be out there," I said. "Then I'd become a part of it. This way, I can stay separate, and keep you sane."

"How on God's green earth did I get so lucky?" he said, leaning in to kiss me gently. "I love you, Laney Tucker."

For a second, his eyes got so intense with emotion I thought he was going to drop onto one knee and propose right there. Instead of feeling some smug satisfaction, my heart started hammering and I thought I might faint. And I knew right then that if he asked, when he asked, I wasn't going to say no.

November

twenty-three

Brody

The fans did not hate my new act. The moms did not stop buying, and the fangirls did not stop screaming. I still winced when I saw the creepy baby-doll masks at my shows, but there weren't as many. I had a different sound now, one where dressing in costume wasn't half the fun of getting tickets to a show. One where girls were more likely to wear almost nothing than cover themselves in masks. But I had hired Steve back on, and he was in charge of turning away anyone who tried to come backstage in a baby-doll costume. Laney vetoed almost everyone else who wanted to come back, and no one was allowed in my tour bus or dressing room except members of my team.

The backstage area was a little more lax, but groupies rarely made it back, unless they had paid some ungodly amount to meet me in person. Instead of dozens of predatory, eager fangirls trying to drag me out to my tour bus, I ended up meeting pregnant ladies, little old ladies, and kids with their moms—the few kids who still came to my shows. It was a different atmosphere now, but I didn't mind. I didn't miss the groupies, and I no longer loathed myself in the morning.

Instead, I got to go back to whatever ridiculously posh hotel I'd been put up at, trade massages with the woman I loved, take a bubble bath with her, and then make her cum. There was no contest between Laney and anyone else. I had chosen, and I was happy with my choice. All the girls in the world offering themselves up for a meaningless fuck could not compare to the dazed, blissful, freshly fucked look on Laney's face before she fell asleep each night.

After a show at Red Rocks in Colorado, Nash came barreling into my dressing room and grabbed me in a bear hug. He was unexpectedly strong for such a little guy.

"They fucking love you!" Nash screamed. "We're getting you twelve more shows on top of these twelve, and then we're going international, baby! The Germans are already coming all the way here to see you!"

"Dude, are you serious?" I asked from the steel bars of Nash's arms.

"Would I fuck with you, my golden goose?" Nash asked, releasing me. "I gotta go, my phone's blowing up. Seattle in three days. I'm catching a flight there first thing. You and Laney stay, enjoy Colorado. I used to love this place, when I had the fucking time to see it. I'll catch you on Wednesday evening when you get in. Rest up Thursday for the show that night. Doctor's orders."

I saluted, and Nash dashed off.

"Congratulations," Laney said, slipping her arm around me. "I guess I'm going to get to see the world this year after all."

"Oh, babe, I'm sorry," I said, pulling her into my arms. I took her face between my hands and kissed her softly. "I know you wanted to travel, and you're doing this instead. This is no good…" I trailed off and kissed her again, then broke into a grin. "But yeah, baby! We're going to Europe. I'll make sure I get some time there to hang out, not just work."

"It's fine," she said. "You're the one working. I'm just along for the ride. And anyway, it's kind of cool to see how things work from this side of the stage. Although less glamorous than I expected."

"I told you it wasn't all hookers and blow," I said, though I felt a little guilty for making it sound like backstage had always been full of rich old ladies and kids with their moms. *Just 5 Guys* had been different, though. We'd been teenagers. There had been some jostling for position in the beginning, then a competitive edge when it came to showing our sexual prowess. It wasn't just about quantity, but quality, consecutive scores, what you could get the groupies to do. Which, it had turned out, was pretty much anything. Out of resentment, I'd gotten pretty creative at times, not even finding it especially exciting.

I shook the thoughts away and pulled Laney to me, letting her anchoring effect settle me. I didn't need any of the twisted shit I'd done with groupies. She was enough.

"Hey," I said. "Thank you. For coming with us, for putting up with all of this. I wish it was just us, at home, without all this shit."

"It will be," she promised.

"I could walk away from it all right now," I said. "I'm set for life, Laney. If you wanted to, I'd go home and marry you tomorrow."

She laughed nervously. "I'd need more than a day to plan a wedding."

"Fuck everyone else," I said. "The wedding is for their sake. I just want to be with you forever. I don't care about that."

She pulled away slightly. "But I do."

"Then I'm going to make it happen," I said. "I'm going to give you the best fucking wedding anyone has ever had. There won't be a single thing that you didn't plan and choose and want in the whole wedding. Not one single thing." I kissed her nose and then released her when Stacy called that I had some photographers waiting.

"Let's just finish your tour, and then we'll talk about that," Laney said. "I don't want to ruin your focus."

"Too late for that," I said, slapping her ass. "You're all I think about, babe."

"Aww, but you've got a whole career in front of you. I can't let you go the way of O-Town," she teased.

I laughed and kissed her again. I'd voiced that fear to her once, but now, I didn't think I'd care much. Those guys were probably happily married by now, with families, and the only photographers waiting for them were at the Sears Portrait Studio. Suddenly, that sounded much more appealing than the hungry reporters wanting the scoop, always digging for dirt, trying to stir up drama between us—*why did you and Ms. Tucker break up? Was that a baby bump I saw when you were together at Starbucks? Was she still engaged when you got back together?*

But the hungry reporters waited, and my job was to appease their bloodlust.

* * *

Laney

After the two days in Colorado, still snowless but chilly, we rode to Seattle in the tour bus. From there, we would go on to Salt Lake City, then to L.A., where Brody had a house I had never seen but could imagine was ridiculously ritzy. I was ready to stay a few days and relax, though. Already, I was tiring of the hours of monotony on the road. We spent time in the bedroom, played our guitars and sang together, which at first made me feel terribly self-conscious and corny. When we were in high school, we'd played together all the time—for our families, at church, even at a couple of fall festivals in town. But I had barely touched my guitar since Brody left.

"How do you stay in practice?" I asked one day when we finished playing. "You're so much better than me."

"You're just a little rusty," Brody said. "I play all the time. It's the only thing that relaxed me when you weren't around."

As much as I liked being with him, the bus was boring. I wanted to be out on a horse in the chill of autumn, pushing Pegasus across the field, not in a bus sitting in construction zone traffic for hours at a time. In here, things felt too enclosed, too claustrophobic. I'd thought the city was bad, but now I longed for Chicago's busy streets.

Finally, we made it to Seattle. Brody tried to convince me to go out with Nash and him for dinner, but I just wanted to be alone in the hotel room and take a long bubble bath. I didn't much care for Nash, even after he'd given our relationship his okay. The fact that he thought we needed that irritated me. After weeks on the road, everything irritated me.

The break from everyone recharged me, though, and by the next night, I was ready for the show. By now, I had the routine down. Calm Brody's nerves before the show, then sit in the front of the VIP section, keep the groupies away while his manager and publicity department kept the bloggers, fans, photographers, and reporters busy. He always needed a little space to undress and de-stress after dancing his ass off for an hour and a half, usually in three different costumes, one of which was leather. I didn't know how he didn't pass out from heat. After his half hour of winding down, he talked to VIPs, other celebrities, and on rare occasions media.

The Seattle show went off without a hitch, despite some thunder outside almost loud enough to drown out the performance. I was looking forward to riding back to the hotel in a cab, which he promised we could do if we used the Hummer as a decoy, sending someone else off in his usual vehicle. I didn't mind going along on his tour, doing things his way most of the time. But when I had the chance to be a tourist, I was doing it right. It was so *classic* to ride in a cab in the rain in Seattle.

Brody was still in his dressing room changing when my walkie-talkie crackled. I'd taken to stationing myself at the entrance to the backstage area, like the world's most unlikely security guard, to catch any groupies that charmed their way past Steve. Despite his weakness for curvy, exotic women, I couldn't help but love the guy. He'd fully admitted this weakness, with some shuffling and maybe even blushing, when he'd given me the walkie.

"Got one headed back," he said into the walkie.

I stood from my stool and peered down the little hallway, but I didn't see any skanks yet. "Roger that," I said, feeling all official.

"She might be a little unhinged," Steve said. "That was probably a mistake. She can't hear me, can she?"

"No," I said with a grin, returning my walkie to the table beside me. I turned down the volume just as a hand fell on my shoulder, making me jump a mile.

"Oh my gosh, you scared me," I said, swatting at Brody.

"Just checking on you," he said, leaning in to kiss my temple. "I've got to go take selfies. You know the drill."

Brody's face was probably the most selfie-captured face in the world. It was kind of his calling card, like Taylor Swift with her cats. He had made himself an accessible celebrity by taking selfies with fans and posting them all over social media. He even had someone check through Twitter, Instagram, and Snapchat to repost all the selfies fans posted with him. It had become someone's full-time job at this point.

He kissed me one last time before Nash grabbed his arm and steered him to the first people he needed to greet. I could hear Nash's rapid-fire instructions, reminding him who he was meeting and what he was supposed to say to them.

My attention was diverted by the girl emerging from the hallway at last. It had taken her long enough. I replayed Steve's words and wondered if she'd stopped to pee in the hallway or something equally weird. One thing I'd learned in my short time on tour—fans were batshit crazy.

The girl blew by me without so much as a glance. She wasn't the groupie type. She looked more like a druggie, with a dirty, tattered trench coat, straggly dark hair, and pasty skin with a few breakouts that looked raw and angry, as if she picked at them too often. Suddenly I was reminded of crazed fans who attacked singers, and I leapt off the stool and followed the girl, who was blowing through the crowd with no regard for anyone she pushed out of her way.

"Hey," I said, grabbing her shoulder and spinning her around. I wasn't about to let some psycho pull a knife on my man.

"Fuck off, lady," the girl said, jerking her arm away. When her coat swung open, she wasn't carrying a weapon at all. She was just a bony, sickly-looking pregnant girl who couldn't have been much more than a teenager.

"Brody's meeting with some fans," I said with measured calm and a reassuring smile. But I didn't take my hand from the girl's shoulder. "Are you here for an autograph? He'd be happy to sign something for your baby boy or girl. He'll even autograph your belly if you want."

I found it hysterical how uncomfortable Brody got when the pregnant ones requested a signed belly, and I couldn't help but enjoy watching him squirm.

"An autograph?" the unkempt girl scoffed. "Are you fucking kidding me? I don't want an autograph."

"Hey," Brody said, sliding up beside her. "Everything okay?"

"No, obviously, it's not," the girl said, gesturing at her belly. "I need some money."

"Okay," he said slowly. "Let's see what we can do for you."

"No, you moron, I don't need a handout. I need you to take care of this. This is your fault, *Brody Villines.*" She snarled his name like it hurt her to say it. "This is your baby."

twenty-four

Brody

I stared at the girl for a full ten seconds, unable to speak. A hundred things were trying to burst out of my mouth at once. I knew for damn sure I'd never fucked this girl. She looked like shit. She wasn't even the kind of girl who came to my shows. This chick was more grunge than pop, the furthest thing from a baby-doll I could imagine, with not an inch of skin showing anywhere from the neck down and not a trace of makeup on her pale face.

She stared at me expectantly with these sullen, expectant eyes.

Violet eyes.

FUCK.

"Brody, I need you to come—." Before Nash could finish his sentence, I spun on him.

"Get out!" I screamed. "Get the fuck out. Everybody, get out. Get out! The show is over, get the fuck out of here."

Nash took a step back, looking as speechless as I had been a minute before. When I got stressed, I cussed at people, I saw a shrink, I hid in my dressing room and refused to come out. Throwing a tantrum backstage was not my style. That was more Jace's style. I was the holding-shit-in type, not the meltdown type.

To his credit, Nash recovered in a record two seconds, grabbed my elbow and shoved me roughly toward my dressing room. "Calm the fuck down," he barked. "You don't yell at your fans, Brody-boy."

"Get them out," I growled, planting my feet and refusing to budge. "I need you to get them all out of here now."

"All right, everybody, show's over," Nash said, turning to the backstage area, where the fans had clustered to stare uneasily at me. Nash blocked me with his body as if he were making sure I didn't lunge out and attack someone. "Brody's not taking selfies tonight. Sorry to disappoint you. See this fine lady on your way out and she'll get you a free ticket with backstage passes for the next show." He pointed to Stacy, who smiled her best publicity smile and gestured for them to follow her. A few of the girls were squealing to each other in delight and jumping up and down, while a few others were grumbling because they couldn't make the trip.

Security ushered them out after Stacy. Steve appeared and looked around, then nodded to where Laney was standing with the pregnant chick. Before I could communicate my intent, one of the beefy security guys reached the girls.

"Don't you fucking touch me," the girl warned, yanking her arm away.

What was her name? Had I ever known it?

"Ma'am, I'm sorry, I'm going to have to ask you to leave."

"And I'm going to have to ask you to go fuck yourself. I'm not leaving until I get what I want."

It probably wasn't my baby. It couldn't be. I always wore a condom.

Didn't I?

"No selfies tonight, ma'am."

"Selfies? What the fuck is wrong with you people? I'm not after a selfie, I'm—."

"She stays," I said, stepping between her and the security guy. "They both stay."

With one look from Laney, I knew she understood. She understood that I'd fucked this girl, and that it really might be my baby. Because if I hadn't, I would have thrown her out like the psycho she was.

I couldn't meet Laney's gaze again.

"Come back to the dressing room," I said quietly. "My tour bus isn't here."

Discarded clothes from the night's performances lay scattered across the floor of the dressing room. It was small and unglamorous, barely more than a closet. When I had to do quick changes, it worked, though. And I had a team to dress me between sets. Now I kicked aside the white leather pants and jacket I'd worn during my first set and turned to face the others. Steve had stayed out, minding his own business, but Nash had come in, along with Laney and the pregnant chick.

The dressing room was brightly lit with fluorescent bulbs, which washed out the girl's already pallid skin and made her look even worse. Whatever the pregnancy glow was supposed to do, it wasn't doing it for her.

Nash started barking at me right away, scolding me for yelling at the fans.

"I thought you wanted me to be grown up," I interrupted with a smirk. "Isn't this what grown up rock stars do? Throw tantrums?"

Nash stopped yelling and took a breath, his eyes hard with anger, and ran his hand over his gelled curls. "What is this all about? Who the fuck is this?"

"Yeah, Brody Villines," the pregnant chick said. "Aren't you going to introduce me?" Now she was smirking, obviously aware that I didn't know her name. Of course I'd never asked her name. I never asked any of them for names.

"I'm sure you don't need my help with that," I said. "You've already come in and disrupted the afterparty. I wouldn't want to steal your thunder."

"Afterparty? That's what you call an afterparty? God, you're even more pathetic than last time I saw you."

"Go on, introduce yourself. The floor is yours. You've got everyone riveted."

"Fine," she said, rolling her eyes and adopting a sugary, sarcastic tone as she went on. "I'm Uma. It's ever so nice of you to let me into your exclusive private party. It's not every day I rub elbows with the rich and famous. I guess I'm supposed to be falling on my knees begging to blow you at this point. Isn't that what you said, Brody?"

"So you're one of his 'baby-dolls'?" Laney asked, her voice even. "And you're pregnant, and you're claiming it's his. Do you really think you're the first person who's ever tried to say Brody knocked her up?" She gave Uma a pitying look.

"Bullshit," Nash cut in. "No fucking way. Is that what this is about? Brody, you handled this like a fucking child. So some chick says you knocked her up? Big fucking deal. Let me guess—she wants some money?"

"Hell yes, I want some money," Uma said. "He owes me. And I obviously don't have any." She gestured to her tattered trench coat and dingy grey t-shirt. She was skinny, too, her elbows jutting at the fabric of her thin coat. She pointed a finger at me. "I've been trying to get in contact with you for months. You're going to take care of this."

"Aren't you…a little…uh…big for that?" I asked, gesturing to her belly. It wasn't like she was about to pop out a kid right there, but she was obviously pregnant.

"No, no, no," Nash said. "We're not even going to discuss this. Get the fuck out of here."

"Hey, no problem," the girl, raising her hands. "I could have talked to the magazines months ago, when I found out. I could have splashed it all over social media, like that chick did to the Biebs. But up until now, I've been classy."

"If that's what you call it," Laney muttered.

"Listen, lady," Nash said. "You've never even met Brody before. You're just a crazy fan. Nobody's going to believe you."

Uma's eyes darted to me, and for the first time, she looked a little uncertain. An edge of desperation crept into her eyes. "Brody?" she asked, her voice a little higher than before. She swallowed loudly enough for all of us to hear it in the silence.

"Don't say anything," Nash said. "I'll get security to throw her out, and if you're worried she'll smear you, we can get your lawyer on the phone. Right now, you don't know this chick from Adam, and anything she says is libel."

"It's not libel if it's true," she said, but her eyes stayed on me, still pleading. "And I don't have anywhere to go. I was in this band, and of course the second I started showing, they threw me out. And then I was going to stay with my cousin, but her parents sublet the house while they're off in Europe or some shit…" Her voice broke and she stopped abruptly, swallowing her words.

"Nice story," Nash said, reaching for his phone.

"I'll get a DNA test."

"Hold on," I said, raising a hand to stop Nash from calling security.

"Jesus Christ," Nash said. "It's like managing a toddler. You really going to believe every sob story that comes through the doors?"

"I'm leaving," Laney said. "I can't hear any more of this."

I turned to her, and Nash picked up his phone again, and Uma went on chattering about the DNA test. All I wanted to do was run the fuck out of there. Rewind the clock to the beginning of that night, when everything was going right and everyone was happy. Or better yet, rewind to the last night I'd played with *Just 5 Guys*, so I could talk myself out of grudge fucking some holier-than-thou hipster chick with violet eyes.

The fucked up part was, if she hadn't been the last groupie I'd fucked, I probably wouldn't have remembered her at all. That, and those crazy purple eyes.

Laney pivoted on her heel and walked out of the dressing room with measured steps, her head held high. I didn't know if I should follow or if she wanted to be alone. I didn't know if I should leave Nash alone with this other chick. I sure as hell didn't want to be alone with her.

In a matter of moments, I'd lost the one person I wanted to keep forever. It wasn't really a contest.

I strode out of the dressing room. "Laney," I called, jogging to catch up with her in the backstage area, which felt huge and cavernous now that it wasn't filled with other people. Her back stiffened as I approached, and she didn't turn toward me.

"Laney." I grabbed her arm and spun her around, only to see her face streaked with tears.

"I can't believe I fucking trusted you!" she yelled, slamming her palms into my chest and knocking me a step back. "I can't believe I thought you'd changed."

"Laney," I said. "That was before we were together. It was ages ago. She's nobody."

"Yeah, well, that nobody just ruined us. I hope it was worth it."

Something caved inside my chest, but I wouldn't give up that easy. "Don't say that," I commanded. "I'm not letting you go. We can figure this out."

She dropped her head and swiped under her eyes, but when I tried to put a hand on her shoulder, she reeled away. "Don't touch me, Brody. You better not touch me right now."

"I'm sorry." I didn't know what else to say. She'd never understand. Hell, it was hard for me to even understand now that I'd been away for a while. But I remembered what it had been like, the endless parade of groupies who all blurred together, the illusion that they could make me feel something, anything, when all along I should have seen that the only person who could touch my heart was gone.

She took a shuddering breath and wiped her cheeks with both hands at once, swiping away all emotion. "I'm going back to the hotel," she said. "I need to be alone. I'll be there when you get back. You should go talk to that girl. If it is yours…" She broke off and shook her head. "Give me at least an hour."

"Laney, please…" I reached out again, then dropped my hand before she could shrink back. That had nearly killed me the first time she shrank away like I was someone she didn't know, a stranger. I didn't think I'd survive it again. "Just promise you'll be there when I get back."

"I said I would," she said. "I'm not the liar here, Brody."

"I never lied to you."

"Yeah, well, it's a little late to brag about that one. Outright lying isn't the only way to be dishonest."

"I wasn't—."

She held up a hand. "I don't need to hear it. I've heard more than enough tonight."

Watching her walk away was like watching her rip my guts out while I was helpless to stop her. It was all I could do not to punch through a wall, throw tables and chairs and mic stands and speakers, scream until the fucking stadium burst apart at the seams and blew shrapnel all over Seattle.

"Wow," Uma said behind me. "That was cold."

I hadn't heard her come out, but I turned around, all my anger melting into something else, something that rested uneasily in my bones, something that felt too much like hollowness. Like loss.

twenty-five

Laney

I didn't need a bodyguard. I didn't need the rented Hummer to come and whisk me away, guarding me from throngs of fans. By myself, I was no one, unrecognizable unless someone was looking for me. I ducked my head against the rain, trying to hail a cab. But it was after the show, and everyone had already grabbed all the cabs when they spilled out of the stadium. I pulled my jacket closed around me and walked briskly to a covered bus stop a hundred feet down the sidewalk.

Inside, a crumpled McDonald's bag lay wadded up on one end of the bench. The Happy Meal toy that must have come in in the bag—some kind of action figure—lay face down on the wet pavement just outside the shelter, no doubt dropped as the kid approached the bus. I wondered how old that kid had been, if it was a boy or girl, if it had cried when the missing toy had been realized. Anything to keep my mind off that other kid I couldn't stop thinking about, the one inside that girl.

Uma.

Of all the ways I'd imagined Brody's past coming back to haunt us, that hadn't been among them. I'd worried that I'd never measure up. I'd worried that I would always worry that I'd never measure up. I had worried about him cheating again. That had been the big one.

But never this. And never with a skank like Uma. She wasn't even pretty, with her raggedy clothes and oily hair. I'd never understand how he'd slept with a girl who looked like that, even if I understood everything else. How could he have chosen that, even tons of that, over me? And why did that hurt so fucking much?

I'd heard of guys "slumming it," but usually that meant some football player was sleeping with a poor-but-hot girl with a reputation. This gave the expression a whole new meaning.

I kept circling back to that. To how on earth Brody could have ever wanted to have sex with that girl—even meaningless, anonymous sex. Because face it, even a blind man could have seen that he had no idea who the girl was when she showed up.

The trouble was, he'd remembered. He'd remembered, and it must have been true, because he hadn't told her to fuck off.

I sighed and hunched my shoulders as I stood under the bust stop. In truth, I wouldn't have wanted him to boot the girl. That was the thing. The worst thing. I couldn't tell him to throw her out and pretend he'd never seen her. She looked so desperate, a runaway teen with collarbones jutting through her stained t-shirt and sunken, desperate eyes. If Brody had told her to fuck off, even if it turned out he hadn't gotten her pregnant, I would have been horrified.

You couldn't just say fuck off to a starving pregnant girl, even if she had fucked your boyfriend.

A bus came by, but I didn't climb on. I just wanted the shelter, not a ride. A few passengers descended the steps and climbed off the bus—three laughing college students who made me miss Piper, an obese black woman who looked so weary that she might not be able to take one more step, a young hipster couple with a pair of toddlers strapped to their chests. I looked away, my throat tightening.

Brody was going to be a father. At least he thought so. And that other girl was going to be the mother. Not me.

Not that I wanted a baby. I wasn't ready for that. But someday, I wanted a lot of them. After growing up an only child, I'd always wanted a big family. And not too far in the future. If I was going to have four kids, as I'd always planned, I couldn't wait until I was approaching middle age to get started. I'd had it all planned out. I would marry Paul at twenty-five, after two years of grad school, and we'd start having babies a few years later.

Piper told me I was crazy to want to get married so young. But in the south, that wasn't young. Most of my friends had gotten engaged in college, like me. A lot were getting married now that they'd graduated. Waiting until after grad school was considered cautious. Piper lived in a different world now, and for the first time, I worried she might not understand.

Somewhere along the way, I had gotten comfortable. I had started to believe Brody would never break my heart. I'd forgotten all my own schemes, broken all my rules. One day, when his tour was over, I'd imagined going back to Kentucky with him and settling down. Not having kids now, but not in the distant future, either. He'd finish out the contract with his label for two more albums, and I'd go on tour with him. But he wouldn't want to do that forever. From all that he'd said, he was growing weary of it already.

At last, I called Uber and got a ride back to the hotel. "Did you see the concert?" the driver asked. He was a young guy with a beanie and a beard. "It's that new guy everybody's talking about, right? Brody Villines? The indie popstar?"

"Yeah," I said. "It was quite a show."

Back at the hotel, I climbed onto the elevator and scanned my keycard to go to the suite. No one could access it from the lobby unless they had a card, which kept fans from trying to follow Brody up to his room. On the top floor, I exited the elevator car and stepped into the suite.

A few soft lamps lit the living area, which suddenly felt strange and formal without Brody. We'd lounged around most of the day, watching TV, making love, talking. Now, it was only me with my thoughts. I opened the fridge and surveyed the minibar, but I didn't feel like drinking. I didn't feel like anything.

I sat down on the couch and searched for the remote. A flash of memory came back to me, the moment earlier that afternoon when I'd knocked it to the floor while flexing my foot, my toes curling as I cupped the back of Brody's neck, pulling his face deeper between my thighs as I came.

Suddenly, I wanted to wipe the memory from my mind, go back and wipe all the memories of him from my mind. Not just the recent ones, but all of them. My whole life was flavored by Brody's sweetness, his nearness. My memories, my very soul, was intertwined with his, twisted together like two trees that had once thought it might be a good idea to grow close together. My whole life was filled with Brody's presence and his absence. Even the places he hadn't touched were filled with the longing for him.

It would never go away. He would never go away. Even if he let me go, I would never be rid of him. He'd come back the same way his past had come back for him, haunting, nagging, demanding attention, consuming my soul.

Because I could think of no other way to cleanse myself, I climbed in the shower. Even there, my body held the memory of him. In every soft space, around every curve, nestled into the crook of my neck and elbow, buried deep inside where no one would ever see.

Not like that other girl. Someone would see where Brody had been inside her. It was big and obvious, a growing part of her. Somehow, that was both better and worse. That girl had proof. All I had to show for my pain was a luxury hotel room. I didn't even have a ring to take off and throw at him, that symbolic gesture to signify the end in grand fashion.

No, this heartbreak was as quiet and lethal as the last one.

twenty-six

Brody

"Where's Nash?" I asked, fighting every urge to turn and run after Laney, to chase her down and claim her, to tell her that I'd never be done with her. That didn't matter to her, because she was done with me. After this, she would be.

"He's having a meltdown on the phone in your dressing room," Uma said, pulling out a folding metal chair from one of the plastic folding tables where an orange plastic watercooler sat. It was much less glamorous now that it had been cleared of the VIP trappings.

I pulled out another chair and sat, dropping my head into my hands.

"I'm not making it up, you know," Uma said after a while.

I lifted my head. "How could I have been so fucking stupid? I didn't use a condom. I didn't, did I?"

Uma bit at a hangnail.

"Jesus. Nash always fucking told me. *Wear a fucking rubber. Wear a fucking rubber.* That's all I ever heard. *You can fuck all the groupies you want, but wear a fucking rubber.* And I always did."

"It was in the moment," Uma said. "We weren't thinking about it."

"And you weren't on birth control? You didn't think to go get the morning after pill?"

She shook her head, her limp hair falling in her face.

"Can I ask you something? Are you on drugs, Uma? Because you look like shit, no offense."

Uma rolled her eyes and shook her hair back. "That's not offensive at all," she said sarcastically. "And no, I'm not on drugs, unless you call generic brand antacids drugs, and then, yeah. I'm downing an industrial sized bottle of those a week. But I mostly puke them all up anyway, so I'm not sure I can blame the shitty store brand for its ineffectiveness."

"Fuck. I'm sorry."

"I asked my doctor, well, the time I went to see one, and they can go in with this super long needle and get some DNA before it's born."

"Holy shit," I said, my head swimming at the thought of that needle.

"They said it was risky, though, and I might lose the baby. And you know what's fucked up? I thought, sweet, I definitely want to do that. But I couldn't afford the fucking test."

"Jesus, Uma."

"Yeah, I don't think He's too fond of me right now."

I dropped my head back into my hands. "Fuck," I muttered again. It seemed the only word adequate for the situation.

"Sorry about your girlfriend. I'm guessing that's what she was. I'm right, right? That's why the groupies aren't lined up outside your dressing room waiting to blow you."

"She's more than a girlfriend."

Uma's eyes widened. "Shit, fiancé? Wife? Nah, I would have heard about that in some gossip rag."

"I don't want to talk about it."

She shrugged and slumped back in her chair. "Well, I'm sorry I scared her off. And trust me, I'm not here to get in the way of any of that shit. It's not like I want to marry you."

The very mention made my adrenaline kick in. She couldn't force me to do that. Even a pregnancy scandal was, well, it was bad, no way around that. Still, celebrities had kids out of wedlock all the time.

I just knew what my mother would have to say about that.

I dropped my forehead on the edge of the table, and a dull pain thumped into my skull. So I did it again, and again, and again. There was something satisfying about punishing myself in this small way for the gigantic, irreversible, fucking disaster I had made of my life. One girl. One night. One condom I hadn't used.

"So, look, I'm sorry about your girlfriend and everything, and I'm not trying to be a bitch, but I'm thinking you'll be okay," Uma said. "You're a guy, and you're like twenty-something, and cute in that boyband way, and famous, and you probably wipe your ass with hundred-dollar bills. I think she'll forgive you, and if she doesn't, you'll find someone else."

"I don't want someone else," I snapped, slamming my fist down on the table.

Uma jumped. "Okay, you're obviously not hearing me. So I'm just going to go ahead and be a bitch here. I know this is a lot to absorb in one night, so I'm going to pretend you're not a completely selfish, self-centered douche, because you didn't call me a liar and get security to throw me out. But I'm homeless here, Brody. I have exactly…"

She reached into her pocket and pulled out a handful of change and crumpled dollar bills and dumped it on the table. "Three dollars and change. I'm stuck with this freaky alien thing growing inside me like a parasite. And guess what? I'm nineteen, so I'm going to be a teen mom. A homeless teen mom. I'm not even going to be able to buy diapers, so I guess I'll just walk down the street and let her crap all over the sidewalk. So as tragic as your fight with your girlfriend is, I'd really like to get back to that money thing, if you don't mind."

Damn, I really was an asshole. I needed to pull my shit together and think about someone besides myself right now. Not my specialty.

"Okay, you're right," I said. "Are you, uh, too late?" I gestured to her belly, unable to say the awful word.

"You mean can I get an abortion, so you don't have to deal with it? Yeah, I think so. But I don't really know. I figured I'd do that, but I didn't have the money for that, either. I mean, what do I know about being a mom? I don't even *like* kids. So then I tried to find your number."

That made me laugh, a hollow sound that lacked any hint of mirth.

"I get it," she said. "You can't have your twenty million fans blowing up your phone. Or your Twitter or… I assume you just don't check those at all. You probably have people who do that for you, right? And what's one message, like, *Hey, Brody, I'm that girl you fucked after your last show. I need to talk to you.* You probably get a hundred of those a day."

I laid my head down on the table. I wondered if she ever stopped talking. I needed a shower, and a massage, and a call to my shrink. But more than anything, I needed Laney. I could feel the raw, scraped out feeling in my chest where she should be. I should be with her. Not here with some stranger. I should just cut her a check and tell her to disappear.

"Where are you staying?" I asked without lifting my head.

"Well, I was crashing at my drummer's house until recently," Uma said. "But then her boyfriend made a pass at me, because I guess that's a whole 'nother level of creepy no one tells you about this whole pregnancy thing, is that for some freaky reason I don't understand, guys are suddenly hitting on me. Like, different guys. Apparently, that's a thing. Some guys think it's hot. Don't ask me why, I know I look like shit without you telling me. Anyway, since I'm not in the band anymore anyway…" She shrugged and bit at a hangnail again. Her nails were short and ragged, red-rimmed, as if she'd bitten them down to below the quick.

"Let me get you a room in our hotel," I said. "You can order some food."

She gave me a suspicious look. "You're probably staying in the fucking Hilton or something. I bet that's like, two hundred bucks a night. I could use that money for something else."

"I'm not offering you money right now," I said. "Not until I've talked to my people more. But I don't want you sleeping on the street, either. And you look like you could use some food and a shower. No offense."

She rolled her eyes, but she pushed herself up from her chair. “You’re surprisingly un-douche-like this time,” she said. “Your girlfriend has trained you well.”

“Don’t even fuck with me right now,” I said. “If it turns out you’re lying…”

“I’m not lying,” she said, rolling her eyes again. “And I think you know it. I hadn’t slept with anyone in months before that. That’s probably why I was desperate enough to be susceptible to your douchebaggery. You hit the window.”

“The what?”

“The window of opportunity. You know, that sweet spot between getting it regular and getting used to not getting any, when you’re especially horny and you really don’t care who you’re going home with, you just need a good fuck.”

“Huh.”

“Right, I guess you wouldn’t know,” she said. “You’ve probably never gone two consecutive nights without bashing the gash.”

“Let’s just go.”

But before we could leave, Nash came storming out to grab me. “Where do you think you’re running off to?”

"I need to see Laney."

"Fuck Laney," Nash said. "We need this taken care of tonight."

"I'm getting Uma a hotel room," I said. "I think whatever you have to say can wait until morning. I need to be with Laney."

"You can't get this broad a hotel room," Nash said. "That's an admission."

"I believe her," I said with a shrug.

"Oh my fuck," Nash screamed, throwing up his hands so violently that his phone went flying across the room. "You're going to believe every groupie that says she's pregnant with your baby, you're going to have a fucking caravan of tour buses following you around. Why don't we just make that your act, huh? *Brody Villines and the Pregnant Groupies.* Are you fucking retarded?"

"Oh, wow," Uma said. "So, that's offensive."

"Look, Nash, I fucked up, okay? In the five years we had the band, I fucked up one time. And it was with her."

Nash's voice lowered and his eyes narrowed into slits. "What do you mean, fucked up?"

"I didn't wear a condom."

Nash began spluttering incoherently with rage, his face going redder and redder until it was almost purple.

"I need to be with my family right now," I said. "You do what needs to be done on the business side. You always tell me to stay out of that. So I'm going home to Laney."

Ignoring Nash's tantrum, I ducked back to the dressing room, where I grabbed my ski cap and jacket. Suddenly, I was sure that Laney wouldn't be back at the hotel, that she'd be gone when I got back. The caved-in feeling inside me increased, like everything in my chest was crumbling. I almost ran outside, only to be slammed by a sheet of frigid rain.

"Welcome to Seattle," Uma yelled over the downpour. I tried to shelter her with my arm as we ran to the rented H2. I jumped up into the back seat and reached down to take Uma's hand and pull her up. We were both nearly soaked after the run through the rain, though it had only been ten seconds, tops.

"I can't believe you drive a Hummer," Uma muttered when she'd caught her breath.

"Well, I do."

"Actually, I can believe it," she said. "I just can't believe I'm riding in one. God, this thing probably costs as much as a house. And the gas it takes… I feel guilty just sitting here."

"Would you rather be out there in the pouring rain?"

"No," she admitted, then turned to the window. "Thanks."

At the hotel, I got her a room, told her to order room service, and split. I couldn't wait to get away from her. She was everything I'd tried to forget when I started over.

A new sound, a new lifestyle, a new girl.

One girl.

Love. Excitement. Hope.

All that had come to a screeching halt the moment she showed up like a symbol of everything in my life I'd fucked up.

twenty-seven

Brody

My stomach might rebel at any moment, hurl the contents of my lunch with Laney, so many hours ago. I should have been starving, but all I could think about was Laney. Laney, and how heavy the weight inside me had grown, as if I were turning to stone from the inside out.

I'd been standing outside the door to our hotel room for five minutes, unable to make myself open it. If I found it empty, I didn't think I'd come out of it alive. I'd transform overnight into one of those prima donna rock stars who trashed their hotel rooms and refused to take the stage the next night.

But if I didn't go in, I'd never know. Never know how it ended.

Before I could punk out, I swiped my key card and pushed the door open. A wave of Lysol scent billowed out in my face, so thick I could see it hanging in the air. But it wasn't empty. Thank fuck it wasn't empty.

I stepped inside, and there she was.

She was standing on tiptoes, spraying the wall behind the TV with some kind of cleaning product.

"Hey," I said.

"Oh, hey," she said. "Just cleaning up a little."

I glanced at the Walgreens bag on the couch, cans of Lysol spray and tubes of Clorox wipes spilling forth.

"How long have you been doing this?" I asked. "You're going to give yourself brain damage breathing in all this."

"It's just Lysol."

"I think you're supposed to spray it in a ventilated area," I said carefully. "You have no idea how strong it smells in here."

"I'm almost done," she said, moving to the little kitchen area, where she began spraying the island liberally.

"Laney, come on," I said. "Why are you doing this?"

"I just needed to clean up a little, I told you."

"Laney, this is crazy," I said, waving away a cloud of disinfectant fog that drifted from the island.

"Oh, so now I'm crazy," she said, slamming the can down on the island.

Shit. Bad word choice. I held out a hand and tried to explain. "No, that's not what—"

"I'm crazy for being pissed that the man I love fucked some other girl and couldn't even bother to wear protection? I'm crazy to wonder how many other girls you didn't wear one with, and that the first thing I did when I realized you were going around having unprotected sex with girls whose names you can't even remember was to call and set up an appointment to get tested?"

"It was one girl, Laney. One time. I swear it."

"*That you remember*," she exploded. "You didn't even remember her! You told me you always wore one. So now I find out you didn't. How many others don't you remember?"

Fuck. What if she was right. "I—I'm pretty sure."

"Pretty sure doesn't fucking help when the test comes back positive, does it, Brody?"

"Laney, no. That's not going to happen. She's not like that. She wasn't a groupie."

"Oh, right. She was a real girlfriend. You *really* cared about her. It meant something. That's why you couldn't remember her fucking name?"

"Okay, I didn't say she was a girlfriend," I said, holding up a hand. My eyes were starting to water from the fumes, and I couldn't think straight. "I said she's not a groupie. I'm sure she doesn't have any diseases."

"Oh, really? You're sure? Like you were sure you wore a condom with all your sex-doll sluts? Or you're *pretty* sure, kind of like you're pretty sure there's not some other groupie going to show up nine months pregnant or dropping herpes scabs all over the floor."

"You have every right to be pissed."

"You're damn right I do. And I am. Oh, you have no idea just how pissed. You come back here and defend that girl? Defend *yourself?* You have no right, Brody."

"You're right," I said. "I'm sorry."

We stood there looking at each other across the island, a distance of only a few feet, but it felt like a thousand miles. All I could do was apologize, and even I knew it wasn't enough. Words couldn't make this right. They couldn't stop the woman I loved, who knew me from the day she was born, from looking at me like I was lower than dirt, less than a stranger. Words couldn't fill the chasm that had opened in my chest as it opened between us.

Laney took a deep breath and coughed.

"You're not crazy," I said, circling the island. "It's just hard to breathe in here." I took her face in my hands and kissed her gently, hardly daring to touch her, hardly daring to believe she'd let me.

She pulled away, turning her shoulder towards me. "I'll tell you what makes it hard to breathe, and it's not a fog of Lysol. It's having a random stranger walk in and tell you she's nine months pregnant with your boyfriend's baby."

"She's not nine—never mind. You're right. That was fucked up. I'm sorry you had to be there."

She spun on me, her eyes flashing. "You're sorry I was there? Why, because then you could have hidden it from me?"

"Because then I could have protected you from it," I corrected. "I could have told you myself. So you could understand."

"Oh, that's rich," she said, moving further away still. "You think I don't know how babies are made, Brody? I understand, all right. I think you're the one who doesn't understand."

"Just… Stop moving. Listen," I said, following her to the living room, where she paced like a caged lion.

If only I could think up the words, the right words. They always came when I wrote songs, but now, every word I said only dug my grave deeper. Still, I had to try. I wouldn't give up. I'd dig myself six feet under before I'd give up on her. "What don't I understand? Talk to me, baby. Yell at me, throw things at me if it makes you feel better. But we're going to get through this."

She wheeled around and stared at me incredulously. "Get through this? What do you plan to do, Brody? Get a back-alley abortion and pay her a bunch of money to shut her up?"

"Is that what you want me to do?" I asked quietly. In that moment, I knew that if she asked, I'd do it. I would do anything for her. If she asked me to hire a hitman and dispose of Uma, I'd fucking do it. Nothing would keep us apart.

"No, it's not what I want you to do," she said, resuming her pacing. "I want you not to have fucked every girl in

America. I want one brain cell in your tiny little brain to have told you not to stick your dick in every fangirl who said yes. I want to go back in time and make it all disappear."

She hadn't said me, though. She hadn't said she wished we hadn't gotten back together or that she'd never met me. Which meant she wasn't done. There was still hope. I would find a way to make us both happy. All Uma wanted was money, and I'd give her all of it if she'd let me go on with my life. I'd pay for everything in the world to make my baby daughter happy, give her every luxury, the best nannies and private schools, trips around the world that didn't include me.

She wouldn't be my daughter. She'd be as distant a thing as Uma. A mistake.

DNA.

"Maybe I did get carried away with cleaning," Laney said when I didn't answer. She sagged onto the arm of the couch, her shoulders slumping, her eyes draining of their fire. "Let's go out somewhere and get some food. I feel sick."

"Okay," I said, not daring to say anything more. Not yet.

While Laney went to get her shoes, I opened the windows as much as they would open, which was only a crack.

Luckily, the penthouse suites also had a small balcony, so I left the French doors open, not caring if some rain blew in and wet the carpet.

We left the suite in silence, huddled together under Laney's umbrella, which blocked me from view. Our Uber driver was a curvy blonde chick with a southern accent who immediately alerted us that she had pepper spray mounted on the ceiling, and pointed to the little mount, aimed directly at us. "I've never had to use it on a couple, but I tell everyone who rides," she said. "Full disclosure. I did use it on some drunk college guys once."

"We're safe," I said, then wanted to ram the words back down my throat.

"Oh my God, are you Brody Villines?"

"Yeah."

"Can you sign something for me?" she asked, then looked at Laney in the rearview. "Is that okay? I mean, it must suck to have a famous rock star for a boyfriend. Mercy. I don't think I could handle it."

"It's fine," Laney said dully. Usually, she could laugh it off or make some flippant remark, smiling magnanimously while I signed autographs. Now it was like she couldn't be bothered. A knot of dread began to build inside my gut, thrumming my heart like an electric guitar.

I signed the cocktail napkin the driver found in her purse, and she recommended a quiet local pizzeria where we could eat tucked away in a back corner so no one would notice us. When she let us off, she took an awkwardly angled selfie with us, leaning back between the front seats while we leaned forward.

The pizzeria was kind of a dive, a place where you took a girl like Uma, not Laney. I didn't eat at that kind of place much anymore, but it was quiet and empty that late, and that was good enough for me. We seated ourselves in a back booth. The Uber driver was right about it being dark and private.

Our waitress, a tattooed chick with royal blue hair, black fingernails, and the pallor of a vampire, appeared as soon as we sat down. She slapped down two one-sheet laminated menus, grinding her gum between her teeth like Jace after an all-night coke binge. "Want anything?"

"Give us a minute," I said.

She sighed and stood tapping her pen on the edge of the table while we looked at the menus, then flounced off to get our drinks. She barely cleared five feet even in her chunky fuck-me boots, above which a slice of thick, pale thigh showed below the hem of her bouncy black skirt.

"She's a dream," Laney said.

"Uh huh," I said, scanning the pizza menu.

"But hey, maybe that's what you get off on. I mean, she's probably closer to your type than I am."

"Laney, stop. You know that's not true."

She glared across the table. "Don't tell me what I know."

I sighed and pushed my menu away. "Fine."

"Obviously, you like the wild ones."

I grabbed the edge of the table and leaned forward, locking my gaze with hers. "I like you, Laney. I fucking love you. That hasn't changed. I know I fucked up, okay? I'm not stupid. But that was before we were together."

"Oh, no, Brody," she said with a sweet smile. "You fucked up long before her. When we *were* together."

"So you're punishing me for that now, too? I thought we'd gotten past that. And I know this sucks. I know that. I know you're pissed. But how can you hate me for something that happened when we weren't together?"

"Because," she said. "Maybe I am crazy. I mean, look at me. I smell like a disinfectant factory, and no matter how hard I scrub that hotel room, or myself, I can't scrub away that crazy feeling."

"What feeling?" I asked, reaching for her hand.

Before I could touch her, the waitress slammed tall, red plastic cups of soda down on the table and straightened. "What's it gonna be?"

While Laney ordered, I studied her, trying to decide what she had meant. I had a feeling of my own, a feeling that I didn't want to label. After Laney ordered, I pointed to a random slice on the menu, knowing I wouldn't be able to eat but thankful that the waitress didn't know who I was. She'd probably never heard a *Just 5 Guys* song in her life.

When she was gone, Laney sighed and slid her hand across, surprising me. I took it in my own and held it like a treasure, cupped between both of mine.

"Maybe it's wrong, but I care that, hello, you're going to be a dad. I'm sorry, I'm probably as hopelessly old-fashioned as my mother, but I don't want to stand in the way of that. If that makes me crazy, then yeah, that's exactly what I am. I'm crazy, and I'm pissed, and I fucking hate the fact that I lost you to another girl again."

"You didn't lose me," I said, squeezing her hand until she looked up at him. "You never lost me, Laney. I'll make it right with her. But it doesn't change what we—what you and I—have. You and me, Laney. That's all I want. All I've ever wanted."

"Me, too," she said, her voice so soft and broken it scared the fuck out of me. I wanted to cover her pretty lips with my own, keep her from saying what she said next.

But I didn't, and she said it, anyway.

"Maybe I didn't lose you," she murmured. "But you lost me."

twenty-eight

Laney

When we got back to the hotel, the room had aired out some. I was too exhausted to be embarrassed about the psychotic cleaning episode. Some people drank, some people trashed their guitars on stage, and some people cleaned.

I fell into bed already ready to pass out. Maybe it was all a dream, and I just had to go to sleep and wake up to erase it.

Brody slid in beside me and turned to face me. "It doesn't have to be this way," he said, adjusting his head on the pillow. "It doesn't have to be over."

"Then how come it is?"

"That's your decision, Laney," he said. "You're doing this. Not me."

"Then maybe it's Uma."

"Not Uma," he said, his hand moving to my hip. "She's not part of the equation, and she never was. It's me plus you, just like it's always been."

"Well, maybe me plus you equals a giant mess that just isn't meant to be."

"Don't say that," he said fiercely. "You plus me equals us. And that's it. You can't change a mathematical fact."

"Yeah, but *does* me plus you? Or does me plus you, plus the memory of all the girls you've been with, plus the past that never really goes away even when I pretend it's not on my mind, plus a fucking child, equal a big fat clusterfuck? I'm not ready to be a mom. I mean, if it had happened to me, if I'd gotten pregnant, of course I would keep it. But now? Like this? What are you going to do, Brody?"

"I don't know," he admitted.

"What does she want?" I asked the ceiling.

"She wants money."

"How much money? Is she getting an abortion? Or does she want you to pay for her medical bills, and she'll put it up for adoption? Or does she want to raise the kid, so you'll have to keep paying her millions in child support for the next eighteen years?"

"I don't know," he said again. "I wanted to come back and talk to you. We didn't talk that much."

This ridiculous fear shot through me, that maybe they did something else. But that was beyond ridiculous.

Wasn't it?

He had been with her before, found her attractive for incomprehensible reasons. They had a history, too. And she wasn't big yet, her belly just a little rounded, probably only showing because she was so skinny.

"So what does that mean for us?" I asked, turning my face toward him at last.

"I don't want things to change," he said. "Nothing has to change."

"It's a little late for that."

"It doesn't have to be."

"You can't just pretend it never happened. This is part of you now. Part of us."

"Not every part of us is going to be beautiful," he said, pushing up on one elbow to look down at my face. "If we're together for the rest of our lives, there will be ugly parts, too. But I'll love them just as much, because they'll be parts of us, and I love every part of us."

I didn't know it was possible for a heart to melt and break at the same time until that moment. My throat tightened, and my chest ached so badly I wanted to hurl into the fetal position and scream at the unfairness of this world, this life, this man.

When he leaned in, I pressed my lips to his instead of turning away. It wasn't frantic, like the time under the tree. His familiar hands moved over my body just the way I liked. He knew how to touch me, how to kiss me, with his lips brushing across my ear and down my neck, his hands moving gently over my breasts, squeezing my nipples, sliding down my belly and into my panties.

I ran my fingers through his soft brown hair, tugging at the fringe at the nape of his neck. I knew how he liked to be touched, too. Over the past few months, I'd let myself believe it would last. I'd let myself be happy. But now, even as he slid my underwear over my thighs, I couldn't keep thoughts of Uma at bay. She came barreling in, like she'd charged into the backstage area to ruin our lives. Suddenly, all I could see was that pale, bare face with the eyes like grape jelly. I hated grape jelly.

Brody rolled on top of me, his lips sealing with mine again as his thigh nudged mine apart. Had he done that to Uma? I could feel him against my opening, hard and hot and throbbing. "Are you ready?" he whispered into my ear, his warm breath sparking embers inside me.

I nodded mutely. While he stroked my hair back and kissed me softly, I reached down to guide him in. But when he pushed into me fully, tears slid from the corners of my eyes.

"What's wrong?" he asked, pulling back to look down at my face.

"Don't stop," I said, gripping his hipbones to keep him close. "Keep going."

"Am I hurting you? Why are you crying?"

"I just am," I said. "But I want to do this. Please don't stop. Tell me this will always be right between us."

"I promise," he said, brushing kisses across my damp eyelids. He began moving, each stroke slow and deep, and I came almost immediately. But I couldn't help but wonder if it was the last time we'd make love.

twenty-nine

Brody

In the morning, I had dozens of messages from Nash. I ignored them and ordered room service for myself and Laney. We ate in a silence punctuated only by polite comments about the food, requests for salt, and a brief rundown of the next three shows, which would wrap up that leg of the tour. But the conversation was so stiff that I didn't think I even knew Laney anymore. As much as I'd hated seeing her pissed, it was better than this courteous distance.

But here was where I was woefully ignorant. Laney fretted about her lack of sexual experience, and I always reassured her that it was the best sex I'd ever had. And it was. But what I didn't say was that she had a different kind of experience—relationship experience. I didn't know what to do in this situation because I'd never been in it. I'd never even been in a situation a thousand miles from this minefield, where every misstep might blow me to hell.

Was I supposed to leave her alone, let her have her space to come to terms with it? Or would that make her feel neglected? If I pursued her, would she feel loved or hassled?

In the end, I did nothing, because I didn't know how to reach her through that frosty exterior she'd put up around herself. I could only hope it would thaw with time.

When we reached the lobby, Uma was sprawled across a chair, her little belly just a slight bulge in her t-shirt that could have been her slouchy posture. It seemed small for six months, not that I knew anything about it. For a second, I had a surge of hope. It might not be mine after all.

"What is she doing here?" Laney hissed as Uma heaved herself to her feet and strolled toward us.

"I got her a place for the night," I said. "Did you expect me to tell her to sleep on the street in the rain?"

"'Sup," Uma said, hooking her thumbs into her front pockets.

"We're heading out," I said. Spotting the flushed face of the matronly hotel clerk who was watching us avidly, I jerked my chin toward the side entrance. "Why don't you come out to the bus for a minute so we can talk?"

When we climbed onto the bus, I suddenly remembered with perfect clarity that fateful night. Dragging Uma through the bus, throwing her down on all fours. I was such a dick. No wonder Laney wouldn't look at me. I'd known better than to go after her again, had known it would be bad for her. Hadn't I said from the start I'd only break her heart again?

And here I was, with a broken-hearted girl I loved and a pregnant girl whose first name I'd only found out the night before. The sad thing was, I'd treated her better than some of the others. That night we'd been together, I'd given her what she wanted. I'd even made her come.

Most of the baby-dolls were just toys to me, like Laney said when she'd called them sex dolls. They were things, not people. Not real people, anyway, the kind who could get pregnant and make more people. Not the kind who could tear apart the only good thing, the only real thing, I'd had since leaving home at eighteen to join the band.

"So, are you going to give me some money?" Uma asked. "Because it sucks to have to keep asking. I figure maybe five hundred will do, but a thousand would be better. I could use it for a deposit, and then if I get a job, I could keep gigging at night until the baby comes. I just gotta find a band."

"What are you planning on doing with the baby?" Laney asked.

I wanted to wrap my arms around her and never let go. She didn't worry about hurting Uma's feelings, about being delicate.

"I hadn't gotten that far," Uma said.

"What do you mean?" I asked. "If it's mine, then it's three months away."

"Sorry," Uma said, sounding defensive. "It's a little hard to grasp right now."

She was nineteen. Jesus. How the fuck was she going to take care of a kid? She couldn't even take care of herself, and not in the way that most people meant when they said that. She had literally let herself be kicked out on the streets, and though it wasn't her fault, she didn't seem to have any grasp on how much care a baby would need—less of a grasp than me, and that was saying something.

The driver tapped on the side of bus next to the open door. "You about ready?" he asked. "Nash is blowing up my phone."

"Mine, too," I said. "Give us five minutes."

"Have you been to see a doctor?" Laney asked Uma. "After the test, I mean?"

"Yeah," Uma said, crossing her arms over her chest. "Actually, I did. He said everything was fine."

"And when was that?"

Uma suddenly seemed to find the ceiling very interesting.

"Well?" Laney asked, one hand on her hip.

"You wouldn't understand," Uma said. "You're rich."

"Just come with us to Salt Lake," I said. "We can figure shit out, and you'll be taken care of."

"And then what?" Uma asked. "You're going to leave me there?"

"Of course not," I said. "I'll fly you home."

Although since she didn't have a home, I wasn't sure why she really cared. It didn't sound like her friends were going to be there for her, anyway.

"Fine," she said, flopping down on the plush leather couch that ran along one side of the bus.

"She's coming on tour with us?" Laney asked, giving me an incredulous look. "It's not bad enough that I find out you knocked up some groupie, now you're taking her on the road with us? I'm not going to be the wife while she gets to be the mistress. That is not what I signed up for." She whirled and stomped back to the bedroom, rattling the accordion folding door closed.

The driver fired up the bus, and as we pulled out, I finally answered my phone. "What the hell are you doing?" Nash asked. "Trying to give me an aneurism? Why aren't you answering your phone?"

"I told you, I wanted to take care of the personal side of this."

"Yeah? Laney sticking around?"

"For now."

"Tell me you got rid of the crack head."

"She's right here on the bus," I said. "She's coming with us."

To my surprise, Nash didn't throw another tantrum. "Alright, we got your lawyers on it. We'll need DNA tests, and we'll need her to sign some NDAs. And we can get her to a doctor first thing, see if they can still get rid of it."

The way he said it, so off-handedly, like he was talking about a smelly take-out bag that had to be tossed off the bus at the next stop, made my hands curl into fists. That was a baby he was talking about—my baby.

"I don't know if that's what we want to do."

"Oh, so now it's 'we'?" Nash let out that bark of a laugh. "You do realize if she has that baby, you're going to be paying child support for the rest of your goddamn life?"

"I think I can afford it."

"How much is she asking not to spill it to the tabloid circuit? A million? She's probably shooting low, right? People like that never know how much to ask for."

I glanced over at Uma, who was chewing on a hangnail again, staring out the window with glazed, unseeing eyes. "She asked for five hundred."

"See, even less," Nash said, laughing. "Half a mil is even better."

"No," I said, smiling. "Five hundred dollars."

Nash was still cackling when I hung up.

Outside, the Space Needle thrust into the sky above the skyline of Seattle. Laney had wanted to go see it, to walk around and shop the day before, but we'd ended up wasting the day in the hotel room, not knowing it would be the last day we could enjoy each other without this uncrossable distance between us. It was like Uma had said—this thing was an alien invader. Except it hadn't just invaded her body. Now it had invaded Laney and my relationship, too.

thirty

Laney

When I heard the accordion door fold open, I didn't turn from where I was lying on the bed, my back to the door. Even curled in the fetal position, I couldn't make the sick feeling leave my stomach. I didn't know if I could be held responsible for what I said to Brody right now, after he brought his pregnant ex-mistress on tour with him. With each new development, I could feel the wedge between us being driven deeper, pushing us further and further apart.

"Hey."

At the sound of the unfamiliar voice, I scrambled up from the bed. Uma was standing in the doorway, her thumbs hooked into her front pockets in that defensive stance, as if she were trying to look tough and cool.

I tossed my hair and squared my shoulders, trying to look put-together myself. If Brody came in and saw me lying there, broken, it would kill him. I wanted him to see how hurt I was. I wanted it to hurt him.

But I didn't want this girl seeing how much power she had.

"What do you want?" I asked, my tone light, not angry.

"I wanted to talk to you," Uma said. "I told Brody I had special girl insight, and it would be better if I came back here instead of him." She grinned like she was quite pleased with herself.

I waited, wary of what she'd say next.

Uma pushed the door shut and sat down on the edge of the bed, pulling one knee up and facing me, while I still stood on the far side of the bed.

"Listen, I know this is weird. It's got to be, right? I mean, you don't know me from Adam, and here I come on tour with you. What if I rob you? What if I'm some crazy stalker fangirl getting the dream of a lifetime, right?"

"Okay," I said slowly.

"I'm not after your man."

"Okay."

"He's not even my type. I mean, yeah, we hooked up, but it just happened. I don't even like his stupid boyband crap. And he was kind of an asshole when I told him that, and so…

Well, that's my type, I guess," she said with a shrug and a little laugh. "But now? Like, less than zero attraction. Zilch. Almost repellent."

"Why were you backstage if you didn't even like them?"

"I was there with my cousin. Anyway, I just wanted to get that straight between us. Because really. You made him all nice and decent, which is great, I'm not saying it's not good. It just doesn't do it for me."

"You admit you like assholes?"

"Um, yeah. Who doesn't?"

I perched on the very edge of the bed, ready to jump up if things got weird. "Most girls don't actually know they like assholes, and if they do, they won't admit it."

"Why not admit it?" Uma said. "I'm still a freaking teenager. Wow, that sounds weird to say. But yeah. I'm not looking to get married. I want to travel, and play music, and do crazy shit like sleep with some random asshole once in a while. What can I say, bad boys with good dick are my kryptonite."

"Can you not call him that?"

Uma grinned. "Sorry. Point is, one day, when I'm ready to get married, I'm sure I'll want a sweet guy like you made Brody into. But right now, I couldn't want anything *less*."

"But here's the thing," I said, smoothing the comforter on the bed where Brody and I had been sleeping for the past month, had made love countless times. Where maybe he'd impregnated this very girl. "Brody is a good guy. And when you have a baby… Well, everyone knows it changes you. What if you change your mind then? And you have this great guy right there, being a great dad. Because he will be a great dad. And he's the baby's dad. You're going to want him."

"You're talking like I'm having this thing."

"I know Brody's trying to let you make this decision," I said. "But he's the dad. Doesn't he get a say?"

"I hadn't really thought about it," Uma said, frowning at a spot on the floor beside the bed. "Do you think he wants a say?"

"He'll never tell you not to do what you need to do," I said. "But aren't you at least curious what he'd say?"

"No," Uma said. "I wasn't. It's my body. You're curious what he'd say because you love him. But I have no feelings one way or another. He doesn't mean anything to me, and neither does his opinion."

"So you wouldn't be at all interested in what he'd have to say about it? You wouldn't care if he said he wanted to make things right?"

"Like get married? Hell no. Are you kidding? I don't even know him."

I wasn't convinced. I didn't think Uma was lying, but I didn't think anyone could resist Brody. If he wanted her, he could get her to fall for him. And that's how those things always seemed to work out. Once he saw Uma with the baby—his baby—and he loved the baby, and she loved the baby… Fast forward a few months and they'd be sending out wedding invitations.

"You should probably get to know him, if you're going to have a baby together," I said. "Even if you're not getting married."

"Why do you keep saying we're having a baby?" Uma asked, her hand curling around her little belly. "You think… You really think it's too late?" Her voice went high and trembly, and I actually felt sorry for her.

"Honestly? Yeah, I do. And I don't think you'd be able to go through with it even if it wasn't."

"I can't be a mom," Uma said, her striking eyes suddenly filled with liquid. "I don't know the first thing about babies."

I scooted across the bed and sat beside her. "You don't have to be a mom," I assured her. "You have to have a baby, though. There's no way around that. It's in there, and it has to come out. But no one is going to force you to keep it, to be a mother to a kid you don't want. There are a lot of people out there who would want this baby."

Uma sniffed. "You think so?"

"I know so. You're going to be fine."

"Thanks," Uma said with a shaky smile. She wiped her eyes again. "God, you don't even know how much this has sucked. I didn't tell anyone for like, five months. I mean, who was I going to tell? My band? Because that worked out so well."

"Don't you have, like, a family or anything?"

Uma shook her head. "My cousin and her parents, but they're traveling."

"Where's all your stuff?" I asked, realizing that Uma hadn't stopped to get anything before agreeing to go with us.

"I don't have stuff."

"Nothing? Not even a keepsake from your mom, or…clothes?"

"I left my clothes at my drummer's place," she said. "After her boyfriend… I mean, I wasn't *afraid* to go back and get them, but…"

"What about your guitar or whatever? That's got to be worth some money."

Uma snorted. "I got my guitar at a pawn shop. I mean, yeah, I loved it. But it's not worth shit. Nothing I have is worth shit."

Except that baby.

Brody Villines's baby was worth a lot. If she kept it, she'd be set for life from child support alone. But then we'd never get rid of her. I could see it now. If I married Brody, but this girl had his baby, she'd be a part of our lives forever.

The irresponsible baby-mama, showing up at holidays to cause drama, awkwardly inserting the kid into family pictures after Brody and I had a family of our own. I could see Uma in ten years, dumping the kid on us while she ran off to be her wild-child self, chasing after some asshole, never thinking of how it affected the kid. And my own kids growing up thinking Uma was the cool mom, telling me they wished Uma was their mom. And Brody, forever caught between us, pulled in two directions, trying to explain to our kids why one of their sisters had a different mom.

thirty-one

Brody

You're making a big mistake.

Nash's words ran through my head on a replay loop as I sat sprawled in a chair in the clinic's waiting room, chin tucked to chest, hat pulled low over my face. Uma sat on my left, the click of her teeth knocking together every time she bit at the nonexistent end of her fingernail audible in the silence. Only one other couple occupied the waiting room, a pair of actors, and they looked too busy worrying to notice me.

"I can't just let her go alone," I had told Nash the night before, when I'd told him about the appointment.

"Someone's going to recognize you," Nash had warned. "It's going to be all over the gossip columns by evening."

"Then find a way to spin it," I had said. It became a little harder when Laney had opted out of the appointment. Now it was obvious to anyone that Uma and I were there together. It would get out eventually anyway, despite going to the pricey, private clinic in L.A. where confidentiality paid everyone's salary.

"Would you like some cucumber water?" a candy-striper asked Uma, holding out a tray. Everyone spoke in subdued voices here, smiled with soothing, solicitous faces, and pretended stars did nothing so ugly and common as have medical problems.

Uma took a glass and waited for the girl to leave before leaning over to me. "This place creeps me out," she whispered. "Everyone's so plastic."

"It's L.A.," I said. "Get used to it."

"No, thanks."

Just then, a nurse in seafoam scrubs with a sweet, demure smile approached and murmured Uma's name. "Whenever you're ready," she said.

You're making a big mistake.

Uma looked at me, and I looked at her. "I guess this is it," she said, her face even paler than usual.

"I guess so." I found myself biting back a smile. "Ready to go meet her?"

"How do you know it's a her?"

I faltered, my fingers closing around the sleek wooden arms of the chair I sat in. "I—I don't."

You're making a big mistake.

"Right this way," the nurse said when we stood. We followed her down a carpeted corridor and into a room that, no matter how posh, could not look like anything other than what it was. Uma sat on the edge of the exam table, her hands squeezed between her knees, while the nurse asked her an endless stream of questions about everything from her diet, sleep habits, antacid consumption, family history, sexual activity, and urine output, most of which Uma had already answered on the forms she filled out in the waiting room.

Finally, the nurse told Uma to undress while she stepped out. I turned my back while Uma stripped off the black jeans and Stones t-shirt she'd bought in Salt Lake.

"Want me to wait outside while you get, uh, checked?" I asked.

"No," she said. "You have to endure the awkward with me. I didn't get here on my own."

You're making a big mistake.

"If you're sure it won't make you uncomfortable."

"Dude, you've probably seen like a thousand pussies," she said. "I don't think mine's all that special."

I didn't know how to tell her that I didn't want to be there. That I didn't want to see her naked. Suddenly, I was relieved that Laney wasn't there. She would have taken it the wrong way that Uma wanted me there.

You're making a big mistake.

"You're kind of a prude," Uma said behind me. The paper on the table crackled, and I turned back to find her sitting there in the luxurious white cotton gown. "Look at this thing," she said. "You think they'd notice if I took off with it? I'd sleep in this thing. It's fucking amazing. Feel it."

"I'm okay."

"Seriously, you're going to have to get over this weirdness," she said. "Some dude's about to come in here and stick his whole hand up inside me."

"Uh huh."

"Why are you being such a dude? We fucked, Brody. You've seen my vag. You came inside it. How are you squeamish about it now?"

"I'm not."

"Vaginas are not put on earth solely for your pleasure," she said. "They're also for birthing humans. And if that thing's going to rip the bottom off me, you're going to be there to see it come tearing out. So enough with the pretense that this is something sweet and precious. Just because you take me to the most expensive clinic the country doesn't make it any less gory."

The doctor arrived then, a thirtyish woman with her dark hair pulled back in a tight bun. Uma lay back and set her feet in the stirrups, smirking at me. I stood at her shoulder and took her hand as the doctor did the exam. "I understand you want a DNA test," she said.

"Yep," Uma said.

"Has someone gone over the risks with you?"

"Yep."

"Everything looks good with you," the doctor said after a few minutes of poking and prodding. "We'll get you down for an ultrasound in just a few minutes."

When she left us alone again, Uma sat up.

"I don't think we should do the DNA test," I said, holding her hand in both of mine. The thought of a needle that long made me a little woozy. "Not if there's a chance you could lose it."

"Don't tell me you're worried about the little alien," Uma said, rolling her eyes.

But I had thought about it, not just because Nash had reminded me how it would look if I gave up my baby for adoption. "Are you sure…you don't want her?"

"Um, yeah," Uma said. "Aren't you?"

"I don't know," I said, running a hand through my hair.

"What, Brody Villines is going to be a single dad?" she asked. "Give me a break. You're not going to give up the next eighteen years of your life any more than I am."

"It just seems like there's gotta be a way we could make it work."

"What about Laney? Have you asked how she feels about this?"

I hadn't. We'd barely spoken since Uma showed up. But somehow, it didn't feel right. She was the most important thing in my life, but this was important now, too.

December

thirty-two

Laney

More and more tour dates kept being added, until we finally ended the twelve-show tour after thirty shows. Nash was always hounding me before, but he barely acknowledged me anymore. Brody was always busy with his choreographer, or his vocal coach, or Nash, or his agent, reporters, magazines, interviews with YCE and MTV and VH1. Almost every night, he had a show somewhere. I kept to myself, or sometimes hung out with Uma. She wasn't Piper, but she was a familiar face. And I didn't hate her—I couldn't, really.

Finally, the tour ended, and we had off a few weeks, so we went home for Christmas. Though I had told my mother about the recent developments, I hadn't seen her since summer. The moment I saw the tender, pitying look on Blair's face as she pulled me in for a hug, I knew my worst fears weren't all in my head.

"How are you?" Blair asked, holding me at arm's length to study my face. "You look thin."

"I'm—awful," I admitted. Before I could stop myself, I burst into tears. Blair didn't make her little comments this time. She pulled me into the living room and sat down on the couch and held me. And that was worse because that meant she knew it was over. She knew something that even I hadn't let myself admit. I'd been holding on, denying everything that was right in front of me. Going along with it, hoping I'd wake up and the nightmare would be over.

That evening, when I got back from a long ride through the brown fields, I came out of the stables to see a little red Corvette whipping around back to park on the pad behind the house, spraying gravel as it went.

I took off running and came around the corner of the house to see a thin figure with a shock of long, bright red hair, as familiar as my own mother.

"Piper," I cried, throwing my arms around my cousin in a crushing embrace.

"Oh, ew, you're all sweaty and you smell like a horse," Piper said, but she was laughing.

After getting her settled in, I had to share her with the family for a few hours. We covered the usual topics—the weather, the health of all the relatives, church, football, college, and local gossip, excluding mine, of course, since I was there. Finally, I was able to convince my mother that it wouldn't be rude if we took a short walk, and Piper and I set off on foot.

"God, I miss this place," Piper said, throwing her arms up into the chill afternoon. Even the sun felt cold, the rays short and pale compared to the long, lazy summer afternoons with the golden glow lingering over everything. Now, a wind whipped across them, singing through the brown grasses and bending them double, stinging our faces.

"Me, too," I said. I glanced sideways at Piper and picked a tall seed stalk from one of the grasses. "I might stay."

"For how long?"

"I'm not sure yet."

"Does Brody know?"

"No," I admitted, chewing at the grass stem.

"Well, you can come to New York and stay with me," Piper said. But I knew I couldn't do that, at least not for long.

Piper had fashion school, and she lived in a tiny, cruddy apartment with a roommate. And I'd had enough of sitting around while someone else did their thing. Not that I didn't want Brody to have fame and glory. But sometimes, it got boring making my life about someone else. I wanted to have my own life, too.

"Maybe I'll travel, like I planned to," I said, though that seemed empty now, too. Now that I knew what it was like to be with a man I loved, the thought of traveling alone had lost the allure of escape that it had held while I'd been at school, thinking of the long breaks I could take from seeing Paul. Travel had been an excuse to escape a bad engagement that never should have taken place. But now, I knew I'd want Brody there with me, and he didn't want to leave Uma.

We turned down a little footpath that led to a dip in the land where my father had hired a crew to come in and dig a pond for the horses. We walked the winding, overgrown path in silence until we came out on the grassy bank of the pond.

"I can't believe we used to swim here," I said. The water was murky, the edges filled with dead grasses, each blade fuzzed with pond gunk.

"We probably drank so much horse pee," Piper said, laughing. "My mom hated it when Blair let us swim here."

I wrinkled my nose at the thought. "I don't blame her."

After a minute of silence, Piper said, "So are we going to talk about Brody? Or is that off limits?"

"Nothing's off limits," I said with a sigh. "I'm just… I don't know what to say anymore."

"He's still hauling around the pregnant chick?"

"Yeah."

"And she hasn't breathed a word about it?"

"No. She doesn't hang out with us in public. It gets more intense every day, though. People take pictures of us at Starbucks at five in the morning. It's exhausting."

Piper gave me a sympathetic smile. "At least they're not taking pictures of him with Uma."

"Yeah," I said, tossing down my chewed grass stem.

"And he's still with you. He loves you. And he says there's nothing going on, that it's just about the baby. Do you believe him?"

"I do," I said, huddling into my jacket as another stream of icy wind raked across the fields, tugging at my hair.

"That must be hard."

"You'd think so," I said. "But not really."

"So… I don't get it. Did you want him to leave her on the streets?"

"Of course not."

"What do you want him to do?"

"I want him to go back in time and not fuck every fangirl who threw herself at him. Especially not her. And especially not without protection."

Piper huddled into her white down jacket, her red hair almost glowing against the coat and the dull backdrop. The sun seemed to spotlight my pretty cousin, and for the first time in years, I felt a stab of jealousy. Piper wasn't just pretty, she was free. She'd made her own life in New York, uncomplicated by boys.

"You can't have that," she said. "Try again."

"I don't know," I said. "That's the problem. I can't ask him to kick her out. I don't want to. I feel sorry for her. But I also feel like he can't ask me to be okay with it."

"No," Piper said. "You have to decide that for yourself."

We walked back across the field in silence.

thirty-three

Brody

"Mother," I said carefully, my fingers tense on Uma's stiff spine. "This is Uma. I've told you about her. Uma, this is my mother, Virginia."

Uma bobbed her head. "'Sup."

"Well, hello, dear," said Virginia, looking down her nose at Uma. "You can just call me Mrs. Villines."

I gritted my teeth and glared, but my mother pretended not to notice. Uma started to turn, but I flattened my hand against her back to keep her from bolting.

"It's good of Brody to bring you by to meet us," Mom said. "I understand you have no reliable family of your own to spend the holidays with."

"They're traveling."

"And on Christmas!" Mom said. "Imagine that. Some people have no sense of the value of tradition."

"Mother," I warned, shooting her a meaningful look. "I think she'll be fine here. I know how welcoming you are to guests."

"Of course. We can't let you starve, what with your condition. There's always room for one more plate at the table." She smiled primly at me. "Will Laney be joining us, too?"

"She's having dinner with her family," I said, knowing full well that my mother knew this. Any chance to bring up Laney, though. Mom had been doing it for years, since we broke up. Nettling me. And now she had a new victim.

"Let me show you to your room," I said, urging Uma forward with my palm still on her back.

"We thought she'd rather stay in the downstairs guestroom," my mother said. "So she won't have to deal with the stairs. A lot of babies were lost that way in the past."

"Mom," I said through clenched teeth. I knew the reason for keeping Uma downstairs had nothing to do with the risk of falling and everything to do with keeping her away from me. But I didn't want to argue. For all I knew, Uma wanted to be as far away from me as possible.

I led her down the back hallway to the downstairs guestroom, a cold and dark little room that was almost never used. Although clean, it had a dusty smell to it from sitting so long unused.

"This place is insane," Uma said, dropping her duffle onto the floor just inside the bedroom door. "How many rooms does it even have?"

"I don't know," I said, by now used to Uma's tendency to marvel at all things extravagant. She didn't do it quite as often as when we'd first taken her aboard the tour bus, but now and then, she'd still wonder aloud how much things cost, a habit that Laney found tasteless and embarrassing.

Uma seemed to recover from her momentary slip into curiosity, and she fell back into her usual sullen state after a few seconds. "Your mom hates me."

"She doesn't know you."

"You don't know me," she pointed out.

"I know you're having my baby."

"Do you hate me?"

"What?" I asked, drawing back. "Of course I don't hate you."

"Because I kind of came along and fucked up your relationship. Everything would be better if I'd never found you. Admit it."

I shifted, uncomfortable under her stormy gaze. Her violet eyes had gone dark as a bruise. "I don't think that's something you should be worrying about."

"Oh, no, don't worry, it's bad for the baby," she said in a mocking voice. "Don't drink coffee, Uma, it's bad for the baby. No tea, either. Or soda. I can't even eat a fucking ham sandwich."

"It's only two more months."

She plopped into the leather chair in the corner as ungracefully as possible, her legs splayed, her face shadowed by a belligerent glare. "I thought you were going to tell me not to get worked up, it's bad for the baby."

That day at the clinic, when she'd gone for her first appointment with me, things had gone fine. I'd vetoed the DNA test, saying that even if it turned out to be someone else's, I was going to take care of her until she had it. I didn't want to risk giving her a miscarriage with the test, which had to go into her amniotic sac and extract DNA. Uma had been grateful then, saying I was a good guy. I'd been wondering ever since that day what had gone wrong.

We'd seen the baby in the ultrasound. Uma had just stared at it, not making her usual smartass comments or calling it an alien. After the ultrasound technician had left us alone, Uma had burst into big ugly-cry sobs. I'd sat on the table and held her until she finished, which felt like forever, but was actually less than five minutes. She'd been withdrawn afterwards, but was back to her usual self by the next day.

We'd talked about the possibility of getting her an apartment in Seattle, since we were still traveling. But I didn't want her disappearing on me, and Nash had suddenly changed his tune, sure that she'd spread the story all over the internet if I left her alone. Uma had seemed amenable enough to the idea of sticking with us, saying she'd always wanted to travel. But she'd grown more and more hostile to Laney and me as the weeks passed. I kept telling myself it was just the pregnancy hormones.

After Christmas Eve dinner, Uma immediately disappeared back to her room again.

"She's really something," Virginia said, arching one manicured eyebrow at me.

"Yeah," I said. "She definitely is."

Virginia's eyes narrowed. "How is Laney taking all this? You traveling with her and your mistress? I'd never have imagined her the sort to put up with that."

"Mom, please don't call her that. She's not my mistress. It was a one-time mistake."

"I should hope so," Virginia said, pointing her nose in the air. "That's not the kind of girl I expect you to settle down with."

"I'm not going to marry her."

"Then what are you going to do with her?"

The sound of the door slamming caught my attention, and the arch smile on his mother's face said that she'd known Uma was there even when I hadn't. She really could be horrible.

"Well? Aren't you going to go chasing after her?"

I shook my head and left the room, but I went to make sure, anyway. Uma's room stood empty, her coat crumpled on the floor at the foot of the leather chair. I gathered it up and went to retrieve my own coat before going in search of her.

I found her on a footpath through the gardens out back, combing her fingers through one of my mother's purple moorgrasses, its blades golden as a head of tawny hair. She didn't turn at my approach, so I cleared my throat.

"Hey."

"This is crazy," she said. "I can't believe you live like this. I can't believe anyone lives like this while people are literally dying of starvation, and lack of medical care, and freezing to death. I feel like I've stepped into some alternative reality. I can't seem to wrap my head around it."

"Are you pissed about what I said?"

"It's weird though," she went on as if I hadn't spoken. "I got used to it on the bus so fast. But that's one tiny vehicle. I mean, it's a big vehicle, but it's easy to feel like you're just riding around in this tiny sliver of luxury, but you can still be part of the world. You step outside, and it's all still there. This place…"

"Uma."

"Yeah?" she asked, her head snapping around, as if she were waking from a dream.

"You left your coat." I held it out, and she slipped her arms into the sleeves of the garish orange faux fur she'd chosen when she went shopping. Without Laney and I, of course. Nash didn't want me to be photographed with a pregnant woman if possible, and Laney always had to be there if we went somewhere together, in case it set off rumors.

"This can't be real," Uma said, gesturing to the manicured gardens circling the "natural" pool, where water trickled from a tiny stream all year round. Of course, it was powered by a pump at the start, but my mother didn't like to mention that to guests when they came to walk the garden with her. Unlike Laney's mother, she took no part in the gardening, unless taking credit counted.

"It's a different world here," I admitted. "I was pretty sheltered growing up. But that's not a bad thing for a kid."

"I keep thinking I'll wake up," Uma said, turning back to the grass and combing its wide, arching blades with her fingers. "I'm waiting for it. I've been waiting since last June, when I found out. Like any day my real life will kick back in.

And this is just another weird part of the nightmare, like one of Alice's adventures in Wonderland. This is the opposite side of the coin from sneaking into my bandmates' cars when they were asleep so I didn't have to sleep on the street and get raped. It's less plausible, but here we are. The pretty side of Wonderland."

I looked around, hunching into my jacket when a particularly nasty gust of wind stung across my face. "Are you pissed about what I said to my mom?" I asked again. "You don't want to…? Do you?"

"No," Uma said dully.

I tilted my head, studying her. Was that why she'd gotten so surly lately? Maybe she had thought about getting married. Laney had said it would happen, that it was impossible to think otherwise. And though I did think otherwise, maybe I was wrong. I'd never learned how to read women. I'd never had to. With the exception of Laney, I'd never pursued anyone. They came to me, their intentions clear.

I'd been too nice to her. If I was an asshole, standoffish and rude, she'd get the picture. It was hard, though, while she had that baby inside her, to be a dick to her. In a moment of weakness, I'd even called Quincy for advice, because of all the members of *Just 5 Guys*, Quincy loved women the most. But he'd just laughed at my dilemma and said, "Hell yeah, dude. You got yourself a harem."

Uma put a hand on her belly, a flicker of pain crossing her face. "The thing about Wonderland," she said. "There's always a dark side. It might look all magical and shit, but around the next corner, there's a queen waiting to chop off your head."

"What was that?"

"The queen?" Uma asked, giving me a funny look.

"No, that," I said, gesturing to her hand, still on her little mound of a belly. "You made a face. Is something wrong? Does it hurt? Are you having contractions?"

"Calm down, Daddy, I've still got two months," she said. "Although I wouldn't be surprised to wake up with that woman standing over me with a knife, ready to rip it out so she can get rid of me."

"She's not that bad," I said.

"I'll take your word for it. But I figure it's better to have no mother than a bad mother."

"She's not a bad mother," I said. "She's a good person. She has her ways, but she'd never hurt a fly. Or you."

Uma rolled her eyes and kicked some of the smooth, decorative gravel my mother had trucked in to cover the garden paths. "Yeah, because it might hurt her precious grandbaby. I thought Southern women were supposed to be shrinking violet, seen-and-not-heard types."

I laughed. "You obviously have never been to the South before."

"Yeah, well, I guess I wasn't missing much. I think I'd take a shrinking violet over an evil queen."

"You'll get used to her."

Uma grimaced. "I hope not."

"Stop avoiding the question. Why'd you grab your stomach like that?"

She looked ready to argue, but then she shrugged and turned back to walk along the path to the small arbor with a narrow bench under it, big enough for two lovebirds to sit cozily under the wisteria drooping from it in early summer.

"It's just moving around a lot. It seems to like the cold air," Uma said, looking out at the stream twinkling in the cold winter sunlight as it wove its way gently into the small pool lined with mossy stones.

I squeezed in beside her, and she sighed and scooted over to allow this invasion, though she looked ready to make one of her cutting remarks. I swallowed, trying to work up the nerve to ask the next question, the one I'd wanted to ask a dozen times now. But every time I started talking about the baby, she got pissed and turned away or went in the bedroom to be alone. I never got this far.

"Can I… Do you think you'd let me touch it sometime?" I asked at last. "It doesn't have to be now. But maybe sometime before it's born?" The thought of that, the birth, always made something inside me turn into a sentimental cornball, like I might actually cry.

Uma sighed. "That would be weird."

"Yeah, you're right." I forced a little laugh. "It's your body. I wasn't trying to say, like, I wanted to touch you. It's just, sometimes I wonder if you remember it's my baby in there, too."

"How can I forget?" she asked bitterly. "I'm living in your tour bus with you and your girlfriend. Why else am I there? It's not like either of you actually like me. I know you're just waiting for it to pop out so you can kick me to the curb."

"That's not true."

"You don't have to lie. I know I'm only there because you're too guilty to make a pregnant lady live on the streets. I'm not stupid."

"What if we got you an apartment?" I asked.

"Where?"

I shrugged. "Seattle. LA. Wherever."

"I thought your manager wanted to keep tabs on me."

"There would be some confidentiality agreements to sign," I admitted, shifting on the seat that was suddenly too small for two people.

"I knew it was too good to last," she said. "I guess it's a blessing, in some ways. I got to be spoiled and pampered for a while. I kept reminding myself it was temporary. To enjoy the shit out of it, but not to get attached."

"And her?" I asked, nodding to her belly. "Are you attached to her?"

"I can't let myself do that," she said, turning to stare out at the shallow pool of water again. After a minute, she turned back and lifted her jacket and the hoodie she wore beneath. Her little belly was so strange and unnatural looking that it shocked me for a second. Since the ultrasound, it had gotten bigger, and that had been the only time I'd seen it. She wore hoodies almost every day, which disguised most of the bump. And it wasn't like a little belly fat. This was harder, rounder, all in one place. The rest of her body was still thin, though not as painfully thin as it had been when she first came to us.

"Go on," she said. "Touch it if you want to."

"I thought—."

"Just get it over with," she snapped.

Hesitantly at first, I reached out, halfway expecting her to slap my hand away when it got close. My fingers prodded gently against her belly, which was softer than it looked. From the way it looked, I'd expected it to feel like a melon, but it wasn't that hard. Not soft like a belly fat, either, though. For a minute, my fingers moved as if up the neck of my guitar, trying to find the right note for my other hand to play.

As if in response, someone played the note back to me. It wasn't me, and it wasn't Uma. I jerked my hand back by reflex, and Uma laughed and dropped her shirt. My hand flew out to stop her, but she'd already pulled down her thick jacket, covering the bare skin from the punishing wind. All I wanted was to touch it again, longer, to feel it move, to explore that mystery that Uma took for granted every single day. I wanted to put my whole hand over her belly, both hands, to feel it move as if by magic. There was another human being in there. A little person.

It blew my mind. For the first time, I really saw what was ahead. It hadn't sunk in yet, not fully anyway. My mother said you were never ready, even when it came. But this was different. This was a human being that no one had wanted to create, that no one wanted now that it was here. And that didn't seem fair. It hadn't asked to be given life. It hadn't asked to be born into the world at all. But here it came, more unprepared than we were, into a world that didn't want it. A world where there was no place for it.

thirty-four

Laney

As was tradition, the Tuckers and the Villineses went to church on Christmas Eve. I hadn't been avoiding Brody, but I hadn't been exactly communicative, either. As our families crowded into the small hall of the church, exchanging warm greetings to the members whom we hadn't seen since the last Christmas Eve, Brody's eyes found mine across the group.

"Hi there, Laney," Grandpa Othal said, reaching for my hand. He was mostly recovered, though Brody said he still had a nurse come in a few days a week. The corner of his mouth still tilted downward, but only the far corner, and his handshake was firm, if not as firm as it once had been. The biggest change was the cane he kept clutched in one hand, leaning heavily on it now.

"Hi," I said, giving him a quick hug. All these people, our families, melded together like one. I knew it would break my mother's heart if I didn't marry Brody. It would break my own heart. But how could I?

"Hey," Brody said, squeezing between Piper's father and Grandpa Othal to take my hand. After everything, his touch still made my blood sing.

"Hi, Brody."

"I tried calling you last night."

"I just needed a little time."

He laced his fingers through mine and held our hands to his heart. "I don't like the way that sounds."

"Where's Uma?"

"She says she doesn't believe in church," Brody said. "And it would be hard to introduce her to people, anyway."

I nodded. "Hard to explain that one away."

"So what was that comment about needing space? What does that mean?"

I should have known he wouldn't let me off the hook that easily. He was never one to stand on propriety, not when it came to me. Like he'd said, he'd always been honest with me, at least in word if not in deed. But after enduring his deeds, I wasn't quite as forthcoming with my own feelings.

"Let's just have a nice Christmas," I said. "We can talk about this later."

Brody untangled his fingers from mine and dropped my hand. Instantly, my fingers groped at the chill air in the church atrium, searching out the warmth and safety his hand promised. But it was an empty promise. He'd never be safe. No matter how closely I held my heart, how much I vowed to protect it, he could shatter it with a snap of his fingers. I'd tried not to fall in love again, had told myself I could handle being close to him. Famous last words of a fool.

I ignored the wounded look on Brody's face and ducked off to the restroom. When I came back, they'd left me a spot in the pew next to Brody. I glared at my mother, who returned the look with an innocent smile. When I sat, Brody took my hand. "I want to talk to you, too," he said.

A chill ran through me, despite the stuffy, overly heated air in the church. I'd said the words first, I reminded myself. But it didn't stop a knot of dread from pulling tight inside me. I knew what I should do, the right thing to do. I also knew that if Brody did it for me, because I wasn't strong enough to do it first, it would destroy me.

"After Christmas," I said.

"Okay," he said. "The day after tomorrow, then."

The service started before we could pick a time and place, but I knew. It killed me that I knew, that we knew each other so well. It was like we'd never been apart, like those years had never happened.

But they had happened. And Uma was living, breathing, walking proof of that. And soon enough, the baby would be. It would remind me for the rest of my life what Brody had done. I knew that I was a terrible person for resenting that innocent, unborn child. But I did, nonetheless.

thirty-five

Brody

The Villines' Christmas Dinner was the family gathering of the year. All the aunts, uncles, cousins, nieces and nephews packed into the high-ceilinged dining room, filling in every seat at the long table and the ever-expanding kids' table. My father sat at the head of the table, with his wife on his left and his father on the right, as it had been since Othal became a widower and the traditional dinner had moved from his place to ours.

Beyond Othal sat his son and his wife, then the daughters and their husbands. Beyond Virginia sat her sons, arranged from oldest to youngest. Now that my two older brothers were married, their wives sat beside them. I usually sat at the end of this line, with various cousins beyond me. When we arrived at the table this year, I shot my mother a questioning look, not sure if I had been downgraded for bringing shame to the family. Of course, it probably wasn't the first time a Villines had knocked up a woman without marrying her. But it was the first time he'd brought her to the family dinner table.

"Come sit here, dear," my mother said, pointing to the chair next to hers. "I thought we could enjoy each other's company this year, since it's likely to be the last Christmas you're unmarried."

I shuffled around the table, knowing that despite what Virginia said, this was more of a punishment than an honor. She was keeping me close, since I'd been a bad boy when she let me wander.

"And Uma, I've set an extra plate at the end for you," she said, gesturing to the seat to the left of the foot of the table. The seat of disdain, usually reserved for the lowliest niece or nephew, the one who had just moved up from the kids' table that year.

But Uma didn't know that, I reminded myself as she scooted in next to my cousin Ned, always near the foot of the table since he'd grown his hair past his shoulders and gone to art school. She didn't know she was being insulted. I wasn't sure if that was worse or better than if she had known.

Everyone else knew, which made her the butt of an inside joke known to everyone but her.

"I can't believe you sat her there," I muttered to my mother. She gave me a haughty smile and gestured to my place card, my name printed in silver calligraphy. My money had probably paid for those cards, for all of this. But to Virginia, that didn't matter. I was her son, her property, like the rest of the family. She ruled supreme, and if she sent my child's mother to the lowliest seat, that was her right as queen of the household. Like a good, obedient son, I sat at my mother's left without argument.

"Looks like somebody sucked up to Mom this year," Richard said, scooting into the chair next to me.

"Trust me, it wasn't intentional," I said. "I have no interest in stealing your spot."

"Could have fooled me."

"Leave him alone, Richie," his wife said. "He's the baby, she just wants one year with him before some other woman steals him away. You get her left side every year. You can share one time." She spoke to him in a sugary, cajoling way, like he was a spoiled child.

"I think it's less about him being the baby and more about him making the moolah," said Jim, the middle brother. His wife grimaced and smoothed her napkin into her lap.

Both my brothers had married women approved of by our mother. Women like Laney, smart and attractive, poised, from good backgrounds. Women who were supposed to keep them in line, I figured. My mother might have been content sitting on my father's left side, but everyone knew she belonged at the head of the table. Only her love of tradition kept her from assuming her rightful place.

"That must be it," Richard said. "You don't have a family to take care of yet. And if I was a betting man, I'd say you're not sitting there because Mom thinks you'll be married next year."

"Brody's never getting married," Jim said. "I don't blame you, man. Enjoy it as long as you can."

His wife had to go check on one of their kids at the kiddie table, who had spilled Christmas punch on her white skirt and was shrieking in horror that she'd gotten dirty. A toddler started crying then, and one of the other toddlers fell out of his chair, pulling the table cloth, which upset several more cups of punch.

"Next year, we'll get a nanny and put that table in the other room," Mom said, sipping her wine and watching the commotion with indulgent irritation on her face.

I glanced down the table to where Uma sat, expecting her to be staring in horror at the scene, imagining her own life as a mom. Instead, she was talking to my cousin, seemingly oblivious to the preview of her future playing out before her.

When the shrieking had subsided, Othal led us in the blessing, Dad carved the turkey while Jim carved the roast and Richard carved the ham. The food was all taken to the kitchen, where the night's staff had gathered to load the plates before bringing them to the dining room. The table was too crowded for the food, and a buffet didn't work with so many people having to make the trip through the line.

I recognized one of the waiters as a girl I'd taken selfies with in town, and I hoped she didn't spread our family dynamics around on social media.

"Who's that?" I asked my mother when the girl had returned to the kitchen.

"This really isn't the time to be asking about yet another girl," Virginia said, an edge in her voice.

"I'm just not sure you know how careful you have to be about who you let into the house now. People take pictures, souvenirs…"

"It wouldn't be the first time the help has stolen from me," Virginia said. "It won't be the last."

"I just know she saw me in town one time. She knows who I am."

"Everyone knows who you are, dear. I'd think you would be used to that by now. You know I like to hire locals who could use a little extra around the holidays."

I stuffed a bite of ham into my mouth to keep from reminding her that she was keeping them from their own families on Christmas evening. But if they took the job, I supposed they were willing to make that sacrifice. Lots of people ate Christmas dinner in the middle of the day, anyway.

"I could have hired your little guest," Virginia said with a nasty smirk. "She could probably use the help. But that unsightly bulge would be unappetizing."

I clenched my fist around my fork.

"In our day, you kept that hidden as much as possible," Virginia went on.

"It's all the baby-bump watchers on social media," Richard's wife said.

"They were in the magazines before that," one of the aunts said. "Remember that Demi Moore magazine cover? That was the start of it all."

"Shocking what people will do for attention," Virginia said.

"Nothing shocking about that," Richard said, shooting me a disgruntled look.

Dinner could not end soon enough. Finally, though, the plates were cleared, and the relatives moved off in little groups. Some went to the den to play cards and drink scotch, some went outside to play croquette or walk the garden paths, some of those with younger children packed up early and left, much to Virginia's consternation. "They'll be sitting further down the table next year," Richard muttered, elbowing me in the ribs as we three brothers headed out beyond the wall to practice our golf swings in the open field beyond the fence.

"Dad's talking about putting a real course out here," Jim said. "That your Christmas gift, Brody?"

I shrugged. "I don't know. They take what they need from my account."

"Damn, no wonder Mom had you sitting by her," Jim said. "You're her sugar daddy now."

"That'll change when you have your own wife sucking your bank account dry," Richard said. "She'll nip that in the bud real quick."

"How are things with Laney?" Jim said. "Still together?"

"Of course," I said. "Why wouldn't we be?"

My brothers exchanged a look.

"So you got the wife and a little something on the side," Richard said. "Now I heard of that. But I never heard of anyone getting the wife to be okay with the thing on the side!" He and Jim burst into laughter and back slaps.

"There's nothing going on between Uma and me," I said.

Jim pounded me on the back. "Just giving you a hard time, little brother."

I considered a moment, then said, "The problem is, I don't think I'm making either of them very happy. I'm not sure what to do about it."

"Stop trying," Richard said, and he and Jim burst into more laughter.

I didn't know why I bothered. This was the way it had always been with us. My older brothers giving me shit, never advice. I'd always be their little brother, a joke to them, no matter how much money I made.

"Seriously, little man," Richard said, slinging an arm around my shoulder while Jim lined up a shot. "The minute you start worrying about that is the minute they've got you by the balls. And once they do, they never let go."

The ball sailed high into the air, and they squinted as they watched it arc slowly against the stark blue of the winter sky. "It's true," Jim said. "Enjoy being single, man. Don't rush the inevitable decline. Everything goes downhill after you get married. I think that's what ages a man, not years but marriage. Kids. Nagging wife. Lack of sex. Shutting up to keep the peace. I'm thirty and I've already got grey hair coming in. I feel fifty."

Far off, I saw a figure walking away quickly, head tucked against the chill air, hands stuffed in the pockets of the pumpkin orange coat.

"I'm gonna go," I said, shoving my club into Richard's hand and taking off at a jog across the field.

"Don't do it," Jim yelled behind me.

"Never chase after a girl," Richard called. "Let them come to you."

"Save your balls!"

Ignoring their further taunts and laughter, I continued jogging. When I came to the path, Uma had almost disappeared behind a swell of land, so I kept going. At last, I caught sight of the line of weeping willows between our property and Laney's. In winter, even my favorite tree looked ghostly and drab with the leaves gone, the branches nothing but bare grey twigs bowing their heads in despair.

Uma stood with her back to me, looking up at the line of eerie trees, their draped branches swaying and rattling together like teeth. The wind had carried off plenty of the underlying carpet of fallen leaves, but a sparse golden brown circle still lay beneath each tree. A plume of breath puffed up from Uma's mouth, and after a second, the smell of it hit me, the stinging, burnt smell of smoke.

"What the fuck are you doing?" I asked, grabbing her shoulder and spinning her around to face me.

She jerked away before raising the cigarette to her lips and taking a slow drag, her eyes locked on mine. Rage exploded inside me, hard and quick like a bottle rocket. I ripped the cigarette from her fingers and threw it on the ground, grabbing her forearms when she moved to sidestep me.

"What the fuck," she said, yanking at her arms. "Let me go!"

"Why the fuck are you smoking? You want to poison our daughter?"

She went still, and the words hung between us, suspended on the line of our locked gaze. *Our daughter.* Neither had ever said the words before. It was her pregnancy, her baby. Sometimes, I called it mine. But never ours. It was not an option to think of it that way, as something shared between us. Because that was something too big for two separate people who didn't care about one another, two strangers, to share.

"Brody," she said slowly. "She's neither of ours. We're going to find her a good, loving family that actually wants her, remember?"

"I remember," I said bitterly, dropping her arms and turning away. "Of course I fucking do."

I stalked away, to the tree with the long branches. I ducked through them and approached the trunk. This time, I didn't want to sit on the cold dirt beneath the tree. Instead, I stood at the base and dropped my forehead against the trunk.

One day, my daughter would want to know why I hadn't wanted her.

All the good answers were taken. They didn't apply to me. I wasn't too young, and I could take care of her financially. In all the time since I'd found out, not one person had asked me what I wanted to do. It had been assumed. The most I'd gotten was input on whether I wanted to see if Uma could still get rid of it. But I wasn't sure I could let someone take my baby, raise her, and tell her I hadn't wanted her. How could I let someone take her if I *did* want her?

Suddenly, the fact that I didn't love her mother seemed the smallest, most inconsequential reason in the world. Uma didn't want her, so everyone assumed she'd go to an adoptive family. But what if I wanted her? Not one person had given me credit enough to think that I might want my own child, that I was capable of taking care of her. Not my family, not Nash, not Uma, and not Laney. That hurt the most. If she wanted to have a family with me one day, shouldn't she believe I was capable of being a father?

thirty-six

Laney

I walked Pegasus for a while, getting him warm and limber before I let him really go. The day after Christmas was no warmer than the previous two days, but the icy wind had let up, and the sun had warmed the fields during the day. At midnight, though, the heat had gone, and my cheeks burned with cold as I rode. The full moon overhead lit the way for Pegasus as we crossed the mile to the gazebo in what felt like no time at all.

When we arrived, the gazebo was empty. I walked Pegasus for a few minutes, letting him cool down before I looped the reins around one of the posts of the gazebo. I started rubbing him down while I waited. For a second, I considered what I would do if Brody didn't show up. But this wasn't last summer, and Brody wouldn't stand me up. Unless…

I shook the thought away. It had been easy not to be jealous of Uma in the tour bus, when she slept out on the couch while Brody slept in the bed with me. Now that he was at home with Uma, and I was at my house, I had no way of knowing what would happen while I wasn't around to make sure it didn't. And even though I was certain enough that Brody wasn't cheating on me, there would always be that shadow of doubt, even when I knew better, just like there had been three years ago. He'd always sworn nothing happened, but I knew there were ways to cheat without putting your dick in someone.

Finally, footsteps thumped onto the steps of the gazebo, and I jumped and spun around to see Brody appearing out of the darkness as if out of thin air. Absorbed in rubbing down my horse, I hadn't been watching for him on the path.

"Hey," he said, his breath coming in short little plumes in the cold night.

Leaving Pegasus to graze, I joined Brody and sat on the bench of the gazebo, snuggling deeper into my jacket. Brody leaned down to press his cold lips to mine, but I pulled away after only a second.

"What did you want to talk to me about?" he asked, sitting on the bench beside me. I'd always liked how he got right to it with me, not bothering with all the meaningless chit-chat of polite conversation.

"I've been thinking," I said, taking a deep breath before plunging in. "And I don't think I'm going to go back on the road with you."

"What?" he asked, drawing back, his eyes filled with shock and hurt.

"I wanted to travel," I said. "That's why I took this year off. Not just travel here, but go to Europe, New York, Hawaii. And now it's halfway through my year off, and I haven't gone anywhere except on tour with you. Which was fun, I'm not saying it wasn't. But this is something I need to do, Brody."

"And I need you, Laney," he said, taking both my hands in his.

"You don't need me there," I said, swallowing the ache in my throat. "You performed for years without me waiting backstage. And if that's what you're worried about… If you don't think you could stay faithful without me there…"

"It's not what I'm worried about," he said sharply.

"Good," I said. "Then it won't be a problem if I'm not there. Because if that's the only thing keeping you from cheating, then it's going to happen one way or another. I'm not always going to be there to chase off the groupies."

"I'm not like that anymore. That was years ago. I was a kid then. I was a fucking idiot, too, not to know what I had. I'm never going to lose you again. You're mine, Laney." He leaned in again, his lips brushing mine, then pressing harder. He turned to match his movements with mine, his warm tongue sliding past my cold lips, filling my mouth with heat. After a minute, he slipped from the bench to the floor and reached for his belt. I reached for the button on my own jeans, but Brody took my hand.

Suddenly, my heart was thundering in my ears, and I thought I might pass out. Oh, God. He was on his knees.

"I love you, Laney," he said, kissing the back of my hand. "No matter what happens, no matter where in the world you are, if you're in Europe and I'm here, or you're right there where I can see you during a show, you're always going to be my girl. And I will always be your man."

"Oh my God," I whispered, sure I was going to cry. This could not be real. It was what I had wanted all along, but it was all wrong.

Wasn't it?

"These past few months have been… I don't even know how to describe them. But I can't imagine that would be easy for any couple, no matter how long they've been together. And you've been there, Laney. Strong, and graceful, and kind, even when you didn't have to be. When anyone would understand the reasons you wouldn't be. And as crazy as it sounds, that's what made me know more than I've ever known before, that you're the only person I ever want to be with, no matter how crazy the situation, no matter how tough, how awful or unexpected the challenges. I want to be with you for every one of them, Laney Tucker. I want to marry you."

I'd known it was coming, but my heart still burst inside my chest like a bomb going off when he said those last words. A muffled pop sounded, and he opened the box. He hadn't been reaching for his belt. He'd been reaching for his pocket.

In the moonlight, I could see it perfectly, the huge princess cut diamond glittering with a thousand edges in the cool light. I could see his fingers shaking as he took it out, pulled off my glove, and fitted it on my finger. I could see the hope and love and pride pooling in his eyes. But I couldn't speak.

I was frozen on the outside while a million thoughts and feelings flashed through me at lightning speed. I had wanted this from day one when he came back. I had wanted to say no, to hurt him. But I didn't say anything.

Brody slid his hand over my cheek, rising and pulling me closer, his lips sealing with mine again. His tongue moved into my mouth, slow but sure, and his fingers slid through my hair. A chill wrapped itself around my body, hot anticipation contrasted with the cold night. Brody pushed me back, kneeling on the bench to lay me down. He unbuttoned my jeans, his mouth slipping from mine to my cheek, his breath hot against my neck. A gasp escaped me as his teeth squeezed my earlobe, his warm breath filling my ear, his lips closing around my earlobe, sucking gently.

He slid a hand into my jeans, caressing me in slow, steady strokes, until I was wet and aching for him to join with me, stretch me, fill me. I shivered when his mouth moved down my neck, his breath tickling the fine hairs on my skin.

"Brody," I whispered, lifting my hips to let him slide a finger all the way in. I rocked my hips against him, pressing my mound into his palm. My hands moved over his shoulders and back in frantic, hungry motions, tugging at his jacket. He eased my legs open further and fed another finger into me slowly, pushing them as deep as they would go, his palm massaging my clit in rhythm with the stroke of his fingers.

"Fuck me," I cried out, grasping one of the bars of the gazebo railing.

"Not yet," Brody said, his fingers sliding into me in quick, deep thrusts, until I couldn't hold back. I raised my hips and he pressed deep, pulsing his fingers forward as my walls clenched around him and I came with a cry.

When I finished, he slid my jeans over my hips, lowering himself onto me. His mouth found mine again, and he pressed his lips against mine. "I want to do this forever," he whispered. "No matter what happens, this is what I want. You and me, forever. The way it always has been and always will be. This is the one thing I know I can't live without. You, Laney Tucker."

I pushed his jeans down over his hips, our jackets pressing together like a pillow between us on top, our bare skin pressed together below. I could feel his hard cock throbbing against my bare skin, ready to open me all the way. Reaching between us, I grasped his shaft, still hungry for more after one climax. His cock jerked in my grasp, his skin hot against my cold fingers as I guided him into my slick opening. The air raked icy fingers across us, but he burned into me as he breached my entrance, pressing into my tight, wet flesh inch by inch. Raising my hips, I spread my thighs, hooking one foot behind him to push him deeper.

"Don't rush," he whispered, holding out from giving me his whole length. "We've got forever after tonight."

"Give me everything," I whispered. "Do it hard. Now."

With one slow, powerful motion, he pushed into me so deep I scooted up the bench. Bracing my hand on the gazebo railing, I lifted to give him deeper access, wanting him to be rough, to fuck me hard and fast until it hurt.

"Like that?" he said, smiling down at me, grinding his pelvic bone against my clit.

"Yes," I gasped, rocking my hips faster, wrapping my leg tighter around him, dragging him into me with deep, quick thrusts.

"Like this?" he said, driving into me hard again, bracing his hands on the bench above my shoulders, slamming into me harder and harder until I arched up, crying out as my body squeezed him even tighter. And then the pleasure crested and broke, and I cried out again, bucking against him as orgasm gripped me. Brody growled and ground himself deeper, and I felt a twinge of pain as his cock pulsed thicker, and then his completion spilled inside me, filling me to my very depth.

As his warmth spread inside me, little pulses throbbed through me, answered by his quick intake of breath and an answering pulse of his cock. For a second, all I could think was that I wanted all of him, every inch, every part. I loved this man so much it hurt, so much that the loving itself broke my heart open and spilled out my soul. I wanted to be his forever, to have a piece of him forever. To have him inside me the way that Uma did.

"I'll take that as a yes," he said, leaning down to kiss me softly when we'd both caught our breath.

Moments before, I'd been in the throes of bliss I'd never dreamed possible. And he was still there, still inside me, still thinking his dreams had come true. He was still in it, not knowing that suddenly, my mind had turned to the knowledge that was always there, even when I managed to forget it for a moment. It was always waiting to sneak back in at the most inopportune moments. Waiting like the dread that had been hanging over me for a month, ready to drop in the moment I woke up, allowing me only a few seconds of peace before it descended into my mind where it sat, eating away at me, day after day.

I pushed him off and sat up, gathering my jeans from around my ankles and pulling them up, my underwear cold and damp. The sex was still so good, it seemed wrong that the rest was so fucked up. It seemed like I shouldn't be able to feel this way still, that he shouldn't be able to fuck me so good and make me come so hard when everything else was dying. But I wasn't Uma. No matter how good it was, I deserved better. I deserved more. Bad boys with good dick weren't my Kryptonite.

Brody was.

"What about Uma?" I asked. "Is she just going to disappear when the baby comes? You're tied to her for the rest of your life, whether you want to be or not."

"Laney, I've told you, it's not like that," he said, pulling up his own jeans. "We'll get her an apartment until it comes, and then…"

"And then she's still there. In our lives. It's always there. What you did before, and now her."

"I thought you were okay with this. You said you didn't hate her."

"I don't hate her, and I'm not angry. But I'm hurt, Brody. I know it shouldn't matter. It doesn't make rational sense, but there it is. It hurts me that you did that, even if it wasn't when we were together."

"That's not fair," he said quietly. "You got engaged to someone else. You were going to marry someone else. Yes, I fucked other women, but you *loved* another man. And I've never held that against you."

"I know," I said, running my palms down my thighs and taking a deep breath. "In my head, I know it's not fair. I've tried talking myself out of it. But my heart doesn't care. It still breaks for what you did, even if it has no right to. If that makes me a horrible person, then that's what I am."

"You're not a horrible person," he said, standing to pace the wooden planks. "But what do you want me to do?"

I paused at the question, the one that always tripped me up. I'd asked myself a million times, Piper had asked me, Blair had asked me. And now Brody was asking me. But I still didn't have an answer. "I'm not going to tell you what to do," I said. "You know what you should do, what's the right thing for you. But I can't be around her anymore. It hurts too much."

"You don't have to be. She won't come on the road with us this time."

"But she'll be on your mind, all the time. Worrying about whether she's going to spill it to a gossip column, worrying she's going to disappear, or do something stupid and hurt it… I'll see you thinking about her, and it'll be worse than when she's there." I stopped and drew in a shaky breath. "Maybe it's you I can't be around."

"Don't say that," he said, running a hand roughly through his hair. "What can I do?"

"Nothing," I said softly. "Every time I look at her, I have to think about you doing something so intimate with her, something more intimate than I've ever done with anyone else. Not just fucking her. But being inside her, coming inside her. And I just, I can't endure it anymore. I tried, I did it for months. And I was miserable. I don't want to be miserable, and I don't want to hate you for making me miserable."

"Laney, you can't do this," he said, sinking onto the bench seat beside me and taking my hands, his eyes so desperate that just looking at them sliced through my heart like a sharp blade. "Don't say what I think you're saying. Tell me that's not what you're saying."

Tears pressed at the corners of my eyes, stinging until I couldn't hold them back any longer.

"How can you ask me to choose between you and that baby? Between the love of my life and my daughter?"

I shook my head, the tears coming faster now. "I'm not asking you to choose."

"We'll find a way," he said, snagging my hand and pressing it to his lips. "I choose you, Laney. We'll get through this together. I promise."

"You can't 'get through' having a baby," I said, pulling my hand away to swipe at the tears streaming down my cheeks now. I stared straight ahead while I spoke, determined to get through this even if it killed us both. It was something I had to do for both of us, even if it hurt me as much as it hurt him. "You're going to have a child. It's another human being. You won't be through this for eighteen years. Not even then. You're going to be a father for the rest of your life. And she's going to be its mother."

"Laney, look at me," he said, turning my chin toward him. He wiped my tears away with his thumbs, held my face between his hands. "I love you. I'm not going anywhere. I'm not giving up on you."

"I'm sorry," I said, my voice trembling. I pulled off the ring and pressed it into his hand. "I shouldn't have taken this. I can't take it. You might not be going anywhere, but I am."

I stood, my legs like dead weight, and trudged from the gazebo. Brody called after me, but when I climbed up onto Pegasus, he let me go. Did that mean, as the old wisdom went, that he really loved me?

It didn't matter. I was leaving. I pressed my eyes shut and gave the horse his head, knowing that, like me, he would always find his way home.

January

thirty-seven

Brody

Uma and I were sitting upstairs in my room on New Year's Day, staring out the window at the rain, when my phone rang. Everyone else had gone home, and my parents were at their traditional Sunday afternoon card game, so Uma had been persuaded to come upstairs. She still insisted that my mother hated her, and since it was obviously true, it had been hard to convince her to leave her dark little room at all during the past week. She spent her time wandering the garden paths or sitting under the magnolia trees out front.

"Hey, Brody-boy," Nash crowed into the phone so loudly that I shot a look at Uma, knowing she could hear him, too.

"Hey, Nash," I said warily. I hadn't expected Nash to be in good spirits, not after the complications I had dragged him into during the past few months.

"Or should I say, Brody Villines, solo artist and owner of this week's number one single *and* number one album on iTunes?"

"No shit?" I asked, unable to contain my smile. When I tried to convey the smile to Uma, though, I found her staring out the window again. Laney would have been in my arms by now, whispering congratulations into my ear, kissing my neck, promising me a private celebration later.

But Uma was not Laney.

"No shit," Nash confirmed. "Must be kids using all those gift cards they got for Christmas. And they're using them to get your music."

"So much for a little EP that only die-hard fans would buy."

"Yeah, yeah, get your lady something pretty and celebrate later. Right now, let's talk tour dates."

I glanced at Uma again. Her chin rested on her hand, her other hand curled loosely around the bulge in her belly. She was the closest thing to a lady I had now, and I could just imagine her scorn if I asked her to help me celebrate the success of my 'lame-ass' music. I wanted to run straight to the Tuckers' to tell Laney, but of course I couldn't do that anymore.

The knowledge punched a hole straight through my chest. If I couldn't share my triumphs with her, what was the point? The whole act seemed suddenly trivial. With *Just 5 Guys*, I'd had friends to share every moment with. The glory was split five ways. Now, it just seemed hollow and lonely. What was success if you had no one to share it with?

But there was no point in staying here alone, either.

"How many shows do I have to do?" I asked with a sigh.

"You're going to love this. We've got twenty-four, all this month."

"What?" I asked, jumping to my feet. Uma didn't even blink. "I thought I told you I wanted to take it easy this time around."

"You gotta get while the getting's good. Today you're hot. Tomorrow, maybe not."

"Don't schedule any more," I said sharply. Rain sluiced against the window in front of Uma's unflinching eyes.

"Brody, Brody, that's just one month. We've got the rest of the year before you'll need to put out another album."

"I'm not touring the rest of the year," I said. "I'm going to have a baby, Nash. I'm going to be a father."

I'd never said it before. Never believed it. But the conviction in my voice made even Uma snap out of her trance and turn to give me a sullen look.

Nash barked out that abrupt laugh.

I couldn't give either of them the answer they wanted. I didn't think I could speak if I tried. The weight of the words I'd just spoken had hit me full force.

I was going to be a father. *A father.* The thought was terrifying, but exhilarating, too.

"And I'm just now hearing about this?" Nash yelped into the phone, bringing me back to the present.

"I'm just now hearing about it," I said, my eyes locked on Uma's. She shrank back in his chair, one hand protectively cupping her belly, staring at me like I'd said I was going to rip the baby straight through her belly and steal away with it. "I've got to go."

Nash yelled something into the phone, but I ended the call and tossed the phone onto the bed.

"What was that about?" Uma asked, shifting away from me as I moved toward her slowly, as if she might fly at me at any moment. Or take flight.

"It's my baby, too," I said.

"Okay…"

"I think I should get a say in what happens to her."

"Okay…"

For a second, the silence was cut only by the steady thrum of the rain on the roof, an endless drumbeat overhead. "I think we should talk about this," I said. "Like equals. Not like it's your baby, and I'm going to support whatever you do. Because I'm not."

"Since when? You were all too happy to let me do this alone," she said, jumping to her feet.

"Fuck you, Uma. No, I wasn't. You keep shutting me out. I've never told you to do anything alone. I've kept you by my side since the moment you showed up, even when it cost me my relationship with Laney. I'm done being on the sidelines. You need to let me be involved."

"It's a little late for that now."

"No, it's not."

We stared each other down for a minute.

"You want her, don't you?" I asked. "Admit it. You say you don't, but you don't want to share her with anyone. Not even me."

"I let you feel her move."

"Once. In two months. I'm not going to be your sugar daddy, just throwing money at you when you want it. I want to be part of her life."

"How does Laney feel about that?" Uma asked, a sneer pulling at her lip.

"Laney left."

Uma sank back down into my chair. "What do you mean she left? When?"

"She left me," I said, wilting onto the edge of the bed, all my conviction spent. At the mention of her name, a pit of emptiness opened inside me, threatening to consume me like a black hole. "Right after Christmas."

"Why didn't you tell me?"

"I didn't want you to think it was your fault, or that it had anything to do with you."

"Dude, I'm sorry. That sucks."

I rubbed my palm over the ring box, still in my front pocket. "Yeah."

"So what now?" Uma asked, twisting the chair back and forth, slouching down in it so her stomach protruded upwards like a little mountain.

"I don't know. I guess I'm supposed to go on the road. I have tour dates this month, but I'm not going on more. Not for a while. I want to…I think I want…" I broke off and swallowed hard. "I want to be part of her life, Uma. Not just a paycheck."

"How are you going to take care of her?"

"I guess the same way people have always taken care of babies."

"But what do you know about it?"

"Not much," I admitted, watching the flat grey sky outside spit rain into the cold afternoon. "But you'd be there…"

Uma pushed herself upright in the chair. "I don't want to be a mom, Brody."

I blinked at her, drawing back. She was so possessive of that baby growing inside her. "You don't?"

"No," she said. "I've thought about it…God, like, nonstop. I mean, how could I not think about it? But I probably know as little as you do about it."

"I'll get you some books. I'm sure most of it comes naturally, and we'll figure out the rest as we go. The same as every other parent."

Uma narrowed her eyes. "You're talking like we'll be together."

"We can raise her together, as long as we want. I'll take care of you. I want to. This is scary as hell, Uma. You don't have to go through this alone. Let me be there. Fuck the apartment. Come on the road with me. I'll do right by you, if that's what you want."

"Like… Get married?" she asked incredulously.

I took a deep breath and touched the box in my pocket. But I'd never give that ring to anyone if I couldn't give it to Laney. "I'm from the South, Uma. My girlfriend dumped me so I could do the right thing. I have nothing left to lose. And if we're keeping the baby, shouldn't we at least discuss the possibility?"

"Wow, Brody. That was downright sappy. But as tempting and heartfelt as that proposal was, I'm only nineteen. And no offense, but I don't actually like you all that much."

I inwardly sank with relief. "We can still keep her," I said. "I'll be a good dad, Uma. And you might not feel like it now, but you'll be a good mom."

"How do you know?"

"Because," I said, gesturing to her bump. "I don't think you can help it. It's instinct to take care of that baby you carried."

"You obviously don't watch the news if you think every girl has the instinct to be a good mother."

"I think you do."

"You don't even know me," she said, jumping up to pace the room. Outside, the unremarkable winter rain continued falling in a steady, unending drizzle.

"I can fix that."

"And where do you think we're going to live? Here? Together? What would your mother say to that?"

"I have a house in L.A."

She stopped pacing in the middle of my floor and spun to face me. "You do?"

"Yeah. I do. And one in the Hamptons. I only come here to see my family."

"Can't imagine why you'd want to miss that," she said, rolling her eyes.

"They're family." I shrugged. "So. What do you say?"

"I don't know, Brody," she said, slouching onto the edge of my desk. "This is a big decision. You're asking me to keep this baby, to be a mom for you."

"No," I said, holding up a hand. "That's not what I'm asking. If you don't want to be involved, I'll do it myself. I can hire a nanny. I want to do this. With or without you. I'm just giving you a way to make it work, too, if you want to be a part of her life." The more I talked about it, the surer I got.

"What about the music?"

"I'll always make music," I said, my gaze settling on my guitar in the corner. The usual pull began, an itch in my fingers, the moment I gave it attention. "It's part of me. But I don't have to make money off it. To be honest, that takes the joy out of it."

"Yeah, I can see that," Uma said. "If you sell out."

"I didn't sell out."

She snorted. "You're the definition of a sell-out. Unless you always wanted to be a singing, dancing marionette. And I've heard you noodling around on your guitar. You're not terrible. Not *Just 5 Guys* level terrible, anyway."

I bit back the resentment building in me. "Gee, thanks."

"You really have changed," she said, a grin spreading across her face. "Last time I goaded you, you threw me on the floor and fucked me like you meant it."

"I wouldn't put it that way."

"I would."

We smirked at each other a second before I remembered who I was talking to. I tore my eyes from hers, focused on the bulge in her middle. "I'm sorry," I said to her belly.

"I'm not," she said. "If you're going to do it, you might as well mean it. And if you can't mean it, you can at least get your money's worth."

I suddenly remembered her asking for a refund of her ticket price if she didn't enjoy it. She'd gotten a whole hell of a lot more than the cost of a ticket, even a front row seat. But I wasn't going to let her distract me now.

"I meant what I said. I want to keep her. I'm not okay with giving her away to strangers."

"And what if I am?"

"You can't make that decision if I want her."

"I wouldn't," she said, coming to sit beside me. "But… What if I can't do it? There's somebody out there who would do it for love, because she wants to. I'm just doing it for duty."

"That will change when you see her," I said, taking her hand. "When you hold her and see her face. And I'll be here to help, every step of the way. I promise you that much, Uma, even if I can't promise you all the things I should."

"And what happens when you meet someone you *can* give all the things you should?" Those stormy, violet eyes that made her so recognizable flashed a challenge at me. "You know, the one you actually want to marry? What happens when one of us wants a real family? The other one gets stuck with her?"

"We'll work out a schedule. We can be good parents without getting married. Lots of people do it. Come with me, and we'll work everything out. You'll be taken care of, and so will she. Let's just try it, Uma. It's the right thing to do, for her."

"For her," Uma echoed faintly.

thirty-eight

Laney

"Are you thinking about he-who-must-not-be-named again?" Piper asked, bringing me back to the reality of the bitterly cold day in Central Park. I'd gone to New York with Piper for New Year's Eve to watch the ball drop in Times Square. It was one of those things I'd imagined doing since Piper went off to school there, something for my bucket list. But then I'd just… Stayed.

I knew I'd have to leave soon, but I hadn't decided where to go. I was anchorless, untethered from school for the first time in seventeen years. Until now, the tour schedule and Brody had filled my time. As pathetic as it sounded, without him, I wasn't sure what to do with myself. In my first two weeks in New York, I'd already visited all the main attractions and started to see the ugly, barrenness of the city. Hence the trip to the park, where I could get at least a breath of nature, even if it wasn't the sprawling fields of home where there was so much beauty it could drown you.

"Maybe I am thinking about him," I said, peeling the wrapper further down my vendor hotdog to take another bite. "It's getting better, though. I promise."

"I have some news," Piper said, crumpling her own wrapper into a ball. "I got accepted for an internship in Paris next summer."

"Paris? Oh my God, Piper. Congratulations!"

"I know," Piper said. "It's huge. I was so excited I almost puked when I got the letter. I'll be working for a real designer, getting a fashion show together."

"I'm ninety percent happy for you, and ten percent dying of jealousy," I said with a little laugh. Maybe it was more than ten percent. I was going to grad school, true. That was my dream. But Piper was going to be working with models, moving on with her glamourous career—and in freaking Paris!

"You can come visit," Piper said. "You can share my futon there, too."

A twinge of guilt twisted in my belly. I didn't think Piper meant it as a reminder that I needed to move on, but I took it that way.

"Hey, Red," a guy jogging called to us. "Do the carpet match the drapes?"

"Ugh," Piper said, rolling her eyes. "I can't wait to get out of here, if only for a month. I bet people in Paris aren't nearly that rude."

On the overcast day, Piper's hair seemed even redder than in sunlight, the one bright spot in the whole grey city. It hung around her shoulders in a perfect curtain, straight and even. Suddenly, she looked so grown up, like a real adult about to fly off to Paris on her own and have a glamourous summer of adventure.

"Let's go get our hair cut," I said. "Or at least give me the name of your salon and your girl."

"But you love your long hair," Piper said, looking sideways at me. It was true. I'd always worn my hair long and wild, ever since I'd been a little girl dreaming of being a cowgirl. But I'd turned twenty-three now, graduated college. I needed to stop looking like a fantasy.

"It's time," I said, reaching back to feel my ponytail. It still hung almost to my waist, like a little kid's.

"If you're sure," Piper said. "But first, I have somewhere better to take you."

I balled up the paper around the uneaten portion of my hotdog, now ice cold, and tossed it in a trash can on our way out. Piper got a cab and took me to a tiny shop, completely unremarkable from the street. I could have walked by it a hundred times and not seen it. There it was with a little sign in the window that read *Paperie.*

We stepped through the door, and a little bell tinkled, just like something back in Kentucky. Only this was way better than the Office Depot where I went to get school supplies.

"Welcome to my zen space," Piper said.

While Piper flipped through bins of tabbed folders set up on tables like a record store, I scanned the planners. When we'd been in high school, we'd been the career girls at our private school. We didn't giggle over boys in the bathroom, or play sports, or rebel by rolling up our skirts to show a few extra inches of leg and sneaking off campus to smoke cigarettes at lunch. We planned the future, made endless lists, decorated planners, made scrapbooks of all our extracurricular activities. In short, we were private school nerds.

Since then, I had let the assumption that I'd been the popular cheerleader sort help me along in rushing for my sorority and stoking the fantasies of my now-ex fiancé. But Piper knew exactly what nerd-girl Laney needed to zone out. We left with bags of stationary and planners, giggling like the girls we had been the last time we did this.

By evening, the joy had worn off. We weren't kids anymore. Sure, it was still fun to do crafty stuff. But the world wasn't so simple I could organize away my worries anymore.

I told myself I'd done the right thing. If I filled out a planner for each of the next eighteen years, Uma and Brody would be in each one, or they would be in none. They came as a package deal now. Even if she took the kid back to Seattle, and Brody only had to send her a check every month, I would resent her. And I didn't think Uma was going to go away that easily. Or that Brody would be happy to be nothing but a paycheck to his kid.

"Hey, you got what you wanted," Piper had told me when we left Kentucky. "He asked you to marry him, and you said no. You got him back, didn't you?"

It was true. From the start, I'd set my sights on a ring. I'd wanted to make him fall in love, to make him ask me to marry him. Brody had done exactly what I wanted—probably what I knew he'd do. Because even when he was in pictures with girls hanging all over him, even when he was breaking my heart, when he was famous and had groupies lining up for a chance to get in his pants, when I hadn't seen him for years, I knew Brody. I still knew him better than anyone on earth. I'd known exactly how to play him and get what I wanted because I knew under all the fame, he was still a good guy.

What I hadn't put into the equation was myself. I had gotten exactly what I wanted. I had broken Brody Villines' heart. I just hadn't expected it to break mine, too.

February

thirty-nine

Brody

One night in mid-January, I climbed on the bus after a show to find it quiet and apparently empty. The tour schedule was relentless and grueling, and I barely saw Uma. But she was always there when I got on the bus at the end of the night. She might be huddled on the pullout bed, sleeping, but she'd be there. Tonight, I didn't see her anywhere, and a curdled feeling settled into my gut when I didn't find her in the main room.

She still maintained that my music was shit, and unlike Laney, she wanted nothing to do with it. When we did see each other, half the time I was on orders not to speak at all, having to rest my vocal cords as much as possible between near-nightly performances. Just one of the joys of working for Nash.

With Nash, I often had to remind myself. My shrink said it was all a matter of perspective, but that was bullshit. I had to do Nash's bidding, while Nash did whatever the fuck he wanted with my career.

The only exception was when it came to Uma and the baby. There, I wouldn't budge. I was taking care of them, no matter how many times Nash told me I'd lost my fucking mind. I was not going to let anything happen to my daughter.

After checking the bus bathroom and the cockpit, I'd pretty much exhausted my options. I checked my phone, a surge of bile collecting in my stomach. She hadn't called. What if she'd skipped out on me? I yanked open the accordion door to my bedroom, meaning to grab a half-assed disguise, and stopped short.

Uma was curled up on my bed, on top of the blankets, still in her clothes. For a second, I wasn't sure what to do.

Get my shit together, that's what. She was the mother of my unborn child, not a fucking tiger. Although sometimes that comparison might have been fitting. Though I didn't miss the party atmosphere of *Just 5 Guys*, without Laney the bus was lonely as hell. Uma kept to herself, staring moodily out the windows or pacing up and down the bus to stretch her legs. When she did talk to me, it was usually to bitch about something or snap at me for something I'd said. Luckily, she seemed to sleep more and more the closer she got to having the baby, which meant less bitching and snapping.

I thought about waking her but decided against it and crawled into bed instead. In the morning, she was stretched out beside me, still wearing her clothes.

After that, in some unspoken agreement, we started sharing the bed. Now that I didn't have Laney sharing the bed, there was no reason not to let Uma sleep there. We had zero interest in each other, so it seemed meaningless, a simple convenience. I didn't want her sleeping on the pull-out bed now that she was big, anyway. She needed to be comfortable. When I offered to sleep on the couch, she shrugged and said I might as well be comfortable, too. So that's where we were when, one night in early February, as the bus traveled from Dallas to Memphis, I woke up with a start to find warm liquid seeping through my pajamas. I sat up and moved away, fumbling to switch on the light.

"Uma? Did your water just break, or did you piss on me?"

She sat up slowly, looking confused, and peered down at the wet spot spreading across her pajama pants. "I don't know," she said slowly.

"What do you mean, you don't know? Can't you tell?"

She scrunched up her face for a moment, then shook her head. "No." While she went to the bathroom, I went to talk to the bus driver.

Uma came back from the bathroom holding a towel to herself a few minutes later. "I think it's the water," she said. "It doesn't seem to be stopping."

"We're going to pull over at the next hospital."

"Where the fuck are we?" she asked, pulling up the shade on the tiny window.

"Someplace in Arkansas."

"This better not turn into some freaky version of *Deliverance,*" she said, peering out the window. "I don't see anything out there. I seriously doubt they have a hospital in… Hold on, I see a sign for the next town coming up. *Osceola.*" She said the name like it was another name for a toilet full of shit.

"We'll just see, okay?" I said, pulling her back onto the bed. "How are you feeling?"

"Aren't you afraid I'll get this junk on your bed?"

"Nah. I bet that's, like, one of the cleanest things there is. Your baby is stored in it, so it's gotta be safe. Like formaldehyde."

"Yeah, it's also taking dumps in there," Uma said.

I wasn't sure about that, but I didn't say anything. I really didn't want to know. I was kind of fascinated by all the pregnancy stuff, not that I'd admit it to anyone else. It was cool reading about what new things my baby girl was doing in there each week. But when Uma said things like "prolapsed uterus" or "mucous plug," I got a little nauseous. I had to admit she had a stronger stomach for the gory details than I did.

"Can we please not stop here?" she asked. "I think... I'm having some cramps. Maybe we should go to a real hospital."

Blood rushed in my ears. I'd thought I had prepared for this, but now that it was happening, it didn't seem real. Maybe it wasn't. Maybe the baby would come out black or Asian, and I'd know I'd been had. But it would all be over. That thought gave me enough strength to tell the driver to keep on to the next town with a good hospital.

"What if I can't do this?" Uma said, her face twisting into a grimace.

"You can," I said, returning to my seat beside her on the edge of the bed. "People have been doing this since the beginning of time."

"People weren't here in the beginning of time," she said, clutching the edge of the bed and leaning forward, her face pale.

"Well, since people have been here, they've been making more people," I said.

"People have also been dying of this since there were people."

I pulled the blanket up around her shoulders and started rubbing her back in slow circles. "You're not going to die."

She looked up at me with eyes frantic and terrified. "What if I do?"

"You won't," I said, taking her face between my hands. "You are going to be just fine, Uma. You and the baby. You'll see."

She closed her eyes and leaned in, and I kissed her.

After a second, she gasped and pulled away, her hand circling the huge round of her belly.

"Yeah, this is it," she said. "It's definitely coming."

Eight hours later, it was still definitely coming. We were in a small hospital in a private room with the most uncomfortable chairs in the world. I had tried to doze in one, but it was useless. I hadn't been able to stop thinking. This seemed like a long time to wait. What if something was wrong? The nurses and doctor had assured me that it wasn't that long, and that she'd be fine, even though the water had broken so long ago. Still, it seemed like years. In the movies, the water always broke, and the baby came before the mother could even make it to the hospital. This was better than if I'd had to deliver the baby myself in the back of my tour bus. But shit, if I'd known it was going to take this long, we would have gone on to a bigger town than Faulkner, someplace with a big hospital and surgeons who could help if things went wrong.

Someone tapped on my shoulder, and I turned to see a young nurse holding out a little pad of paper and a pen. "Do you think you could sign this? For my sister?" she asked, looking like she hated to ask a favor, but she sure wasn't going to miss the opportunity to ask for one. I sighed and signed the pad.

Uma was dozing, half asleep now that they'd given her an epidural to cut the pain. When the nurse skipped off, I turned back to the window that overlooked a parking lot, the few cars glinting in the first rays of morning sun. That was the thing about having the most famous face in the world. Even in a tiny town I'd never heard of, everyone had heard of me.

Not for the first time, I wondered if this would get out to the media. It probably would. I'd told the nurses Uma was my cousin, and there was that confidentiality thing, but news always seemed to leak out. I was so sick of it all. Sick of signing autographs, taking selfies. Sick of living for other people.

I turned back to the bed. Uma's eyes had opened. In the morning sunshine, with her hair spread out on the pillow, she seemed more real. Everything was revealed on her face, and she looked frightened and trapped, like an animal in a snare. Not like a mother about to greet her baby for the first time.

"Are you in pain?" I asked, adrenaline surging through me as I shot to my feet, panic gnawing at my nerve endings. "Is the epidural wearing off?"

"Chill, dude," she said. "It's fine. I'm fine."

"Do you need more ice chips?"

"I'm hungry as fuck," she said. "But I don't guess they'd let me have a Big Mac."

"Probably not," I said, taking her hand and relaxing a bit. "It's nice to see you still have your sense of humor."

"They're ripping out my twat, not my brain."

"I don't think you have to give them your twat, either."

"I might as well. No one's going to want me after a baby comes tearing out of there. It'll be like, *Want to come over? I've got a hallway for your hotdog.*"

I sank back down in my chair, still holding her hand. "I'm sure that's not true."

"Really? Who's going to want to fuck me then? You? Ha. You don't even want to now, and everything's still intact."

"You don't want to, either."

"Yeah, but it would be nice to think someone would find me attractive again someday. But after seeing a baby pop out of there, I don't expect you to want anything to do with that."

"Did you want me to?" I asked, shifting in the chair that had suddenly become, impossibly, even more uncomfortable. "I mean, we did kiss…"

"Yeah, thanks for the pity kiss, but sorry, that didn't really do it for me."

"If you're worried about it, I don't have to watch."

"Yeah, fuck that. You put this thing in me, you're damn sure going to watch it come out. You don't get to sit outside and have a cigar and have everyone pat you on the back while I'm in here bleeding and screaming and tearing in half."

"Okay, I'll watch," I said, holding up my hands. "Whatever you want."

"What I want is for this bullshit to be happening to you, not me."

"I wish it could," I said, squeezing her hand. "I wish I could take the pain instead of you. I really do."

"Yeah, easy for you to say, since you obviously can't." She turned and glared out at the parking lot, her throat working as she swallowed.

"I'm sorry," I said, putting a hand on her knee. "Someone will want you again, Uma. You're nineteen. Your life isn't over."

"It might as well be," she muttered to the window.

I didn't know what to say, so I said nothing. I checked my phone, hoping against hope that my mother would come through for me this time. Somebody needed to rescue me, that was for damn sure. I had no fucking clue what to do in this situation, how to make Uma see reason or even feel better. Probably not the best time to tell her she was being crazy, but then, what was I supposed to tell her?

My mother would know. Sure, she was a pain in the ass, but she'd done this three times. Maybe she'd change her mind at the last minute, when it became real to her that she had a grandchild. But then, she already had grandchildren. The only thing special about this one was that it was a bastard, as she'd so lovingly put it the last time we'd talked. Even so, I'd texted her when Uma had been admitted, thinking maybe…

Of course, she hadn't texted back. Uma wouldn't have wanted her there, anyway. She needed her own mother, and she didn't have one. Her cousin was back in Seattle, but she wouldn't make it to Arkansas in time for the birth. All Uma had was me, the shitty father of the baby she didn't want. No one who knew what to say to her, or even what to say to women under ordinary circumstances. She needed someone she could be close to, someone she had a connection with.

I thumbed through my phone, stopping at Laney's number. I wanted to call her, to tell her. She wasn't exactly close with Uma, though they'd gotten along better than I'd expected. But her being there would probably have upset her and Uma both.

More than anything, I wanted to call her for selfish reasons. I wanted to hear her familiar voice, to feel her steadying presence beside me, my anchor in any storm life could throw at us. But I also wanted to share this moment with her, to include her in the pride and unbelievable awe of it. I wanted her to be part of the biggest moment of my life so far.

But she wouldn't want that.

In a way, she would be a part of every moment of my life, if only because I had her there in my thoughts. But this time, it wasn't enough. I needed her to be more than a memory, a fantasy.

She had made her decision, though. She'd cut me out of her life. When we'd said goodbye after Christmas, the politeness in her voice had nearly killed me. For good measure, she'd driven the nail into the coffin by saying she hoped we could always be friends. The memory of it still smarted.

Instead of calling, I sent her a text. I wasn't sure what she'd say, what she'd think of it. But I knew that I had to say something to her while still respecting her boundaries and letting her move on with her life the way she'd asked.

Uma said the contractions were starting to hurt, and I was drawn from my thoughts back to the present. I called the nurses to check on her, and then she needed a doctor. After eight hours of waiting while nothing happened, suddenly everything was happening at once.

"I'm sorry, sir, we're going to have to ask you to leave," said a nurse whose name tag said Eden. "Only immediate family is allowed during the birth."

"He's staying," Uma bellowed, her face glazed in sweat. "Either he stays, or I'm walking out right now with the baby hanging halfway out."

She glared so fiercely that Nurse Eden only nodded, her lips tight. After that, they left me alone, focusing all their attention on Uma.

I held her hand while she panted and pushed and sweated and screamed. I was glad Laney wasn't here. If all women had to go through this hell—and it was a hundred times worse for her than the hell I was in—I didn't know how humankind still existed. There was no way I was ever, ever, ever going to put anyone through this again. I didn't think I'd make it through this one. I had no idea how Uma could bear whatever was happening inside her.

And then suddenly, with a final roar of pain, she pushed the head out. I felt woozy, but I clutched her hand tighter. I wasn't going to be one of those guys who fainted at the sight of a baby being born. But goddamn, did I want to.

The doctor told her to push again, and in what seemed like an anticlimactic push compared to the epic last one, she gave a little push and the doctor drew the baby out. It was slimy and red and wailing with a hoarse little cry that echoed through the room. The nurses took it for about thirty seconds and then lay it on Uma's chest. I couldn't tear my eyes from the scrunched up little face. It looked so tiny, like a kitten.

It continued wailing, its little hands working up and down, but Uma didn't seem to hear it. Her arms hung limp by her sides, and her face was turned toward the window, her eyes blank and unseeing. For one ball-shriveling moment, I thought she was dead.

"Don't you want to hold her?" the nurse cooed at Uma.

"Can I?" I asked, already lifting her off Uma's chest. If anyone didn't believe in love at first sight, they'd never held a baby for the first time.

I rocked the little bundle back and forth, and after about thirty seconds, her cries tapered off into sniffles, and then she lay still, looking up at me with eyes the color of the sky on a winter evening. This was someone I could live for, someone I wanted to live for.

Her perfect little bow of a mouth scrunched up as she looked up at me, and her fragile fingers clenched around my thumb when I stroked her palm, her translucent skin so delicate I was afraid to touch it with my guitar hardened fingers, afraid I'd tear it.

With one blink of her tiny eyelids, she shifted the whole world.

forty

Laney

I stood on the lid of the toilet in Piper's tiny bathroom, trying to see my full outfit in the mirror. If I bent my knees and kind of crouched and looked up, I could see all but my shoes. Not that I should care, really, what a stranger thought of me. If he didn't like me, so what? I didn't know him. It was no loss to me. I'd already lost the love of my life and survived it, so what was one blind date's opinion going to do? Nothing.

Clambering down from my perch, I straightened my little black dress. At the last minute, I decided against the pearl earrings. Even the dress might be too much. But he worked on Wall Street, which sounded so glamourous to my country ears. I didn't want to look like a hick who wore ragged jeans on a first date.

I'd probably worn ripped jeans on my first date with Brody.

Pushing the thought away, I ran my hands over my torso, my slender waist, the swell of my hips. After ditching the pearl earrings, I settled for a pair of simple studs and a ruby teardrop necklace. With my blonde hair now cut just below my shoulders, I looked much more New York and much less Kentucky cowgirl. I stepped back from the mirror. I was ready. Designer heels, a pair Brody had given me, completed the ensemble. When guilt started to leak in at the edges of my mind, I reminded myself of the text I'd gotten the day before.

5:16am Brody My Love: The baby is here.

Brody had moved on. It was high time I did, too. Starting with changing the sappy name he'd programmed into my phone for himself. And this time, I wouldn't sit around mourning my broken heart any longer than I had the last time. That time I'd had Paul. This time I had…

I wracked my brain, trying to remember the name Piper had given me when she'd said she had a friend I might like. "He's young and self-made," Piper had said, then laughed. "Well, his dad's an investment banker, but he's also made a fortune on his own on top of that."

Piper rarely dated, but she had gone out with one of his friends for a while. She assured me he could make me forget Brody. I doubted that, but still. If Brody was off having babies with someone else, I could certainly go on a date. It wasn't like I was going out clubbing every night. We were just going for drinks. And even if I had been slutting it up all over New York, that was my business. Brody had moved on. My choices no longer affected him.

Outside, I wrapped my coat tightly around myself and hailed a cab, which took a good ten minutes. Finally, I slid onto the worn upholstery seats of an old yellow taxi, my legs shaking from cold. And fine, maybe I was a little nervous. I'd only dated two guys ever. Guys in New York were probably cynical and jaded, nothing like me. Somehow, I'd end up showing my naivete, and he'd go home thinking I was a country bumpkin still in love with my high school boyfriend. God, I was such a fool. What was I doing here?

Before I could reconsider or tell the cabbie to turn around, he was dropping me off at the designated meeting spot, a place called Last Call. It was small and simple, the façade completely undecorated. A sign on the door mandated that ladies must wear dresses and men must wear jackets. Thank fuck I hadn't worn jeans.

I walked in, only to be greeted by one of those New York-beautiful women, the ones who looked like they spent hours polishing every bit of themselves—hair, nails, teeth, skin… Probably a model waiting tables on the side.

She gave me a smile that went nowhere near her eyes. "Are we expecting you?"

"I'm meeting my date," I said, realized I still didn't know his name. "I'm sure he has a table already. I'm Laney Tucker."

God, even my name sounded country.

"Ah, here you are," the woman said. "He did call ahead to tell us to seat you if he wasn't here yet."

I wasn't sure how to take that. It seemed polite, but then, it also seemed like he was giving me permission to sit down instead of standing in the cold entrance waiting for him. I gave the woman my winningest smile. "Can I ask you what his name is again?" I whispered conspiratorially. "Help a girl out?"

The woman did not return my smile. Instead, she gave me a look that was half pity, half contempt. "Robert Mensch," she said. "Right this way."

When I was seated and the snooty hostess had gone, I breathed a sigh of relief. The place was dark and small, with only a handful of tables covered with white cloths, four booths along the wall, all occupied, and an old, polished wooden bar. Potted plants, probably fake, hung in square, walnut boxes around the bar, and the walls featured large framed pictures of European castles.

Five minutes later, the waiter had been by my table twice, and I was beginning to wonder if I should order a drink without Robert. I didn't want to drink alone like a loser, but I also didn't want to sit there alone all night. What if he stood me up? I should have asked the door girl if he'd said anything else, like that he would be late, instead of asking his name. I wasn't about to go back and ask now, though.

Finally, I broke down and ordered a gin and tonic. At least it would take the edge off my nerves. It arrived icy cold and sparkling, and I took a sip, relishing the bitterness. Just as I set my drink down, a tall guy approached the table with a confident, determined stride. He wore dark jeans, a button-down shirt and a blazer. Despite the slight bump on the bridge of his nose, he was attractive, with short dark hair, a slight tan, and dark eyes. Not Brody Villines, but handsome in a more sophisticated way.

"You started without me," he said, sliding into his chair.

"You're late," I said with a shrug.

He grinned, his teeth perfectly straight and white. "Your hair is shorter than in your picture."

I bit back my reply that his hair was thinner than in his picture. No reason to be tasteless just because he'd been late. He probably had a perfectly good reason. I took a long sip of my drink to quell the urge to give him the smart retort he obviously wanted.

"What number is that?" he asked, nodding at my drink.

"One," I said defensively. Were all New York men so confrontational?

He motioned for the waiter and ordered a scotch, neat. "What number is that for her?" he asked the waiter, nodding at my half-empty glass.

My mouth literally fell open in shock. The waiter looked like he wasn't sure if he should answer, but when Robert asked again in that impatient, demanding way, he did. When he'd scurried off, Robert grinned at me. "Hey, you're honest," he said. "You passed that test. After the false advertising of your picture, I had to make sure."

"I guess you're not worried about passing any tests," I said with a serene smile.

"Why would I be?" he said. "I'm a catch. If it doesn't work out, there's ten more of you lined up waiting for me to buy them a drink and take them home, and maybe, someday, give them that hundred-thousand-dollar dream wedding. Isn't that what you want?"

I finished my drink in two long pulls and pushed back from the table. "For your information, I can pay for my own damn wedding. And it sure as hell won't be with a prematurely balding egomaniac without a tenth of the tact and charm of a common Kentucky redneck. Thanks for the drink, though."

"Aw, sit down," he said. "We've barely gotten started."

"I've seen enough," I said, forcing my voice to be light and offhand. I shrugged into my coat and smiled. "Don't worry, I can get my own cab."

Not that he would have bothered to make sure.

When he didn't show any intention of contradicting me, I turned and headed out. It had been a bad idea from the start. I wasn't ready for this, for anyone. Last time, I'd jumped back in and gotten engaged to an asshole. This time, I knew to stop at one date. As the fifth cab sped by without slowing for me, a guy going into Last Call grabbed himself and made a lewd comment. The remains of the snow sat in sludgy grey puddles along the street, and when a cab finally slammed on the brakes and slid to a stop beside me, it sprayed frigid slush across my Louboutins.

I climbed into the taxi, wiped off my shoes with a tissue from my purse, and texted my mother. I was time to go home.

forty-one

Brody

"I guess congratulations are in order," Nash said as he dragged me to the dressing room. "But you barely made this one. Everyone's getting antsy out there. Your opening number's already run through their entire repertoire."

"I told you to cancel," I snapped. "Uma wasn't ready to leave."

"She'll be as good in the bus as at the hospital," Nash said, slamming the dressing room door and ripping my t-shirt off with a swiftness that would have impressed even the most rabid baby-doll. "A bed's a bed."

"It's been two days. I'm not sure I'm ready."

"Does your pussy hurt, too? Jesus, Brody. You're not the one who gave birth."

"I want to be there for her," I said quietly, succumbing to Nash's insistence on dressing me. I didn't want to tell Nash about Uma's odd detachment, like she'd checked out of everything, not just the hospital. I didn't want to admit that I was a tiny bit afraid to leave Uma alone with her own baby. My baby. The nurse had assured me that not everyone fell in love at first sight, even with their own babies. She said it was perfectly normal for it to feel like a stranger, for the mother to take a while to bond. But I had my doubts.

I knew I didn't give my best performance at the Forum. My heart and mind were elsewhere, with the baby. Osceola. Uma had come about in the hospital long enough to tell me how to fill out the birth certificate.

"I think her name is Osceola," she'd said, peering at me almost shyly from beneath her lashes. I'd thought, for a minute, she was going to take an interest. I'd jotted the name down on the form without so much as blinking. I didn't care what we called her. I'd love her just the same if her name was Horse Manure or Cinderella. But I'd paused, the pen raised, before putting down a last name.

"Villines?" I'd asked, my heart pounding in my ears like a bass drum.

She'd shrugged and gone back to staring out the window, and I'd felt a swell of pride bigger than anything I'd ever felt—more than when I'd filled Madison Square Garden, or had my first number one single, or won Best New Artist at the Grammy's. Nothing in my life could compare to holding that baby and gazing at her perfection for hours at a time. But giving her my last name came close. She was mine. By blood, by name, by law. And nothing could take her away.

Except Uma.

Some paranoid little voice in the back of my mind kept asking if I was sure she hadn't been faking it. If, when I got back from my first time leaving her alone for more than a few minutes, she'd be gone with Osceola, leaving nothing but a stain on the mattress to prove it had happened at all.

After the show, I blew off the obligatory schmoozing and went directly to my tour bus. As soon as I opened the door, I heard the baby's wails. They'd grown louder in the past few days from the feeble squall in the hospital. Now, she was giving us an earful when she wasn't happy. And she didn't sound happy.

I hurried to the bedroom, where we'd set up a bassinet beside the bed. Uma was sitting on the bed, propped up on pillows, with her arms crossed over her chest, frowning at the wall.

"What's wrong with her?" I asked, bending to scoop Osceola from her little bed.

"Fuck if I know," Uma said. "I think she hates me. She won't eat. I tried to feed her, but guess what? Even she doesn't want anything to do with my tits."

"I don't think that's the problem," I said, rocking the baby back and forth. "Have you pumped any milk? I can feed her a bottle."

"No," Uma said. "I tried, but nothing comes out, and it hurts like hell. Just get her some formula."

I glanced at Uma, about to argue that breastfeeding was healthier for the baby, but I decided against it. It was her body. Instead, I sent Nash a text asking him to run out and get formula, which went over about as well as expected. When Nash appeared at last, I was sitting on the couch with Osceola, who was only fussing now.

"I'm not going back out," I said, scanning the back of the formula can. "I need some time off."

"We can cut most of the post-show crap," Nash said. "But you gotta do the meet-and-greet before the show if you don't do it after."

I held the baby in one arm while I scooped formula into the bottle, added the distilled spring water I'd warmed while waiting, and screwed on the cap, managing to slop it all over the counter in the process. I'd have to get this one-handed thing down a little better before I called myself a pro.

"I'm not talking about after the shows," I said, glancing back at the bedroom, where Uma remained. "I'm talking about needing a few months. To get her settled, figure out how this whole dad thing works."

"You let the mom take care of it," Nash said. "That's how the whole dad thing works."

"Not for me," I said. Though it was true, that's how my parents had done it. My grandpa had done all the dad things with me, while my dad was a distant, detached kind of figure, rarely home at all. I had a suspicion that was just fine with my mother.

"You've got twenty more dates booked," Nash barked. "People have bought tickets. You can't back out."

"Yes, I can." I plopped the nipple of the bottle right in Osceola's open mouth. She promptly spit it out and started wailing instead of fussing.

"What am I supposed to tell the ticketholders? The fans? The label?" Nash yelled.

"Tell them I'm in rehab, I don't care," I said. "Tell them I had a nervous breakdown, I'm suffering from exhaustion. I don't fucking care what you tell them. Tell them I died, maybe then they'll leave me the fuck alone."

Nash glared, his fists clenching. "You can't do this."

"I'm doing it," I said. "Refund their money. I'm done, Nash."

"Okay, take a few weeks off, spend time with your… Family. We'll talk then."

"I don't need to talk," I said, a flood of relief washing over me when Osceola at last accepted the bottle and started sucking. "This is all I want now. Nothing's going to change that in the next two weeks."

"That might," Nash said when the baby broke away and started wailing again. "We'll see how you feel after listening to that nonstop for a while. In the meantime, I think you can squeeze in these last few shows before you take a break."

I stared at him hard. "Are you deaf? Or just trying to piss me off? I'm fucking done, Nash. I'm not doing another show tomorrow, or next week, or next month. I might never be doing another show again. Now get your ass on the phone and cancel them, and then you can pack up your shit and go home, too, because I won't be needing you anymore."

Osceola wailed and arched her back, and I put her up to my shoulder, patting her back gently.

"You can't fire me," Nash roared. Osceola's body jerked as she startled, then wailed louder, as if to outdo Nash.

Nash went on, yelling over the baby. "I *made* you, Brody Villines. You were nothing but a shit guitar-playing hick when I found you. If it weren't for me, you'd be sitting on a street corner collecting change in your guitar case."

My voice was low but deadly when I spoke. "If you ever scare this baby again, I will fucking end you."

"End me? End *me*?" Nash spluttered. Then he barked with laughter. "I will end you, Brody Villines. This is going to cost millions of dollars, and it's coming out of your pocket. Not mine. Not the label. You are going to pay for this."

"Fine, I'll pay for it."

Nash pointed to the door. "When I walk out this door, you cease to exist," he said. "You understand me, boy?"

“That’s exactly what I want.”

“Are you hearing me right now?” Nash asked, throwing up his arms. “This is the end of your career.”

“No,” I said, slipping Osceola off my shoulder and into my arms. “That career ended three days ago. And I couldn’t be happier.”

I didn’t even look up to watch Nash go.

March

forty-two

Laney

I had been home for three weeks when my mother came in to tell me the news. "Othal Darling had another stroke," she said, sitting on the edge of my bed, cradling Majesty's giant mass in her arms. "They don't know if he's going to make it this time. He's home, but he's got a hospice nurse in there."

"Oh my God," I said, sitting up so quickly my supply caddy toppled over, sending colored pens cascading across my blanket and the floor. The first thing I wanted to ask was if Brody knew.

But of course he knew.

Brody had been home for a few days just a few weeks before, presumably so his family could meet the baby. He hadn't even stopped by to visit me before leaving again.

"We should go and pay our respects one last time," Blair said. "After all he's done for our family and the community."

"Of course," I said, tossing off my blanket. Majesty struggled from Blair's arms and jumped to the floor, where he began batting my pens under the bed.

"I just wanted to make sure you weren't going to throw one of your tantrums, because I'm quite sure the whole family will be with him now," Blair said.

"Mom, it's fine," I said. "We're adults now. I know I'll see Brody from time to time."

But I wondered. We'd gone for years without seeing each other before. It wasn't hard to imagine we'd go for another three before the next time we met. By then, he'd probably be married to Uma and having another baby, and I'd be finishing grad school. And then in another three, I'd be married, too. Even if we both stayed in the area, which was doubtful, we'd only see each other at church picnics, awkwardly saying hello and chatting about the weather and our kids.

I felt my heart withering away and dying a little at the thought of this grim future. But I didn't know what I could do to stop it. I'd let Brody go, and he'd gone, taking Uma with him. I'd done the right thing, letting him make an honest go of things with the mother of his child. And he'd done the right thing, too—the fact that he was the kind of guy who would do that was part of why I loved him so much. If he hadn't tried, I'd have lost all respect for him. So now Uma and he had a baby to raise, and I had a broken heart to tend.

But I could suck it up and be an adult, not avoid him the way I had on the few occasions we'd been home at the same time during the past three years. Othal was a good man, one who had looked out for me as much as he did Brody and his brothers. So I climbed out of bed and made myself presentable, knowing it would break my heart to see Brody happy with his little family, but knowing also that sometimes, you had to break your own heart for someone else's sake.

* * *

I had expected the house to be full when we arrived, but only a few cars were parked in the driveway, and Brody's H2 was not among them. A sick feeling climbed into my throat, a conflicting swirl of relief and heart-rending sadness. But this wasn't about Brody. This was about Othal, a man who had taught me how to spit watermelon seeds along with his grandsons, who had given me tough love warnings when I'd chosen to go to college instead of joining *Just 5 Guys* on tour.

A woman I didn't know opened the door to let my family in. When we stepped into the living room, I stopped short. Brody was there, sitting by his grandfather's side, murmuring to him. He looked up when we entered, and his gaze caught mine. A coil of heat smoldered to life inside me, like a red-hot copper wire twisting down my spine.

I had made a terrible mistake.

Brody broke the connection first, standing to shake hands with my father, then accept a long, tight hug from my mother. Then it was my turn. I swallowed hard, schooling my face into what I hoped was an appropriate expression. Brody stepped toward me, close enough that I could have thrown myself into his arms, told him I was sorry, I didn't mean it. That I wanted to go back in time and fight for him, the right thing be damned.

But it was too late. I'd left him.

"Laney," he said, and he reached out, trailing his knuckles down my arm. The fire from his touch spread up my arm, then down my entire body, consuming me, eating me alive.

Faintly, the sound of a baby crying echoed from upstairs. Everyone fell silent for one eternal moment.

"Come and say hello to Othal," Blair said, hooking her arm through mine.

My knees nearly buckled with relief. I couldn't face Brody right now. I wasn't ready to be a mature adult if that meant pretending I'd never loved Brody or even pretending he didn't affect me anymore.

Mom's grip tightened on my arm, and an ache formed in my throat and behind my eyes. I held onto her arm like it was a life raft, knowing she was holding me up when I couldn't hold myself up, that she was my strength when I had none. Mom wasn't perfect, and she made excuses for Brody because she loved him and hoped we'd end up together. When I needed her, though, she was one hundred percent on my side, by my side, walking me across a room to say goodbye to a dying man like it was what she'd been put on this earth to do.

People could say what they wanted about Southern women and traditions, but my mother was the strongest person I'd ever met. Strong enough to hold up her daughter when her world was shattering, say goodbye to a man who had been like family, and look like a true lady while doing it.

"Thank you," I whispered, even though I knew my mother didn't need or crave acknowledgement for doing what she did. She knew exactly what it took to walk with her head held high in this world that wanted to stomp her into the ground.

When we reached the bed, I took Othal's hand. It seemed only yesterday I'd come to see him in this very bed in this very living room with Brody, when we were setting out for Chicago together. How had so much happened in such a short time? My whole life had begun and ended since then. And now another life was ending, and another beginning somewhere nearby. All of it happened without me, regardless of my feelings or presence. Even without me, Brody was a person, having his own troubles and triumphs.

His world would keep spinning without me. But mine had already stopped turning.

* * *

I wasn't sure how long I sat holding Othal's hand, tears spilling down my cheeks. I wished I could ask him what to do, how to keep living without the person you loved. He'd lost a wife, had lived for fifteen years without her. How did he keep walking across a world barren of her love? How did he keep walking across a world that no longer turned?

I knew I should be happy to have a young and healthy body, but already, I felt old, as if the best of my life was already over and time was slipping by, faster and faster, out of my control. And the more time passed, the further I was from happiness, from those months and years I'd spent with Brody, the only time I'd felt truly alive. Now everyone was here to say goodbye, to remember Othal's life. To mourn the death of his earthly body. No one mourned the deaths that took place silently, inside the heart.

When I finally stood, everyone had left me alone in the room with Othal. I bent and kissed his pale, liver-spotted forehead. "Safe travels, old man," I whispered, smoothing away one of my tears that had fallen on his crinkly skin. "I love you. See you on the other side."

With one final sniff, I composed myself and turned to go.

Uma stood in the doorway of the living room, watching me.

"Hey." She hooked her thumbs into the front pockets of her jeans, shoulders slouching as she regarded me coolly. We were alone. I was stuck talking to Uma. Trapped in my nightmare.

"Hi," I said.

We stood in silence for a minute, avoiding each other's eyes. Uma was wearing a tight-fitting long-sleeved shirt under a puffy vest. She didn't look like she'd been pregnant at all. She looked like a lost kid who didn't know what to say. But her body looked better now, not so sickly. Like she'd probably looked when she hooked up with Brody.

"How's…the baby?" I asked.

Uma shrugged. "She cries a lot."

I couldn't ask what I really wanted to ask, how was Brody taking it? Was he falling in love with Uma when he saw her cradling that baby, his baby, feeding it and loving it as much as he did? What was it like to share something so momentous as the whole of life with him? Had they gotten a DNA test?

I heard a little mewl of a cry from somewhere close by, the kitchen it sounded like, and all I wanted to do was run out of the house and keep on running, leave all this behind. It was too much, too awful, to see Brody with someone else, already with a family, when I couldn't even make it through one date with another man.

"What have you been up to?" Uma asked when I didn't respond.

I couldn't exactly tell her the truth, that I'd run away to New York to nurse my broken heart, to listen to Adele and bawl my eyes out while wearing sweatpants for two weeks straight and eating more ice cream than anyone had the right to do. That I'd overstayed my welcome at my cousin's apartment until she set me up on a terrible date to drive me home, knowing no guy would measure up to Brody Villines, no matter how much money he made or what kind of wedding he could give me.

"I went to New York for a month," I offered.

"No shit?" Uma said, nodding her head and looking impressed. "I've always wanted to go to New York. What's it like?"

It was my turn to shrug. "You know. It's a city."

"Damn," Uma said. "I wish I could trade places with you."

You and me both, I thought.

"What about you?" I asked.

"Well, we moved in here. Did you know that? To help take care of Othal."

"I didn't know."

"Yeah, so Brody does that a lot. I mean, it's his grandpa, I never knew him. So, I stay out of the way. And then there's Osceola."

"Where?"

"Oh, that's the baby," Uma said. "Lots of changing shitty diapers, getting puked on. Glamourous stuff, let me tell ya."

I didn't know how to respond to that, so I just nodded.

"Hey, you want to meet her?" Uma said, hooking her thumb back towards the kitchen. "I mean, she's not very interesting. I've pretty much gone over everything already. Pooping, puking, crying. Oh, and she sleeps. But you can look at her if you want. She's kind of squishy looking, but she's not hideous or anything."

I couldn't tell if there was hope in Uma's voice, but I couldn't shed my upbringing. If someone asked you to meet their baby, or their dying grandfather, or their comatose cousin, you smiled and said, "Sure, I'd love to."

So, that's what I said.

With another shrug, Uma turned and sauntered into the kitchen. I trailed after her, a knot of dread turning my insides to lead. Brody was sitting in a large wooden rocking chair, which had definitely not been there the last time I was in this kitchen. He was holding a little bundle in his lap, his arm curled lovingly around her, while he held a bottle with his other hand. The chair rocked gently back and forth as he hummed softly, smiling down at the thing with a look that shattered my heart all over again.

I knew in that moment I had done the right thing. The right thing for him, for the baby, for Uma. Nothing that made someone look that happy could be wrong. He stared at the baby with this look of awestruck wonder, like it was the most beautiful being to ever grace the earth with its presence. Which, to him, it obviously was.

Uma cleared her throat, and he looked up, his eyes blinking us into focus, as if he'd gone into a world where we didn't exist. I had the distinct impression we were butting in on a private moment, uninvited and unwelcome. And then he smiled, his dark, beautiful lips curving into that smile I knew so well, the smile I'd kissed, the smile that was only for me.

"Come say hi," he said, nodding towards the baby, his voice tender with emotion.

I shuffled forward, my legs feeling wooden and unreal. I peered down at the little face Brody had been looking at, and my heart caught. This wasn't an enemy, someone who had torn us apart. It was a tiny little creature, its eyes the same beautiful, clear blue of her father's. Whether they had gotten a DNA test didn't matter. The baby was all Brody, from the eyes to the soft wisps of light brown hair, the cheekbones and chin. This tiny version of Brody, innocent and pure, had never hurt me or anyone else. She hadn't meant any of the trouble she'd caused. I couldn't hold any of it against her, or Brody, or even Uma. It was no one's fault. It just was.

"Can I hold her?" I whispered, my eyes blurring over with tears again.

"Really?" Brody asked, the hope in his voice just about killing me. "Sure, yeah. Here, sit down." He stood and nodded to the chair, and I sat. Gently, he bent to settle the warm bundle in my arms.

Osceola stopped sucking at her bottle, her eyes intent on my face. She gave a few more sucks, then broke off and started crying.

"I'm sorry," I said, standing and shoving the baby back at Brody. "I guess she doesn't like me."

"Don't worry, she hates us, too," Uma said.

"Sorry. I should go." I turned and fled, ignoring Brody's call after me, ignoring the fact that my mother was now in the den with Othal. I couldn't take another minute in that house. Instead, I slid into the car, laid my head back on the seat, and tried to breathe.

A minute later, the door opened, and Brody slid into the back seat with me. "Mind company?"

"Maybe I do."

"I don't think so," he said, taking my hand. "I don't think you can forget me, either."

Did that mean…?

"Brody, you have a family. You're obviously a great dad. And that's great. Really. I told you, I'm never going to stand in the way of that. You should have that."

"Then what's the problem?"

"Maybe I'm just a little jealous, okay?" I said, pulling my hand away. "Is that what you want to hear? Well, I am. And, yes, you're right, I can't forget. I never said I could. That's not why I left."

"Then why'd you leave?" he asked, his voice hardening.

"You know why," I said, throwing up my hands. "You have your thing, and I'm not part of it. Uma's part of it. Not me."

"Laney," he said slowly. "I've told you a hundred times. There's nothing between us. There never was, and there never will be. Your leaving didn't change that."

I bit back the hope that thrilled inside me and made my voice hard. "Really. You're not together."

"We're really not together."

"Then what about—." Before I could finish, he grabbed my head between his hands and crushed his lips to mine. God, it was like Alice, falling down that rabbit hole. I wanted to fall again, to never stop falling. To let go and throw myself headlong down the rabbit hole, to be consumed by it the way Brody's mouth was consuming mine. The fire had burst to life inside me all at once, devouring me, racing across my skin like a fire across the prairie, obliterating everything in its wake.

"Stop," I gasped, pulling away.

"I'm here," Brody said, staring fiercely into my eyes. "I'm not going anywhere. I quit the tour, Laney. I quit Nash. I quit the business, all of it. And I'm not going back."

"What? How?"

"I'm still the same person I always was. And I'm not going to make you do anything you don't want," he said. "But you're going to see what you're missing one of these days. When you do, you know where to find me."

With that, he slid out of the car and jogged back up the steps and into Othal's house before I could say another word.

forty-three

Brody

We'd been living with Othal for a few weeks when Nash tracked me down. I had avoided his calls for the first two weeks, when we'd been at my place in California. But everyone had agreed that moving in with Othal was a good idea. In his lucid moments, a familiar face would comfort him, and my mother had her own house to tend.

"You've had your little vacation and played house," Nash said when I answered the phone with a sigh. It was evening, Osceola's favorite time to cry unceasingly for no discernible reason. My mother said it was colic, for which there was apparently no cure. Because life was just that awesome.

"Hey, Nash," I said. "How have you been? How's the family? It's so nice to talk to you, too."

Without missing a beat, Nash said, "It's time to talk about going back on the road."

"I told you. I'm not going." I stepped out onto the front porch so no one would hear me arguing. I didn't want Othal to wake up to that, or Osceola to have any more reason to cry than she had. I could hear her inside, working herself up for her evening performance.

"You're contracted for three albums," Nash said. "You don't just break a contract with Nyso Records."

"Then I'll make the albums," I said. "But no interviews, no photo shoots, no tour. I'm done with all that. I want to be left alone. I need my baby girl to be able to have a normal childhood."

"That's not the life you chose, Brody."

"I'm choosing it now."

"You're committing career suicide, that's what you're doing," Nash yelled. "And you're throwing me under the bus."

"We've talked about this," I said. "I'll buy my way out of anything that can't be cancelled. I'll sell my properties if I have to. You're my manager. Get us the best deal you can, and then I won't need you anymore. You're free. Go make a new boyband, or chase down Zane and Jace."

"They're starting a rock band," Nash growled in disgust.

"Good for them," I said. "Listen, Nash. If you want to stay on, I might need you when I'm making the other two albums. But I don't need all the other stuff. You'll get your cut. But you can manage someone who needs it. Right now, the only managing my life needs is figuring out sleep and feeding schedules. I love you, man, but we've outgrown each other's usefulness."

"Send me a fucking post card," Nash grumbled.

"I will," I said with a smile, raking my hair back with my fingers. My hair, which now I could wear however I wanted. I could grow it past my shoulders like his cousin Ned if I wanted. I could wear gas-station sunglasses and dollar-store flip flops. I could really, truly, avoid the paparazzi and live my own life.

"I have to go," I said, the wail from inside almost drowning out my thoughts.

Without waiting for an answer, I hung up the phone and slid it into my pocket, then hurried inside. Uma had gone upstairs, but I could still hear the baby's angry wails. When I reached the room we'd begun converting into a nursery, Uma was sitting on the floor, her hands over her ears, rocking furiously back and forth. Osceola lay in her crib, her fists pumping, her little face scrunched up and bright red. She had a pair of lungs on her, that was for sure.

I scooped her up, but her whole body was tense, her fists tight little knots of fury.

"Make it stop," Uma moaned from her spot on the floor. "I'm going to fucking lose it, Brody. Make her stop."

"It's okay, babies cry," I said. "Go get some rest."

In my room, I checked Osceola's diaper. Dry. Tried to feed her. She refused the bottle. At last, I gave up and walked her up and down the hall, bouncing, rocking, singing. She just kept on screaming. I didn't know how she wasn't passed out from exhaustion. Weren't babies supposed to sleep like twenty hours a day? So how was she still awake, screaming fit to bust a lung, while Uma and I were worn thin as a mic's feedback whine?

At last, sometime after dark, I stumbled into my room and lay her on the bed. Again, I checked her diaper and tried to feed her. Now I knew what Uma meant. She was right. The baby hated us.

In a fit of frustration, I picked up my guitar and ripped my calloused fingers across the strings. The chords thrummed loudly in the small room, and for a startled second, Osceola stopped crying. Her little face scrunched up with confusion. After a few breaths, she started again, but this time more tentatively, like she was working herself up for more.

I sat on the edge of the bed and strummed a gentler note this time.

Again, her crying stopped. I began to pick out the notes for "Twinkle, Twinkle, Little Star," the first song I'd ever played, when I was five years old, sitting on Gramp's knee. A bit of snuffling and ten seconds of halfhearted fussing accompanied the first verse, but by the time I was on to the next round, she'd fallen silent. Her big eyes searched the room for the sound, finding me at last. She mouthed her fist and made another fussing noise, then started sucking on her knuckle, her eyes drifting closed.

"You're really good with her," Uma said from the doorway. I hadn't heard her come in, and my first instinct was to snap at her to be quiet. But when I looked at the baby, her eyes had drifted all the way closed.

"I think she's sleeping," I whispered.

"Sorry I didn't help."

"It takes a village, right?"

"But I'm her mom. I should be able to make her stop crying."

"I couldn't, either."

"You just did." She gave me an accusing look, as if I'd done something wrong.

"Pure luck."

"I don't think so."

I carefully laid a blanket over the sleeping baby. "You should get some sleep," I said. "I'll come get you when she wakes up."

"You should get some sleep, too," she said. "We don't have to stay awake in shifts. She's not going to wake up and escape."

"I know," I said, sitting back down and letting my fingers move softly across my guitar strings. "I like watching her sleep."

Uma stared at me a few seconds, opened her mouth, but then closed it again. She picked at the doorframe beside her.

"You know, you're going to be an all right dad," she said at last. "I'd never have guessed it. But you're not a total piece of shit."

"Did I hear a compliment hidden in there?"

"Don't flatter yourself."

I smiled. "Thanks. You're not so bad yourself."

With a snort and an eyeroll, Uma crossed her arms. "Yeah, right."

"You'll get the hang of it. I'm just making it up as I go. I might look all cool and shit, but that's just me. I can't help it. I was born this way."

She snorted again and leaned her shoulder on the doorframe. "Riiiiight."

"Seriously, though," I said. "I don't know shit. It's all trial and error. I'm not doing any better than you." Except that I was trying, but that was probably not something to include in a parenting pep talk.

"I better get some sleep." She turned as if to leave, then hesitated. "Thanks," she said. "For everything."

"Don't thank me," I said. "I helped make the little tyrant."

Without another word, Uma disappeared into the dark hall beyond my room. I sat up a while longer, plucking at my guitar and watching Osceola, before finally drifting off to sleep at the foot of the bed.

* * *

Sometime in the night, I staggered to the kitchen with Osceola in the crook of my elbow. I walked her while her bottle warmed, then fed her and went back upstairs. I thought about getting Uma up, but her door was closed, so I figured I'd let her sleep. After laying Osceola in her crib, I lay down on the twin mattress we'd dragged into her room. Despite her evening crying jags, the baby had already begun to sleep most of the night, only getting up to eat a couple times and then falling back asleep. Tonight, I fell asleep on the mattress on the floor.

In the morning, I dragged myself up to change and feed Osceola before going to wake Uma. An eerie feeling crept over me when I opened her door and saw her bed neatly made. Uma was not the bed-making sort. I had to swallow the sour taste in the back of my throat a few times before crossing the room to her closet. Some part of me knew what

I'd find. A part of me had been waiting for this moment, expecting it, every day since she'd crashed the afterparty and told me it was my baby. Not ours. *Mine.*

With a great heave, I yanked open the closet door. Empty. Methodically, I opened each of her bureau drawers, as if she might have moved her clothes there. When I found them also empty, I retreated to my own room. My laptop was open on the desk, just as I'd left it the night before when I'd been checking emails, going through some paperwork for Nash and meaning to get back to Zane to congratulate him on starting the rock band and politely decline his offer to join. My guitars sat in the corner on their stands, except the acoustic, which stood leaning against the foot of bed, where I'd left it after playing Osceola to sleep. My wallet lay on the bureau, open to reveal my I.D. and credit card. The only thing missing was the cash.

Uma had balls, I'd give her that.

I sank onto the edge of the bed and looked down at the little person curled against my chest, her fingers clutching my shirt. My baby. My heart.

"Guess it's just you and me now, kid," I whispered, brushing her hair off her forehead. She looked up at me, and her face broke into a big, wet, toothless grin.

April

forty-four

Laney

"Are you still planning to go to Iowa next fall?" Blair asked at breakfast one warm spring morning. It was the first day she'd set the plates outside on the veranda, and I had joined her after a morning ride.

"Of course," I said, sliding a poached egg onto my toast. "Why wouldn't I?"

"I'm glad," Blair said. "That's all. I know how hard the last year has been for you."

"Don't worry, Mom, I'm not going to be a bum or live with my parents for the rest of my life. I'll be out of your hair by August."

Blair reached across the table and took my hand. "I may not always say it, dear, but I'm proud of you. You've handled yourself better than anyone could expect a girl to. The bridge club was talking about it just the other day, and we all think you showed real grace in the whole situation."

I smiled sadly and turned my hand to link it with hers. "Well, I'm glad at least my heart breaks gracefully from the outside. It's pretty ugly on the inside."

"I know that, dear," Blair said.

I chewed my toast for a minute. "You know, I'm not sure I want to be known as the kind of girl who handles a breakup with class. That's like being a woman who can take a punch. I don't think that's anything to be proud of."

Blair pushed her plate aside. "You've very brave, Laney. I hope you know how proud that makes me."

"No, brave is going to Paris by yourself to work on a fashion show. Not hiding in your parents' house because a boy broke your heart yet again."

"Opening yourself to love is always an act of bravery," Blair said. "And doing it after you've had your heart broken is doubly brave. It takes a whole hell of a lot more guts to do that than to take a punch."

"Yeah, well, it doesn't feel brave. It feels like I was a sucker once again."

"Love does make us feel weak," Blair said. "That's why it's brave. Not everyone is willing to make themselves weak for another person. Sometimes it takes more courage to be weak than it does to be strong."

"Can we talk about something else?"

"Of course, dear," Blair said, pulling her plate in front of her again. "I stopped by to see Othal Darling yesterday."

"That's nice."

"He's still hanging in there," Blair said. "His hospice nurse even left. Brody swears that baby of his has healing powers."

Since the spring thaw, I had been doing better myself. The long winter had frozen me, broken me, but all the pieces of ice were now melting into one serene pool inside me. I was going to be okay. Maybe not brave or graceful, but okay.

"You know that girl left him," Blair said.

My head snapped up. "What? When?"

"A while back," Blair said casually, spreading jam on her English muffin like she hadn't been hiding a huge secret that could change my life. "Three weeks, maybe a month. He's been taking care of that baby all by himself. Virginia says he refuses to hire a nanny."

"Why?"

"You know Brody," Blair said with an indulgent smile, as if he were her son. "He's always been stubborn. Same as you. I imagine he wants to prove himself, though to whom, I can't imagine." She arched an eyebrow at me before taking a bite.

"That's so sad," I said faintly. I remembered Uma's protestations, the ones no one had listened to—that she wasn't interested in Brody, that she didn't want to be a mother. Everyone had told her she'd change her mind. Eventually, she must have had enough of it, and done the only thing she could do to make them take her seriously.

"Tragic," Blair said. "Virginia says she just up and left in the middle of the night. Didn't even leave a note. Just—*poof!*—vanished."

"I wonder if she's going to sell her story," I mused. By some miracle, no one had found out about the baby, Brody Villines's secret love child. Although *love child* seemed the wrong term for the situation. I'd seen no love between him and Uma. But eventually, someone was going to find out he had a baby. They had to. No matter how private he was, people could find his houses in Los Angeles, in the Hamptons, in Kentucky.

That was another secret only me and a few other knew. Even Brody's brothers didn't know that he'd bought the family estate from his parents. They'd agreed to sell it to him, not leave it in the will, when he'd given them the money to reclaim their lost acreage and restore the estate to its original size. But his parents would continue to run it and live there as long as they pleased, which would be until his mother's dying breath, if I knew Virginia. I also knew that Brody would never move back in with his parents. What would happen when Othal passed away? Where would he go then?

"Maybe I'll stop by and visit," I said lightly, although my stomach knotted at the prospect. Still, it was the good, neighborly thing to do. After all, Laney Tucker was a good girl.

* * *

Maybe it was still a little chilly for the sun dress I chose to wear to Brody's. And maybe I spent a few more minutes on my makeup than was strictly necessary for a casual visit to an ailing old man and a baby. But no one could fault me for wanting my ex to see me looking nice. After all, I was a pretty girl with my whole life in front of me. A girl going to grad school in the fall, still young and free enough to pull off the dress that showed a little more leg than I would have shown at church.

I slid my Camaro through the gate at Othal's place and parked on the gravel drive in front of his garage. Again, I noticed the lack of Brody's H2. Maybe he'd gotten rid of it now that he was a family man.

The flower boxes in the windows were bursting with grape hyacinths, courtesy of my mother's visits I was sure.

Standing on the front porch, waiting for someone to answer my knock, I felt suddenly silly. My good mood had begun to darken with memories of the long, dreadful days on the tour bus. But then a shadow passed behind the frosted pane beside the door, and after a second, Brody was standing before me in sock feet, jeans, and a royal blue cashmere sweater that made me want to run my hands over the muscles

I could just make out through the fabric. Just to see how soft it was, of course.

"If it isn't Laney Tucker, in the flesh," he said. "Aren't you a cheerful sight. You look just like a flower in bloom."

"Why thank you, Brody Villines," I said, smiling up at him.

"I wasn't expecting company," he said. "Your mother was just here yesterday. So if you'll excuse the mess..." Opening the door wider, he gestured for me to come inside. "Would you like something to drink?"

"I'm okay, thank you."

"I'm afraid everyone else is asleep," he said with an apologetic smile. "Nap time."

"That's okay," I said. "I can wait. I mean, we're friends, aren't we?"

"Sure," he said, eyeing me up and down in a way that made my skin tremble. "If you're okay being basically alone with me."

I swallowed hard. "Maybe I could use that drink," I said. "Is there a tall drink of water anywhere around here?"

He grinned and shook his head. "What are you doing, Laney Tucker?"

"I'm just dropping in on a neighbor. Isn't that what friends do?"

"Sure," he said, still grinning. "Come on, I'll get you some water."

I followed him into the kitchen, where he poured two glasses of water and pulled out a barstool at the island for me. After sitting, I smoothed my skirt over my thighs. I did not miss the flicker of Brody's eyes following the movement, then lingering on my legs an extra beat.

"So," he said, sliding up onto the stool next to mine and resting his elbows on the island. "How you been?"

I tried not to stare at the muscles in his broad shoulders. Had he been working out?

"I've been well," I said. "I'm starting grad school in the fall, so I've been looking into apartments around Des Moines."

"Is that so?"

"Yep." I took a swallow of the cold water, trying to quell the sparks threatening to start a fire inside me. "What about you? What's it like being a single dad?"

"Hard as hell," he said. "I think I found a grey hair the other day."

"Well, it looks good on you. The dad thing, I mean, not the grey hair."

He laughed and leaned closer, like he was about to tell me a secret. "Since we're friends now, I should probably tell you, I've never had a lady friend before."

"Why does that not surprise me?"

"You might have to help me out here," he said. "Do friends do this?" He leaned in and nipped the tendon on the side of my neck.

I let out a yelp of surprise and swatted at him. "No," I said, my face suddenly hot. "They most certainly do not."

"Hmm. Interesting." He smirked at me for a second, his gorgeous mouth twisting in that infuriating way. God, the things that mouth had done to me. Things I wanted it to do again.

"What about this?" he asked, leaning in again, cupping my cheek in his palm while his lips whispered over my other cheek until they met my ear. "Is this allowed?"

I sucked in a breath, trying not to show him all my cards at once. Not wanting him to know that when his lips brushed across my earlobe, ripples of heat radiated across my skin. "Definitely not," I whispered, closing my eyes, leaning my face into his palm to give him access to my throat.

"Then let's try something else," he said, his lips trailing down my neck. He slipped off his stool and stood over me, tugging the strap of my sundress aside and kissing along my collarbone. His lips opened, and his tongue touched my skin. My body responded with an involuntary shudder of longing. Three months. I'd been good for three months. How had I gone three years without this? I was so hot I thought I'd explode.

"Brody," I said, grabbing his wrist when he started to pull my dress down further. "We're in the kitchen. Someone might hear us."

"They're sleeping," he said, his silky voice roughened with desire.

“What if we wake them up?”

“Then you’d better be quiet,” he said, his mouth dipping to my cleavage. Gentle kisses trailed along the swell of my breast until he curled his fingers under the edge of my bra and drew it down. His teeth scraped against my nipple, and I gasped, looking around to be sure we were alone.

“People eat in here,” I whispered.

“Not a problem,” he said, giving my nipple one quick suck.

I gasped and clamped my knees together against the ache swelling between my legs. My fingers curled around the edge of the island. I should stop him. We weren’t even dating. But God, I wanted this.

Brody laughed softly and parted my knees. Dropping to the floor between them, he smiled up at me and then slid his hands up my thighs in one quick motion, all the way up, pushing my dress over my hips. As he grasped my underwear, I lifted my hips, and he tugged them down to my ankles.

I had been so good these last three months. Hell, I’d been good my whole life. Just once, couldn’t I be bad?

Brody's breath was coming fast, as fast as mine. Discarding my underwear on the floor, he wrenched my knees open and buried his face between my thighs. This time, there was no teasing, no playful kisses. He sucked and licked and bit at me, his tongue roughly taking what he wanted. I gripped the edges of the island harder, biting my lip to hold in my cry of bure bliss at his demanding treatment as he forced his tongue into my slick entrance. He yanked me forward to the very edge of the barstool, and I let my head fall back, giving in to the waves of pleasure coursing through me as he fucked me with his tongue.

He mouthed a wordless growl of pleasure against me, and I gasped, hardly able to contain myself at the vibration it sent through me. His fingers spread my folds, and his tongue stroked from my entrance to my swollen clit in one long, hard motion. He pulsed the flat of his tongue against the sensitive bud before he began circling it with just the tip, making shudders of heat wrack my body with each motion. I opened my mouth to cry out, but his hand clamped over my mouth.

"You'll wake the baby," he said, then closed his lips gently around my pearl. With the gentlest pressure, he began to suck, softly at first, then harder, until I was breathing so fast I thought I might faint.

Just when I was about to grab his head and smother him in me, his tongue stilled, keeping gentle pressure on my throbbing clit. He drove two fingers into me at once, deep and hard. This time, I couldn't hold back. My whole body arched, and I cried out as the climax rocked through me. My hands lost their grip on the island, and I clamped one around the back of his neck, pulling him in as he thrust his fingers rhythmically into my tight opening, his lips still tormenting my clit with pleasure. I cried out again, grasping for the edge of the island but succeeding in upending a glass of water instead.

His fingers caressed the magic spot inside me, and I lost all control. My legs started jerking in little spasms, my hips rising as his tongue ran along the edge of my entrance, stretched around his fingers. My walls clenched in waves around his fingers, pulsing along their length as my clit throbbed against his tongue over and over.

I didn't know I was speaking until I heard my voice echoing around the kitchen, chanting, "Oh God, Brody, oh

God." At last, the final shudders finished wracking my body, leaving me dazed and halfway embarrassed. Laney Tucker did not lose control easily.

Slowly, Brody slid his fingers from me and stood. Upstairs, I heard the first mewling cries of the baby. "I'm so sorry," I said, mortified at my inability to stay quiet during that orgasm.

But holy fuck, that orgasm…

"It think it's safe to say you woke the baby," he said, picking up the glass I'd broken.

"It's your fault," I said, snatching my wet underwear off the floor.

"Hey," he said, his hand falling on my waist, stopping me. "I'm kidding."

I drew on my underwear despite the wetness, avoiding his eyes.

"Besides," he said with a grin. "It was totally worth it."

I gave a shaky laugh. "For me."

"Oh, for me, too," he said. "Trust me on that one. You taste like sunshine over the sea."

I could feel heat rising to my cheeks. "I should… I mean, Othal's probably awake, and…" I dropped my voice to a whisper. "Do you think he heard us?"

Brody grinned and grabbed a towel off the stove. "I have no doubt." He tossed me the towel. "Hey, will you wipe that up real quick while I grab the baby? If I let her get herself worked up, it takes forever for her to stop."

Without waiting for an answer, he ducked out of the kitchen. A second later, I heard his feet padding up the stairs. I wanted to leave the mess for him to clean up and run away in shame, but even now, I couldn't do something so rude. After all, I'd broken the glass, and he had his hands full. The least I could do was clean up my own mess.

Just as I'd finished tossing the glass shards in the trashcan and wringing out the towel, Brody appeared in the doorway, the baby sitting snugly in the crook of his elbow. "Hey, thanks," he said, then winked at me. "Teamwork."

"I should probably go," I said, my face warming again. Just looking at him made my heart flip and my lips tug into a smile. "I mean, I'd love to stay and talk to Othal, but I'm not sure I can face him just now."

"Eh, the TV's always on, and he's not wearing his hearing aids," Brody said. "I'm sure you're fine. Unless you want to stay and experiment on me with one of your Pinterest recipes…" The hopeful look on his face nearly broke my heart all over again.

"I don't think cooking for you is on my list of neighborly duties," I said, trying to keep the mood light.

"Really? I think it's customary, when someone has a baby, to bring them a dish."

"What are you doing, Brody Villines?" I asked, echoing his question from earlier. I could not seem to make my mouth stop smiling, and butterflies were swarming in my belly. This had been a huge mistake. Why did it have to feel so damn good to be near him?

"I'm trying to get you to stay," he said. "If you won't cook, then I will."

"You can't cook."

"Exactly my point. You don't want to eat what I can make."

"And I won't have to," I said, straightening the straps on my dress. "My neighborly visit is over."

"Fine, then maybe I won't let you leave," he said with a mischievous grin. "I'll hold you hostage until you say yes."

"Then maybe *I'll* just wait until you're sleeping and sneak out in the middle of the night." No sooner were the words out of my mouth than I wanted to smack myself in the forehead. I could tell by the look on Brody's face, all joking and arrogance gone, that I'd hit him where it hurt the most, unintentional as it was.

"I—I'm sorry," I said quickly.

"Don't be." He went to the refrigerator and took out a bottle, then turned and lit the gas range under a pan already sitting on the burner, half full of water.

I knew I should leave, but I didn't want to leave like this. "Brody…"

"I guess you heard," he said, his back to me. "So, that's why you came by? So you wouldn't have to feel bad, since I'm not tied down to her anymore? And hey, I did promise that would always be right between us. Guess I didn't break that promise today."

"It's not like that," I protested. I hadn't come for a booty call. I hadn't meant anything to happen.

Had I? I mean, I had worn a short dress and gotten myself all dolled up...

"It's okay," he said. "Happy to be of service. But I'm still tied down. I'm tied down to this little gal, and I always will be." He smiled down at Osceola with so much love in his eyes it could have drowned her.

"I know that. I think it's really cool, what you're doing."

He turned to face me, his eyes so intense I had to reach for the remaining glass, just to have something to do with my hands. "My feelings for you haven't changed, Laney," he said. "They never will. I'm going to carry that ring around in my pocket until the day you say yes."

"Brody…"

He stepped around the island and took the glass from my hand, setting it on the counter before turning those intense blue eyes on me. When I started to look away, his fingers closed gently around my chin. "Stop avoiding this, Laney," he said. "It's not going to go away. I'm ready to slide this ring on your finger tomorrow. All you have to do is say the word."

I couldn't bring my voice above a whisper. "Okay."

His fingers moved away from my chin, brushing along my jaw and the side of my neck, sending heat rushing across my chest in anticipation. But the baby wiggled in his arm, and he dropped his hand from my skin and stepped back.

"I'm also never going to change my mind about her," he said, turning off the gas and setting the bottle in the pan of water. "I'm her father. I'm always going to be. She's my responsibility now, and I'm going to give her the best life I can."

"You're really not going back to music?"

"Music is right here with us all the time." He dribbled milk from the bottle onto his wrist before wiping it on the wet towel and inserting the nipple into Osceola's mouth. "Music's always been part of my life, and it always will be. I'm writing some songs, going to do that little EP like I wanted. I'm going to do more than just sing this time. But the band, all that shit? I'm not going back to that."

"What are you going to do, though?" I asked, watching in fascination as Osceola began to suck in earnest, her eyes fixed on Brody.

"This is my job now. And if someday...*when* someday, I'm your husband, that will be my job, too, and I'll love it just as much. But this one isn't going away. Nothing could make me want to quit this."

"I—I have to go," I said, backing away. It was all so much, so intense. The way he talked about Osceola, the way he talked about me... It was what I'd always wanted. Brody, a family, Kentucky bluegrass and horses all around. So why was I still running away?

forty-five

Brody

The funeral was held on one of those warm days at the end of April that felt more like summer than mid-spring. Though it had been a long time coming, and in a way, I had been expecting it, Othal's death had hit me like a gut-punch. The evening Gramps passed, I had almost broken my vow to stay hidden from the outside world, the cameras and eager fangirls. I needed a night out of that house of death and sickness, someone to make me forget who I was. But I couldn't forget because the world hadn't forgotten. They'd started wondering where I was, why I'd disappeared.

Now, three days later, people inside the house were probably wondering where I was as I sat on the wooden bench Othal had built around the trunk of the magnolia tree at the edge of the yard. The same tree where I had taken Othal and Osceola out to soak up sun every day for the past month. This time, instead of a quiet hour on the lush green of new grass, I was spending the afternoon consoling my inconsolable mother. Across the wide expanse of lawn, crowds of guests brought food, consumed food, consumed alcohol, and gave toasts memorializing his grandfather. That's what Othal would have wanted—a big party for his send-off.

Unfortunately, neither my mother nor I were in the party mood after the burial, so we'd escaped to the magnolia tree. Osceola was the only one who seemed unaffected by the tragedy, oblivious and content to sleep in her stroller as she did every day.

"I just can't believe he's gone," Virginia said, dabbing at her eyes with a shredding tissue. "How am I going to go in there and entertain all those *people?*" She said the word as if it were a scourge.

"No one expects you to," I said, putting an arm around my mother. I understood her distaste for people right then. Since leaving the tour, leaving the business, I'd found the outside world more and more unappealing. Othal, Osceola, and I had made a quiet little family. Most of the time, it was all I needed.

As if to prove me wrong, at just that moment, Laney's little white Camaro came zipping up the driveway.

"Her again," Virginia sniffed.

"Mom, you know you love Laney," I said.

"Yes, well, that was before she ran off and left you."

"I've done worse to her." I gave my mother a squeeze before standing. Somewhere deep in her shriveled heart, I knew that she still hoped for the same thing I did. But she wouldn't forgive Laney until it suited her.

"Look after the baby, would you?" I said after a quick check to see that my girl was still sleeping. Mom sniffed in response, but I knew she would. As soon as Uma had disappeared, Virginia had accepted Osceola into the Villines' fold, for better or worse.

I jogged over to the front of the house, where Laney was climbing out of her car.

"To what do we owe this pleasure?"

"Just stopping in," she said, smoothing her skirt over her thighs and shaking her hair back. "I'm so sorry, Brody."

"It was time," I said, because that's what I was supposed to say.

"I wanted to apologize for how crazy I was the last time..." She scuffed her flat white sandal against the gravel drive. "It was stupid of me to run away like that. I guess that's sort of my thing. Running away."

"I've noticed," I said, arching an eyebrow.

"Right. Well, the thing is… I'm not mad at you about the baby. I mean, I'm hurt about what you did. And… God, this is going to sound even more crazy," she muttered, breaking off and taking a deep breath. I waited, and she forged ahead after a pause. "I guess that it hurts to know you did all that stuff with all those girls because I still loved you. So even though we weren't together, it still feels like a betrayal because, to my heart, it was."

"I'm sorry," I said. "I've apologized a thousand times. But I can't fix that now, Laney. It's done. I can't change the past any more than you can."

"I know," she said. "I just wanted to say that. And that… Well, I'm not mad that you have a baby, even though it's not mine. I think it's really awesome what you're doing, actually."

"You're pretty awesome yourself, Laney Tucker."

"I don't know about that. I've made some pretty big mistakes, too," she said. "And I think you've redeemed yourself. At least partially. Taking care of the baby after her mom ran off and all..."

"It never had anything to do with Uma," I said. "You know that. Oceola's my daughter. That's what it's about."

"I know," she said. "But not everyone would give up what you have for her."

"It's not just for her," I said. The words hung in the air between us. I swallowed, searching Laney's eyes before adding, "This is the life I want."

"I want it, too." Her lip trembled, but she met my gaze without flinching.

Damn, I wanted to take that quivering lip between mine and bite it. I wanted to make her come how I had the last time she visited—every night. I wanted to make her breakfast in the morning until I could make one worthy of her. I wanted to be her guinea pig for all her dinners, even the fails. I wanted another stroller with our baby in it.

I pushed the thoughts away. "I thought you were going to grad school in the fall."

"I am," she said. "I am doing that. I'm not going to give that up."

The mood shifted, and I slid my hands into my pockets and squared my shoulders. That was that. "Well, I know Othal would have wanted you to be here. So thank you for coming."

Laney gave me a polite smile, the kind she gave the pastor at church. "It was really good of you to be here for him these last few months. I'm sure he appreciated that more than you know."

"Would you like to go inside and have a drink?" I asked. "Dad's entertaining the masses. I'll be over there with Virginia and Osceola. I've more than fulfilled my duty to the masses."

I smiled, trying to lighten the mood, but Laney just shook her head. "No, I came to see you," she said. "And to tell you that… I think I kept running away, hoping you'd chase me. But you can't anymore. You've grown roots. You can't come to me anymore, so I have to come to you."

I didn't dare let myself hope that statement meant more than its words.

"For what?" I asked, cocking my head. "That last time was… Jesus. Fucking incredible, Laney. I'm not saying I'd take a second of it back, because I wouldn't. And you know I'll be here any time you want to come on over and let off steam."

"It wasn't just that," Laney said, her cheeks getting all pink and cute as hell.

"Whatever it was, I'm down for seconds," I said with a grin. "Any time you want, just holler at me. I won't say no to that."

"You make it sound so tawdry," she said. "It wasn't a hookup, Brody. Not for me. I still… I'll always love you, Brody. I was hoping, maybe, we could find a way…"

"Laney," I said, reaching for her hand. Her words had rammed an invisible knife right through my sternum. "In my heart, you'll always be my girl. But I'm a dad. Osceola's my girl now, too, in a different way. And you don't want to be a mom."

"But I do," she said. "I wasn't exactly planning for it now, but… Neither were you."

"So… You're saying, what, exactly? You want to live here with us? Move in here?"

"No," she said firmly, shaking her head. "I'm not saying that. I'm saying I'd give you another chance. I know if I don't, I'll end up doing what I did last time. I'll marry someone I don't love, and always wonder what would have happened if I'd tried again. But I'm not giving up my dreams for you, Brody Villines. I went on tour with you. I'll come to you and ask, but if you want to be with me, this time, you have to come to where I am. And I'm going to be at University of Iowa."

I didn't even have to consider her offer. I'd already started planning. I didn't want to live in the house where Othal had died. I didn't want to be on the celebrity scene in L.A. or raise my daughter with the snobs in the Hamptons. I wanted her to have a normal childhood, like I had.

I wanted to disappear for a while. And the truth was, I didn't have to think about it at all. I'd cross the universe to make Laney mine again.

"Fair enough," I said. "But you're going to have to do something for me."

"What's that?" she asked, her face suddenly wary.

"You're going to have to marry me."

"I do hope that will happen someday."

"No," I said, wrapping my hand around the box in my pocket. "You're going to have to let me put this ring on your finger and tell the world you're mine." I drew out the box I'd been carrying around since the last time I'd asked.

"What are you doing?" Laney whispered, her eyes wide.

"You can have your moment in the sun, Laney. I'm not going to stand in the way of your dreams or let this shitty celebrity stuff stop you from doing what you want to do. I'll stay home and be a dad while you're off at school every day. But I'm taking care of my family. And that means Osceola *and* you."

"Then you're going to have to wait until I finish grad school," she said, but she didn't pull away when I took her hand.

Slowly, I eased the box open and took out the ring, letting the box fall to the ground at our feet. My heart was pounding out a steady rhythm in my chest, but I managed a smile. "I told you I'd keep asking until you said yes."

"Did I say yes?"

I stepped closer, angling my mouth towards hers as I held her hand gently, like the treasure it was. "Marry me, Laney Tucker."

"Okay," she whispered, her breath sweet across my skin.

My lips brushed over hers. "Say yes."

"Yes."

Her fingers trembled as I slid the ring into place, but mine were steady. I wasn't going to fuck this up. She was mine, and I was never letting her go.

FIVE YEARS LATER

May

Laney

I settled myself into one of the white folding chairs that sat in circular rows around the gazebo and squinted up at the man standing before me.

"What do you think?" Brody asked, dropping into the chair next to me so I didn't have to shade my eyes from the bright, early summer sun.

"I think you're nervous," I said, smiling at him.

He draped an arm across the back of my chair. "Me? Nervous? Never."

"Yeah, I guess I imagined all those times I had to hold your hand and talk you through the nerves when you went solo."

"I'm a little excited," he admitted with a smile. "But come on, Laney. It's been five years since I played a show with these guys."

That was the deal—*Just 5 Guys*, just five shows, five years later. Each of the guys had chosen a venue. Brody's just happened to be in the middle of a field in Kentucky, with the sun overhead and the freshly green grass underfoot. Needless to say, tickets had been scarce.

"Mommy, Mommy, look at me," a high voice interrupted. I turned to watch the little girl on the grass attempt her hundredth cartwheel…that hour. She always managed to make it until she was upside down, and then her feet drooped one way or the other, and she went sprawling onto her back or her belly. Undeterred, she got up and tried again, her shiny chestnut curls bouncing like springs as she moved.

"If practice makes perfect, that girl is going to do the world's most flawless cartwheel once she gets the hang of it," Brody said.

"Go on," I said, elbowing him in the ribs. "Give her another lesson."

He leaned in to give me a quick kiss before jogging over to demonstrate the correct cartwheel technique for Osceola.

I sighed in contentment and slid my feet out of my sandals, burying my toes in the lush grass and closing my eyes, letting the sun warm my skin. It really had been ages since I'd watched Brody play with a band. It seemed such a long time ago that I'd gone on tour with him. Most of the time, I barely remembered that he was famous. For the past few years, he'd only played private concerts for our daughter and me.

Smoothing my hand over my belly, I smiled. This time, I'd get to be a mom from day one, with all it entailed, good and bad.

"Mommy!" Osceola's insistent voice roused me, and I opened my eyes again. She did a silly canter through the grass toward me before throwing herself across my lap. "Am I going to meet my second mommy tomorrow?" she asked, swiping stray hairs off her face with her little hand, the knuckles still dimpled like a baby's.

"That's right," I said, tugging her headband from her hair so I could smooth it back into place.

"Is she as pretty as you?"

"Not even close," Brody said, scooping up Osceola's legs and scooting into his seat beside me again. "And she's not your second mommy, she's your birth mother. Laney's the only mommy you've got, kid."

He gave her round, little kid belly a playful poke, but I caught the edge of seriousness in his gaze when our eyes met. I'd told him how weird it made me feel to see Uma again after all this time, to let Osceola meet her, but we both felt it was wrong to withhold the truth from our daughter.

"What if she tries to take Osceola?" I'd asked Brody when I found out Uma would be coming to the show. He'd promised that wouldn't happen.

If she tried, well, she'd see what happened when you messed with a southern woman. Osceola was my baby girl now, and no one was going to mess with her—not even the woman who had given birth to her. Besides, we had legal documents. I had adopted her a long time ago. I still didn't understand how someone could not want the little bundle of energy and excitement squirming in my lap, but Uma had signed away her rights without a word.

"You're the only mommy Phillip's got, too," Osceola said, lying still for a brief moment while I settled her headband back in place.

"Phillip?" Brody asked, cocking an eyebrow. "Who's Phillip?"

"Phillip's the baby," Osceola said. "Obviously."

"Where'd that come from?" I asked, shooting Brody a look. He better not have started picking out names without me.

"Because he filled up Mommy's belly," Osceola said impatiently. She put her little lips right next to my baby bump, poking them out like she was trying to whistle again, another skill she was determined to master. "Hellooooooooo." Turning her head, she cupped her ear between her hands and pressed it to my belly.

"What's he got to say today?" Brody asked.

"Shhhh," Osceola said. "I'm still listening." After a long pause, she pulled away. "He says he doesn't want to meet our birth mother tomorrow, so he's staying in there."

Brody scooped up the little girl and set her in his lap. "You know you don't have to meet her, either," he said. "If you change your mind tomorrow, that's okay. Granny and Nana both said you could stay at their houses if you didn't want to come to the show."

"I know," Osceola said, squirming down from Brody's lap. "Can we go see the horses now?"

As we walked through the field, I turned to my daughter. "How do you know it's a boy, anyway?"

"Because I want a brother," she said, as if it were as simple as that.

To her, I suppose it was. I took Brody's hand without thought as Osceola skipped ahead, along the trail I had run so many times, on foot and on horseback. For a second, I let the memories wash over me—the trips to the gazebo as a child to play with Brody. Sneaking out to see him when we were teenagers. All the drama of our breakup and reunion. And two years before, after I'd finished my master's degree and he'd finished out his contract and delivered his third solo album to Nyso Records, we'd gotten married there, just like I'd always wanted.

Well, except for the rain that had fallen for three days straight, leaving the fields a muddy, impossible mess on our wedding day. I hadn't fantasized about that for years in advance. Or the sudden downpour during the ceremony that drenched the entire wedding party and all the guests. But hey, everyone said rain on your wedding day was good luck. From what I could tell, they weren't wrong.

As we neared our parents' house, I sighed and laid my head on Brody's shoulder. Every time I came home, it was harder to leave. One of these days, I was going to stay. Now that I was having a baby, it seemed like the right time to settle down somewhere away from prying eyes, a place where time moved nice and slow, and I could enjoy each new phase of my life.

That night, as we slid into bed, Brody reached for me and pulled me close, nuzzling against my neck.

"I can't believe I'm sleeping with the front man of *Just 5 Guys*," I said. "I'm such a groupie."

"Mmm, just don't put on one of those freaky masks," he said, his hands exploring my new curves.

I laughed at the thought of the baby-doll masks. I'd forgotten all about them. In the years we'd been together, I'd put all that aside—jealousy over the groupies in his past, insecurities about his loyalty, and doubts about my own performance. Brody was a good teacher, and I had lots of experience now. And I never doubted his commitment to me and our family. He'd wanted this life before I did.

"Are you tired?" he asked, one finger skimming from my belly button down the slope of my bump to the waistband of my panties.

"Aren't you supposed to conserve your energy the night before a show, like an athlete?" I teased, hooking a leg over his.

"*You* don't have to." He shot me a wicked grin before ducking under the covers and sliding between my thighs.

* * *

Brody

I looked out over the small crowd of expectant faces, many of them familiar. We'd only sold two hundred tickets to this show, which was enough for the field surrounding the gazebo. Virginia would never have permitted such a violation of our property, but the Tuckers were more generous to outsiders.

I adjusted my mic stand and looked down at Laney, standing in front of her chair, just a few feet away from the gazebo and within easy reach if she needed me. That's all I could see—my beautiful wife smiling up at me, the serene glow of pregnancy lighting her up from within.

"I got something very special for y'all today," I said, lowering my voice and gazing into her eyes. This show was for her, like everything was for her now. Her and Osceola and our family.

"It's time we took it full circle," I said when the clapping and polite cheering had subsided. "You know what that means. Our first song will be our first."

I added a wink just for fun, and Laney gave me an encouraging, slightly giddy smile. Almost half the people in attendance were locals, while others were friends and family of the guys in the band. Those fans who had bought tickets were the young elite who could afford the steep price to indulge in an evening of exquisite nostalgia. Family and friends had staked out the front rows, but the rest of the seats were filled first-come, first-served. I couldn't believe how polite and well-behaved everyone was. No pushing and shoving and screaming to get nearer the band. Everyone had grown up.

With a dramatic flourish, Jace counted us in on drums. None of that canned shit this time around. That was a stipulation for this show. Intimate. Remote location. Real music.

Then I spotted a girl standing in the front row on her cell phone. There she was.

Uma.

While everyone else had grown up, she had stayed exactly the same. Her dark hair was still a wild, tangled mess of waves around her shoulders. Her eyes, when she tore them away from her phone and slipped it into her back pocket, were still the same violet shade that had made her so memorable when she came crashing backstage to change my life. Hell, she even wore a black Pink Floyd t-shirt. I'd bet dollars to doughnuts it was the exact same one she'd worn the night we met. Oh well, the girl was only twenty-four. I could cut her some slack. She had plenty of time to grow up still. And her disinterest in children had definitely put Laney's mind at ease the night before.

I turned my attention to the gorgeous blonde standing beside Uma, radiant in her white sundress. Damn, I'd gotten lucky. My wife was hot as hell. I met her eyes and gave her my trademark crooked smile, adjusting my guitar strap before I started singing. Leaning into the mic, I let the lyrics slide out of me without thought, just like I had all those years on the road with the boys.

Be my baby-doll

I ain't even playin' wit' you

I just want a baby-doll

I can hold the whole night through

This was kind of fun. Sure, it was cheesy as hell, but still fun. I even kind of missed it. Not the lifestyle, but the band, the guys. I hadn't kept in touch with them as often as I should have. We'd gone our separate ways, found our own successes, whether that meant starting a family or a new band. But that didn't mean we couldn't get together on occasion to talk about the glory days. Hell, even this once-loathsome song was making me a little nostalgic. It was the right song to kick off the five-date tour, even if we'd all hated it once. We were big boys now. We could put aside our egos for the fans.

Playing for an audience brought an unexpected high. I hadn't played a live show in years. Maybe I'd pick it back up, give the occasional show in Louisville or Nashville, small shows like I'd wanted before I'd left the business. Or drop in and play a song with Zane's rock band once in a while.

As the song moved into the bridge, I slowed down to grind my hips in that way fans had always loved. The choreography was still there, stored in my muscles, waiting to come out when I started singing. But this time, I had a guitar. I could make music the way I wanted now. It was still a rush; I couldn't deny that. Music would always be a part of me. I might even do another solo album—this one on my terms.

After all, I'd worked my ass off to get where I was. Independently wealthy, with the wife of my dreams. A beautiful, perfect daughter I could spoil to my heart's content and another baby coming. We were set for the rest of our lives. We could do whatever we wanted—stay home with the kids, travel, take up painting or raise horses. Just the night before, as we'd lain in bed, Laney had mused about moving back to Kentucky. We'd both always wanted to raise a family in the country, close to our parents. Laney could do most of her work online, and I could do whatever I wanted. Maybe make that country album we'd been talking about since we were kids.

When the song slowed, I caressed the mic stand as I crooned the last lines, my gaze locked on Laney's. I didn't think I'd ever seen her smile that big. I wrapped up the last few notes of the melody and smiled back at her. "That one was for the pretty lady in the front row," I said. "I love you, Laney Villines."

Uma rolled her eyes and shook her head. Laney laughed and blew me a kiss, and Osceola jumped up and down and waved at me as if I were on a real stage instead of ten feet away, in the gazebo where she played whenever we came home to Kentucky. I had a feeling she'd be playing there a lot more often from now on. I just might make a habit of it myself.

The End.

Acknowledgements

Special thanks to my beta readers, Emily, Leona, Kylie, Laurie, Elizabeth, and Sophie, for making this book shine.

Thanks to my editors Kathy Bosman and Tristin M. for all your advice and hard work.

Huge shout-out to my cover designer Ally for making this amazingly hot cover for me.

Lastly, a huge thank you (with guitar riffs and lickable abs on top) to all my amazing readers for taking a chance on this book. Y'all are all the real rock stars of this world!

Printed in Great Britain
by Amazon